CHASING CHARLIE CHAN

A Jimmy Pigeon Mystery

ALSO BY J. L. ABRAMO

Jake Diamond Mystery Series

Catching Water in a Net
Clutching at Straws
Counting to Infinity
Circling the Runway (*)

Other Titles

Gravesend

(*)—COMING SOON

J. L. ABRAMO

CHASING CHARLIE CHAN

For Eric Campbell

Who gave Jake Diamond a leg up
when Jimmy Pigeon no longer could.

THE WISDOM OF CHARLIE CHAN

"Hollywood is famous furnisher of mysteries."
—from *The Black Camel*
Fox Pictures, 1931

"Sometimes better to see and not tell."
—from *Charlie Chan at the Wax Museum*
Twentieth Century Fox Pictures, 1940

"Authors sometimes take strange liberties."
—from *The Chinese Cat*
Monogram Pictures, 1944

CAST OF CHARACTERS

LENNY ARCHER. . . . . .a private investigator
EDWARD RICHARDS. . . . . .a journalist
JAKE DIAMOND. . . . . .an actor
JIMMY PIGEON. .a Private Investigator
FRANK RAFT. . . . . .an LASD detective
BOB TULLY. . . . . .Raft's partner
SOLOMON MEYERS. . . . . .a medical examiner
MEG KELLY. . . . . .a café owner
VINNIE STRADIVARIUS. . . . . .a kid who likes to help
JACKSON MASTERS. . . . . .a prosecutor
RAY BOYLE. . . . . .an LAPD detective
RICARDO DIAZ. . . . . .a three-time loser
JOHN BARNUM. . . . . .a SMPD detective
SAM STEPHENS. . . . . .an LAPD detective
KEVIN TULLY. . . . . .a high school baseball star
HANK FELLOWS. .a newspaper editor
CARLOS VALDEZ. . . . . .friend of Ricardo Diaz
ANGEL RIVAS. . . . . .a young lady in distress
PETER QUINCE. .a high school teacher
PAM WALKER. . . . . .assistant manager at Meg's Café
NATHAN ARCHER. . . . . .a San Diego private investigator
ROGER ROLLINS. . . . . .a former LAPD captain
WILL CADY. . . . . .a killer
JOHN BILLINGS. . . . . .an LAPD uniformed officer
ANNIE ARCHER. . . . . .Nathan's wife
MARIA RIVAS. . . . . .Angel's mother
REGINALD MASTERS. . . . . .a Hollywood legend
NATALIE LEVANT. .a missing person
SETH CADY. . . . . .Will Cady's brother
WILLIAM MASTERS. .a former governor

Part One

FALLEN ARCHER

"Life is a carnival."
—*Lenny Archer*

LENNY ARCHER

When Lenny Archer managed to open his eyes, the first thing he saw was a small black circle with a white spot at its center. As he began to focus the circle became deep red and he recognized the white object. A tooth. Lenny probed the inside of his mouth with his tongue and found the space where the molar and a few of its neighbors had once been. And he could taste blood. Lenny realized he was face down on the floor and made an effort to move. The pain in his lower abdomen was unbearable. He shifted his gaze to the significantly larger red pool that spread from the floor up into his shirt below his waist. Archer let out a ghastly sound, part animal moan and part angry prayer.

"This mope is still breathing," said Tully.

"Put him out of his fucking misery."

"Maybe he'll tell us where he stashed it."

"If he was going to spill, he would have talked before you knocked his fucking teeth out," said Raft. "The guy is a fucking mess. Kill him. You'd be doing him a favor."

Lenny Archer tried to remember where he was, remember what he'd been doing before taking a bullet in the stomach and a kick in the face. He wondered if it really mattered.

Archer remembered sitting at his desk looking over the notes Ed Richards had handed him and hearing the noise in the hallway outside his office door. Midnight, too late for a social call and long past business hours. Archer had instinctively placed the notes in the fold of the newspaper on his desktop and quietly slid open the top drawer. Lenny pressed the remote switch to start the office tape recorder and he pulled out his handgun. And he listened.

Silence.

Archer rose from his chair and moved to the door, his gun in hand, intending to check the hall. He slowly turned the knob, the door knocked him to the floor and his weapon discharged. Then another shot and the terrible pain in his abdomen and the crushing blow to his head.

Archer thought he heard voices, in his mind or in the room, debating his fate. He seemed to remember questions. *What did Ed Richards tell you? What did Richards give to you? Who else did Richards talk to? Who did you talk to?* And each time he had failed to respond he could remember another blow to the face. And then blackness.

Lenny looked in horror at the pool of blood growing larger at his waist. The voices were louder now.

"You'd be doing him a favor," Raft said.

Tully pressed the gun barrel against Lenny's head.

"Bingo, Richards' notes," said Raft.

Tully looked over to the desk. Raft held the notes in one hand and he tossed the newspaper at Lenny with the other.

"Shoot the motherfucker already," said Raft.

"We're still not sure who else knows about this."

"The sooner you kill this fuck, the sooner we can get to Richards. And trust me; Richards is going to spill his guts."

An hour earlier, Tully and Raft had followed Richards to the parking lot of a donut shop on Fifth. The shop was closed for the night. Richards pulled up next to the only other car in the lot. They watched from a distance as he climbed out of his car and moved to the driver's window of the other vehicle. Ed Richards passed some papers through the window, quickly returned to his own car and drove off.

"Follow the other car," Raft had said.

"What about Richards?"

"We know where Richards lives, he can wait. Let's see where this guy goes, who the fuck he is and what he knows."

They followed the second car to a building on Fourth Street and waited for the driver to enter. When they saw the light go on in a second story window, they left their vehicle and moved to the front entrance of the building.

"Fucking private dick," said Raft, checking the names on the mailboxes.

"There are two of them," said Tully.

"Not tonight. Whoever this one is, he's alone up there. Let's go and check his ID."

Tully and Raft stood in the hallway outside the office for a minute, unsure about how to play it. They had pulled out their weapons.

"Sounds like he's coming this way," Tully said.

They heard the footsteps and watched the door. When the knob began to turn, Raft slammed his shoulder into the door. A shot went off. They stepped into the doorway and saw the man on the floor, a gun in his hand. Tully fired a round into the man's stomach and then quickly moved to kick the man square in the mouth.

Raft found the wallet in Lenny's jacket pocket.

Lenny Archer knew he was a dead man. Tully held the barrel of the gun against Lenny's temple.

"It's not too late, Leonard," Tully said. "We call for an ambulance and you survive this mess. All you need to do is help us out a little."

Lenny Archer could feel the life spilling out of the center of his body.

"Is your partner in on this?" Tully asked.

"No."

"You wouldn't lie to us at a time like this, would you, Leonard?"

"No."

"Any last words?"

Archer closed his eyes, felt the lightness in his head and saw the bright light behind his eyelids.

"Life is a carnival," Lenny Archer said.

Tully pulled the trigger.

JAKE DIAMOND

I met Jimmy Pigeon on the set of a film shoot on a Los Angeles sound stage. All I knew about private investigators was what I had found in the Hollywood movies I was desperately trying to break into.

Nick Charles, Philip Marlowe, Sam Spade.

After arriving in LA in pursuit of fame and fortune, I had managed to land several small film roles. Very small. Always a low budget crime melodrama. Always a second-string petty criminal or thug. If it was a prison movie—a man framed and incarcerated for a crime he didn't commit—I would be the slow-witted convict at the far end of the mess hall table eyeballing the hero's mashed potatoes as he laid out plans for escape. If it was a heist film—an FBI agent negotiating the release of hostages following a failed bank robbery attempt—I was the gang member lurking in the background listening stupidly while the boss and his right hand man argued the destination of the getaway jet. On the film shoot where I met Pigeon, it was kidnapping. A private eye was employed by a prominent politician to locate his young daughter being held for ransom. The abductors had strongly advised the girl's father against involving the police. I played the role of the kidnapper with the fewest lines.

Jimmy was a genuine private investigator engaged as a consultant for the production. Pigeon's job was to help the actor playing the PI in the film look more like a real private eye than an actor playing one, which was nearly an impossible task. I watched Jimmy closely while we were on the set together, his character, concentration, style and charisma. I talked with him about his work as often as he would allow between takes, studying his every move as if I would one day be competing for the lead role in *The Jimmy Pigeon Story*. And then something entirely unexpected and unexplained occurred. I found myself much more fascinated with the notion of *being* a private eye than with the idea of portraying one. On the final day of shooting I found the nerve to ask Jimmy what he thought of my wild impulse. Pigeon invited me to visit his Santa Monica office to mull it over.

A week later, Jimmy was sitting at his desk looking at me as if he wasn't sure where to begin or whether or not to begin at all. I sat opposite Pigeon in what he informed me was the *client chair*. I was learning already.

"Well, if nothing else," Pigeon finally said, "Jake Diamond is a perfect name for a PI. Did you come up with it yourself?"

"Gift from my parents," I said. "How about yours?"

"James C. Pigeon," he said. "Since day one."

"C?"

"Not important," Jimmy said. "Why do you want to give up acting? Believe me, it's a lot more glamorous than what I do. And certainly more lucrative."

"There's not enough glamour to go around," I answered, "and I'm weary of waiting for some to get around to me. I wondered if you ever considered taking on a partner."

"Had a few."

"And?"

"How about this, Jake," Jimmy said. "I'll tell you the story of my last partner and then you tell me if you want to leave the bright lights of Hollywood for the dark alleys of Southland."

As he was making his offer, Pigeon had pulled a bottle of bourbon and two small glasses from a drawer in his desk and began pouring.

"Sounds fair," I said as he passed me a glass.

"There's not too much about fair in this particular story, Jake."

Jimmy took a pack of Camels from his shirt pocket, lit one and dropped the package onto the desk between us.

"Light up if you like," Jimmy Pigeon said.

And he began.

JIMMY PIGEON

Jimmy Pigeon sat up in his bed. His eyes were leaking like a faucet. He grabbed a roll of toilet paper from the bedside table. It had replaced the empty tissue box sometime during the night. Pigeon sopped up the tears running down his cheeks. His right nostril was packed as solid as a car full of clowns. Jimmy considered trying to blow his nose but he was afraid of what might spill out of his ears. He had hardly slept all night, the plop plop fizz fizz cold and sinus cocktail he had guzzled before crawling into bed had him up to urinate every thirty minutes. He had arrived home late the previous night from a rare vacation, visiting his sister and her family in South Carolina. Six dreadful days. Everything down there, from the family station wagon to the family kitten, was covered in layers of fine yellow dust. By day two the pollen had settled on his shoes, had found refuge in his nose, mouth and eyes. By day three he could barely breathe. His sister, her husband and the kids seemed unaffected, immune, adapted, empirical validation of some Darwinian theory. Pigeon dried his face again and made his way to the bathroom. He adjusted the water to a few degrees below scalding and he stepped into the shower, making a plaintive wish for an unobstructed nasal passage.

Ninety minutes later, Jimmy took the short walk from his apartment to the office. He looked out at the brown haze hovering over downtown Los Angeles in the distance. It was a sight for sore eyes. As he turned onto Fourth Street he spotted two uniformed officers planted at the front entrance to his office building. Pigeon pulled a business card from his wallet and he quickened his pace. One of the young patrolmen stopped Jimmy at the door.

"Can I help you, sir," he asked.

"Just trying to get to work," Jimmy said, carefully offering the officer his card.

"Please wait here, sir," the officer said. He turned and carried the card into the building.

"Something happen?" Jimmy asked the second uniform.

"Officer Sutton will be right back, sir," the cop said and then nervously added, only for something to say, "there was a high pollution warning this morning."

"Love it," Jimmy said, taking in a deep breath for the first time in nearly a week.

The uniform returned his attention to the street.

A few minutes later, Sutton was back.

"Would you please come with me, Mr. Pigeon," he said.

Jimmy followed Sutton into the building and up to the second floor.

The building superintendent stood in the hall, pale as a ghost. He looked at Jimmy and then turned his eyes away. At the office door, Jimmy immediately noticed the crack in the opaque glass pane which ran diagonally across the hand painted words. *Archer and Pigeon, Private Investigation.*

Sutton pushed the door open. Jimmy's eyes went to the floor. Lenny Archer, his face nearly unrecognizable, lying in what seemed an ocean of blood.

Pigeon sadly looked away and surveyed the room. It had been turned upside down. File cabinet drawers open, papers scattered everywhere. Two men in white lab coats dusting for prints. Two plain clothed detectives staring back at him. The older of the two starting toward him.

"Are you okay, Mr. Pigeon," the detective said. "You don't look very well."

Allergies, Jimmy thought to say, *aversion to violent death.*

"When did this happen?" Jimmy asked.

"I can't say. The call came in a few hours ago. The medical examiner is on his way. We'll know more after he takes a look. Do you feel up to a few questions?"

"Give me a moment," Jimmy said. "I need some air. Can we talk outside?"

"Sure. We'll be down in a few minutes."

Jimmy walked back down and out of the building. He passed Sutton and the other uniform at the door. They had nothing to say. He walked twenty feet from the entrance, leaned against the building and lit a cigarette.

Jesus Christ, Lenny, what the fuck was it about?

Jimmy was crushing the cigarette under his shoe a few minutes later as the two detectives approached him.

"Go ahead, ask," Jimmy said before either could speak.

The older of the two took charge. The other detective took notes.

"When was the last time you saw your partner?"

"Monday evening, a week ago today. I left town early Tuesday morning, got back in late last night."

"Did you speak with Mr. Archer while you were gone?"

"No. I imagined Lenny could stay out of trouble for six days."

"Do you have any idea about why this happened?"

"None."

"Whoever it was seemed to be searching for something."

"No idea," said Jimmy.

"A case you were working on? Something particularly sensitive or dangerous?"

"Nothing I was involved in," Jimmy said. "Nothing Lenny told me anything about."

"Did you usually work separate cases?"

"Most of the time."

"So, you can't really help us on this."

"I'll let you know as soon as I learn anything."

"Mr. Pigeon, it would be much better for all concerned if you left this to us."

Not much better for Lenny.

"I didn't get your names," Jimmy said. "I thought I knew all of the Santa Monica homicide detectives."

"I'm Detective Raft and my partner is Detective Tully. We're LASD," said Raft, handing Jimmy a Los Angeles County Sheriff's Department business card.

"Oh?" said Jimmy.

"We were handy," Raft said. "Can you tell us anything about Mr. Archer's next-of-kin?"

"He had none," said Jimmy.

"Here's the ME," said Tully. "I'll take him up."

Tully started toward the Ford that had pulled up in front of the building. An ambulance turned onto Fourth Street. Tully led the Santa Monica Medical Examiner into the building. Solomon Meyers, a familiar face.

"When can I get back into the office?" Jimmy asked.

"Hopefully by early this evening. Is there somewhere I can reach you before then?" Raft asked.

"I'm not sure where I'll be. You have my card. You can reach me at the office number, hopefully by early this evening. Can I go now?"

"Sure," said Raft. "I think that's all for the time being. You have *my* card, if there's anything we can do."

"Thanks, I'll let you know," Jimmy said and he quietly walked away.

Raft returned to the office. The medical examiner was studying the corpse, the ambulance drivers were waiting for the ME to release the body, the crime scene investigators were dusting, collecting, shooting photographs. Detective Raft called Detective Tully out into the hall.

"Do you think Pigeon knows anything?" asked Tully.

"I don't believe so," said Raft. "Archer and Richards both said no. But Pigeon is a snoop and from what I hear a very good one. And he has a poor fucking attitude. We'll need to keep a close eye on him."

"Do you think they've found Richards yet?"

"I'm sure they have," Raft said. "I imagine that's why the Santa Monica PD was too busy to take this one."

Pigeon spent the remainder of the day alone. He sat for hours at the Santa Monica Pier, watching the ocean. He dropped into a few bars along Third Street, nursing more than one drink in each saloon. A toast to Lenny Archer. At a table in the rear of Murphy's Saloon four men in military uniform, all in their late sixties or early seventies, sang patriotic songs and tipped drinks in honor of the fiftieth anniversary of the allied invasion of Normandy. It was too much celebration for Jimmy to handle. He left the bar and treated himself to a steak dinner before returning to his office.

Someone had tried valiantly to scrub the floor, most likely the building superintendent, but a large faint stain remained. The strong scent of bleach had taken the place of the hideous smell of fresh blood. The office was still in shambles. He knew he would need to call someone in to pick up, to fix the glass pane on the door, maybe drop an area rug down. He knew he wasn't up to it himself.

Jimmy went over to Lenny Archer's desk and opened the top drawer. In the top center drawer of each of their desks sat a small ceramic change bowl filled with coins and paper clips. Imbedded into the bottom of each bowl was a remote switch, a small button which started the tape machine that recorded sound through a microphone hidden in the ceiling light fixture. The tape recorder was hidden in the wall behind a metal vent cover. Jimmy emptied the bowl in Lenny's drawer.

The record button was depressed.

Jimmy went over to his own desk for a screwdriver. He detached the metal grill and he pulled out the machine. He carried it back to his desk and rewound the tape. He lit a cigarette and pressed the play button.

Pigeon could not identify the voices but he could tell there had been two men in the office with Lenny. The dialogue was audible, as were the background noises. The first gunshot followed by a close second. The awful sounds of the beating Lenny had taken. The brutal interrogation, a name mentioned more than once. Richards.

Ed Richards.

Something to go on.

They had found what they came looking for; Lenny had been of no use to them.

And then the final fatal gunshot.

Pigeon replaced the tape recorder and switched on the small portable TV hoping to catch the late local news. He pulled the pint of bourbon from his desk and drank from the bottle. Jimmy caught the lead story, a Santa Monica author and journalist found shot to death in his beach house. The place had been ransacked. The Santa Monica police suspected a robbery turned felony homicide.

The name of the victim was Edward Richards.

Jimmy turned off the TV, slipped the bottle into his jacket pocket and left the office. He stopped at the front entrance to check the mail. He unlocked the box and found two bills and a postcard. The card had been addressed to Jimmy at his sister's place in South Carolina, but the street address had been transcribed incorrectly and the postcard was stamped *Return to Sender*. On the front of the card was a photo of the Santa Monica City Hall Building and on the back side of the card was an eight word message to Pigeon.

Chasing Charlie Chan.
Wish you were here.
Lenny.

VINNIE STRINGS

Jimmy Pigeon had another bout with sleep, the restless night plagued more by elegy than allergy. Pictures and sounds. Lenny Archer's battered face, the clamor of his brutal punishment. Lenny, who only a week earlier, sat at his desk laughing at Jimmy's inability to master call-waiting.

"Fuck, I lost the first caller."

"You need to get a desk telephone with a hold button," Lenny had said. "Meanwhile, just let the answering service pick up the second call."

"If you got your nose out of that book for a minute maybe *you* could pick up the phone once in a while," said Jimmy. "What the hell is it that's so damn interesting?"

Lenny held up the large volume for Jimmy to view.

Homes of the Hollywood Stars, History and Mystery.

"Looks riveting."

"You'd be surprised."

"Do me a favor, Lenny. Take that thing home with you and leave it at home so you'll have both hands free here in the office while I'm out of town."

"I might not even bother coming in while you're gone," Lenny had teased.

As Jimmy dragged himself out of bed Tuesday morning he thought about Lenny's banter. *Staying away from the office would have been a smart idea, Lenny. What the hell were you up to?* Pigeon made a mental note to look for the book Archer had been so absorbed in.

An hour later, Jimmy walked over to Meg's Café on the Third Street Promenade and took a seat at the counter. In the blink of an eye, Margaret Kelly rushed out of the kitchen to greet him.

"You look terrible, Jimmy," she said.

"Nice welcome home, Meg."

"Your eyes are all puffy. If I didn't know you better, I'd think you'd been crying."

"I still haven't purged the South Carolina ragweed," Jimmy said. "How about coffee?"

"Sure."

Meg placed a ceramic mug on the counter and reached for the coffee pot.

"I guess I'll skip asking you how you enjoyed your vacation," she said as she poured.

"Lenny Archer was murdered."

"No."

"Sometime late Sunday or very early yesterday morning. In the office. Shot and beaten and shot again."

"Who? Why?"

"No clue."

"My God, Jimmy," Meg said, resting her hands on the counter for support. "He was here Friday evening. I sat with him for a while. How horrible."

"What did he talk about?"

"Nothing important. Lenny had his face buried in a book; he kept showing me pictures of houses. Errol Flynn lived here, died in the saddle. Jean Harlow lived here; Clark Gable planted the rose bushes. Not my idea of priceless information, but Lenny could make just about anything seem vital. I can't believe he's dead."

"Did he mention Charlie Chan?"

"Charlie Chan the Oriental sleuth?"

"I don't know," said Jimmy, pulling the post card from his jacket. "Lenny sent this."

Meg looked at both sides of the card.

"No, Jimmy," she said. "Charlie Chan didn't come up. What are you going to do?"

"Find out who did this to Lenny and why. Do you mind if I use your telephone?"

"Of course not," she said, grabbing the wireless hand set and passing it to Jimmy.

* * *

Vinnie Stradivarius was a lanky twenty-year-old with a mop of red hair. Two years out of high school and still living with his widowed mother in a house near Echo Park just west of Dodger Stadium. Vinnie had no work other than the odd jobs Jimmy Pigeon tried to throw his way. Pigeon had been strapped with Vinnie since Sarge Stradivarius fell or was pushed off the roof of a seven story building in downtown Los Angeles when the boy was fifteen.

Vinnie's father had been an insurance investigator and a compulsive gambler, famous for being behind in payments to loan sharks from one end of the county to the other. Jimmy and Sarge met at a high-stakes poker match in LA and got to talking after the game. Later, Sarge engaged Pigeon occasionally as outside consultant on insurance fraud cases and Jimmy came to know the family. When Sarge went off the roof his own employers tried to default payment on the life insurance benefits, alleging suicide. Frances Stradivarius reached out to Jimmy. With assistance from a friend in the LAPD and a resourceful attorney, Jimmy managed to have the cause of death officially ruled as accidental and the widow collected double-indemnity; although Jimmy always suspected Stradivarius was assisted over the ledge by someone he owed money to. Over the sixteen months it took to win the case, Vinnie adopted Jimmy as a replacement father.

Vinnie Stradivarius inherited three things from his late father. The subsidy of a substantial life insurance settlement, the nickname *Strings* and the gambling gene. It took a good deal of effort on Jimmy's part to keep the kid out of the same sort of trouble Sarge had fallen into time and time again until his time ran out. Pigeon found keeping Vinnie busy was most effective.

Vinnie Strings owned no alarm clock; he woke up when he woke up and rarely before noon unless his mother had a reason to yank him out of bed. It was nine in the morning when Pigeon phoned the Stradivarius home from the counter at Meg's Café.

Vinnie's mother took the phone call and went to roust her son. She opened the door to his bedroom, where all of the windows were covered by dark shades. Pitch black, the only light coming in from the hall.

"Vinnie, wake up."

Strings half opened his eyes, the silhouette of his mother standing in the lit doorway looked like something from *The Exorcist.* Fran switched on the ceiling light.

"Vinnie, wake up," she repeated.

"Jesus, Mom," Vinnie moaned, blinded. "What time is it? It feels like the middle of the night."

"Jimmy Pigeon is on the phone," she said.

Vinnie came wide awake and found the receiver of his bedside telephone.

"Jimmy. What's up?"

"I need your help here, Vinnie," Jimmy said.

Vinnie loved to help and occasionally managed.

"I can be there in an hour," Strings said.

"Make it two; meet me at the office at eleven."

"Can I fix you something to eat?" Meg asked when Jimmy handed her the phone after the call to Vinnie.

"Just some rye toast," Pigeon said. He picked up his coffee mug and a newspaper from the counter and moved to a booth at the café window.

The death of Edward Richards made page one. Richards had reported for the *Santa Monica Outlook* for less than a year, after three years on the staff of the *Beverly Hills Weekly.* Richards had published several non-fiction books, most notably a biography of the British movie actor Leslie Howard, best known for his role in *Gone With The Wind* and his heroic death in a downed RAF bomber during the Second World War. Funeral arrangements for Richards were noted. Lenny Archer's death made page twenty-six. There was nothing reported to suggest any connection between the two homicides. There was nothing about funeral plans for Lenny Archer.

It suddenly dawned on Pigeon that since Archer had no family, it would be up to Jimmy to handle the details.

Meg came over with the rye toast and the coffee pot.

"What now?" Meg asked as she poured coffee. "You look worse than you did when you walked in."

"I was thinking about Lenny, how alone he was."

"Lenny was far from alone, Jimmy," Meg said, taking a seat. "He had plenty of friends and plenty of women and he always had a good time."

"And no one to bury him."

"I'd bury him, Jimmy. He was your friend and partner. Why would you need to look further than that? If Lenny had no wife or children to lament his passing, it was entirely his choice. Lenny was a charming, funny guy. He is going to be missed and remembered. What's really bothering you, Jimmy?"

"Maybe it has me wondering who will remember me."

"You are unforgettable, Jimmy. Stop being so morbid. I'll help you with the funeral and burial, but what makes you think Lenny's brother wouldn't want to take care of it?"

"Lenny hadn't spoken with his brother in years."

"That doesn't mean his brother isn't interested. He should at least be notified of Lenny's death."

"I wouldn't know where to begin looking for him."

"Jesus, Jimmy, you're a detective. Stop moping. Eat your toast," Meg said and she headed back to her cooking.

Fifteen minutes later, Jimmy returned the empty plate and the coffee mug to the counter. Meg came back out front from the kitchen.

"I'm heading over to Lenny's apartment before I meet Vinnie at the office. I'd like to locate the book Lenny was so wrapped up in and, while I'm at it, maybe learn something about how to find his brother."

"Good, that's more like the Jimmy Pigeon I know and love. Why don't you let me feed you tonight? I have the evening off; I could fix dinner at my place."

"Eight?"

"Perfect," Meg said, "and Jimmy?"

"Yes."

"Find out who killed your friend and partner. Lenny would have done the same for you."

***

Jimmy Pigeon met Lenny Archer at an annual conference of the California Association of Licensed Investigators in San Francisco three years earlier. At the time, Jimmy was living in Los Angeles and working out of a Westwood office. At the CALI conference, Lenny Archer moderated a seminar in surveillance. That night, Jimmy cornered Archer with some questions and they spent hours talking shop; Jimmy sipping bourbon and Lenny guzzling orange juice.

Jimmy complained that business was slow in LA; there was too much competition from ex-cops and larger agencies. Lenny complained he had more work than he could handle.

Two months later, Pigeon's name was added to the door of Archer's Santa Monica office.

Jimmy arrived at the office ten minutes before eleven. He had visited Lenny's apartment. After letting himself in with the spare key he carried in his wallet, Jimmy had searched for the book on celebrity homes. No luck. Pigeon hadn't thought to look for it in the office the day before; he hoped Lenny had ignored his advice about taking the book home. Jimmy did find some documents that might help settle Archer's affairs, but nothing to help locate Lenny's brother.

Jimmy was combing the office when Vinnie pushed the door open. Strings looked into the room and then back at the cracked window.

"What the hell happened here?"

"Lenny was murdered."

"Jesus, Jimmy, that's fucked," was all that Vinnie could think to say.

"I need you to clean this place up, Vinnie. You know where all the files go. Then I want you to find someone to replace that glass."

Vinnie finally noticed the large stain on the floor.

"Oh man, is that blood."

"And I need you to find a rug to cover that up," Jimmy said. "Nothing too fancy."

"What are you looking for?"

"A book. And I can't fucking find it anywhere."

"Can I help?"

"You can get started picking up, Vinnie. There's two hundred dollars on my desk for any expenses. Do you think you can handle this?"

"Yes, I can handle it. I'm not an idiot," Vinnie said and quickly began picking up folders from the floor.

"I didn't mean to snap at you, Vinnie. I'm sorry. It's been a really bad week."

"No sweat, Jimmy, I only want to help."

"And I appreciate it, Vinnie," Jimmy said. The room was beginning to close in on him. He had looked everywhere imaginable in search of the book. "Listen Vinnie, I need to get out of here for a while. I'll check back with you later this afternoon."

"No problem. And Jimmy," Vinnie said as Pigeon moved for the door.

"Yes."

"I'll keep my eye out for a book."

"That would be good. It's a big book, *Homes of the Hollywood Stars.*"

"I love that kind of stuff," Vinnie said as Jimmy left the office.

Jimmy walked over to the newly remodeled main branch of the Santa Monica Public Library on Sixth Street. The young man at the service counter was scanning books he pulled from a large wheeled canvas bin.

Jimmy doubted Vinnie would stumble over the book Lenny had been reading; Jimmy had gone through Archer's place and the office thoroughly. Pigeon was hoping the library owned a copy so he could at least get a look at.

"I'm looking for a book," Jimmy said when the clerk finally looked up.

"You came to the right place."

The nametag on his lapel identified the comedian as WHITMAN DONALDSON.

"A particular book," Jimmy said.

"Could you give me the author's name and book title?"

"*Homes of the Hollywood Stars,*" said Jimmy. "Can't tell you who wrote it."

The kid punched his computer keyboard.

"We have one copy, sir. Checked out."

"Could you tell me who borrowed it?"

"I'm afraid I can't. I could tell you when it's due in," said Donaldson, "but the identity of the borrower is confidential."

Dead end. Jimmy was debating his next masterful move when something in the bin beside Donaldson caught his eye.

"Well, how do you like that?"

"Excuse me?"

"What are those?" Jimmy asked, pointing.

"They came in last night, through the after-hours drop box."

"Could you do me a huge favor, Whitman?" Jimmy asked, pulling a handkerchief from his pocket.

"What kind of favor?"

"Could you grab that book? The one we've been talking about. And please use this to handle it. I'd like to borrow it."

"What's this about? Are you a cop or something?"

"Something. Private eye," said Jimmy.

"No kidding."

"No kidding. Could you help me out here, Whitman?" Pigeon asked, holding out the handkerchief.

The kid tentatively took the handkerchief and used it to pick out the book and place it on the counter.

Jimmy glanced at the book cover and the name of the author below the title.

Edward Richards. No kidding at all.

"You'll need a library card," Donaldson said.

"Never leave home without it," Jimmy said, pulling the card from his wallet.

Donaldson took the card, scanned it and the book, and stood waiting for Jimmy's next instruction.

"Do you have a bag?" asked Jimmy.

The kid reached under the counter and came up with a large plastic bag labeled *SMPL.*

"Perfect, could you place the book in the bag?"

Donaldson did as he was asked and then he handed the handkerchief and library card back to Pigeon.

"We're almost done, Whitman. And I can't tell you how much I appreciate it," said Jimmy. He returned the card to his wallet, slipped out a twenty-dollar bill and put it on the counter. "Now, what if I try to guess the name of the last borrower and you blink your eyes if I guess correctly? Would that help ease the confidentiality dilemma?"

"I guess it could," said Donaldson, slipping the bill into his pocket.

"By chance, was it borrowed by Leonard Archer?"

The kid checked his computer monitor again.

"Yes."

"And you're sure it was dropped off last night?"

"Yes."

"Thank you," Jimmy said, grabbing the plastic bag.

"Please don't mention it," said Donaldson.

Jimmy walked to his apartment. He pulled a pair of latex gloves from a box in a kitchen drawer, moved to his recliner and started through the book. First he checked for markings. Pencil marks, bent page corners, slips of paper. Anything that might indicate Archer's particular interest. Nothing. But Jimmy was certain there was something here. Lenny was already dead when the book was dropped at the after-hours box, someone else had returned it to the library. Who? And why bother, if not to insure that an overdue book wouldn't bring unwelcome attention to the dead man who had last checked it out, the dead man who had written it, or the curious coincidence. Pigeon began to read from page one, hoping for a clue. Twenty pages in, his eyes were burning. Residual effects of the vacation in South Carolina. Jimmy decided to give his eyes a moment's rest. The ringing of a phone woke him. He couldn't feel his hands. He glanced at his wristwatch, almost five; he had slept for nearly four hours. He tore off the plastic gloves and grabbed for the telephone.

"The window guy is over here," Vinnie said when Jimmy answered the call. "If you want the new window painted he needs to know how you want it to read."

"Is he done installing the glass?"

"He's finishing up now."

"Cut him loose, ask him to send a bill. I'll be there in fifteen minutes."

Pigeon used one of the discarded gloves to return the book to the plastic library bag. He rinsed his face at the bathroom sink, slipped into a fresh shirt, grabbed the bag and walked back to the office.

The question of how to adorn the office door window was the furthest thing from Jimmy Pigeon's mind.

Pigeon peeked through the newly repaired office door and caught Vinnie Strings in an unguarded moment; sitting behind Jimmy's desk, hands locked behind his neck, justifiably admiring the fine job he had done cleaning the mess left by Lenny Archer's murderers. Vinnie jumped to attention as Jimmy pushed the door open.

"Good work, Vinnie," Pigeon said. "Very good work."

Jimmy walked across the Oriental rug now covering the area where Lenny had died. He recalled the position of Archer's body and put it together with what he had heard on the tape recording. Archer had moved to the door, had been knocked back, voluntarily or involuntarily fired his weapon and been shot. Lenny kept a small handgun in his desk, the report from Archer's gun was clearly audible but apparently not loud enough to attract outside attention. The second gunshot, and the shot that ended Archer's life, were muted. Pigeon looked around the office searching for Archer's spent bullet. He found the spot, high on the wall above the door, where a small section of plasterboard had been removed. Jimmy guessed Archer had been going down when his weapon fired. Vinnie followed Jimmy's gaze.

"I picked up some plaster and paint," Strings said.

"We'll deal with that later," said Jimmy. "Now I need you to get this over to Ray Boyle at Parker Center."

Pigeon walked over to Vinnie and handed Strings the plastic bag from the library.

"Don't touch the book; we need Boyle to have the lab check for prints. Ask Ray to call me with results. When they're done, I want you to pick it up and bring it back here."

"Boyle will want to know why you're sending it over to him at the LAPD when there's a crime lab just a few blocks from here," said Vinnie, wondering himself.

"Tell him you have no idea and let's leave it at that for now, until I've thought it out some. Be patient, Vinnie, I'll keep you informed and I'll need your help."

"Great," said Vinnie. "I'm on my way."

The suggestion that he would be involved was enough for Strings to temporarily suspend his nagging curiosity.

Vinnie headed out the door, a young man on a mission.

Jimmy debated whether to call to inquire about the police investigation. Detective Raft had made it clear that Pigeon's help wasn't needed or welcome, but at the same time indifference would be suspect. Jimmy decided he would check in with Raft in the morning.

It was after six, Jimmy had a dinner engagement with Meg Kelly at eight. He left the office and as he shut the door he glanced at the newly installed window. He decided that before it read *Pigeon Investigation* he would work to earn the title.

"This is all he had?" asked Jackson Masters, looking over the rough notes that had cost Lenny Archer and Edward Richards their lives.

"That's all Richards gave to the PI. That's all we found in the dick's office. We searched Richard's place and grabbed his computer. And had a long talk with him before he died. He told us it was all he had. I believed him."

"He was researching a fucking book?"

"That's what he said. That's what Richards did, he wrote fucking books."

"What if someone connects the two homicides?" Masters asked.

"I don't see that happening. We were on Richards from the time he stopped at the hotel asking questions about the woman. He never met with Archer before Sunday night."

"Use your head, Frank. Richards had to have *spoken* to Archer before Sunday to set up the meeting and Archer had the library book in his office. There could be telephone records. Archer may have dropped the writer's name. We need to establish a connection before someone else does."

"What sort of connection?"

"Do what you always do, make it look like something drug related," said Masters, tossing the notes into the fireplace. "What happened to Richard's computer?"

"It was a laptop; Tully took care of it with a sledge hammer."

"Will Tully hold up?"

"Absolutely. You should have seen him work on Archer and Richards. Tully's got ice in his veins."

"Throw some evidence around and find a fall guy. I want these two homicides cleared before the old man gets back."

"I might be better if I knew what this was all about," said Raft.

"How long have we been doing business, Frank?"

"A while."

"And haven't you always been well taken care of?"

"Very well."

"I ask you to do something and you do it, am I right?"

"Yes."

"And you do not ask me why," said Masters, reaching into a desk drawer. He pulled out a brick-sized package neatly wrapped in plain brown paper and tossed it to Raft. "Don't spend it all in one place, Frank. And keep an eye on Jimmy Pigeon. I know the man's reputation and he's no idiot."

"No problem."

"That's what you said when I asked you to keep an eye on Ed Richards. Use the back door when you leave. And don't call me, Frank. I want to learn about your progress from the newspapers."

They had been silent during dinner. Meg had waited quietly and patiently for Jimmy to bring up the subject of Lenny Archer.

"That's the best meal I've had in a long time," Jimmy said as he dried the last of the dishes and Meg poured the coffee at the kitchen table.

"How would you know, Jimmy? You told me this morning that everything you've put in your mouth since last Wednesday has tasted like ragweed."

"I simply wanted to let it be known I consider you a remarkable chef."

"The fact that you eat in my café five or six times a week says it all. Lose the dishtowel and sit, Jimmy. We need to talk a little about Lenny."

"I don't know much more than I did this morning, Meg."

"We'll get to that, but first we need to think about what to do when the police release Lenny's body."

"I found papers at his apartment. Lenny served with the Navy; they owe him a military burial. I'll check into the details tomorrow."

"Let me know. I'll plan to be there for the service," said Meg. "Any luck locating the brother?"

"Not yet."

"What do you know about him?"

"Only that they worked together before the falling out. I suppose his brother is or was in the business."

"Do you have a name?"

"It might have been Norman, or Nelson, I can't recall. Lenny stayed away from the subject."

"Well, that's something to go on. I'm off tomorrow morning; I can do some digging around if it would help."

"It would help a lot. Meg, when you saw Lenny on Friday did he say anything about the author of the book he was looking through?"

"No."

"The book was written by Edward Richards, the same Ed Richards who was killed a few hours after Lenny died."

"My God, Jimmy, I'd met Ed Richards. He wrote for the *Santa Monica Outlook*, he came into the café a few times."

"Ever see Richards and Lenny together?"

"No. Do you think the murders were connected?"

"I do."

"What do the police think?"

"I haven't heard."

"Did you tell the detectives about the book?"

"No, I'm waiting to see what their investigation turns up," Jimmy said. "And I want to talk with Ray Boyle first. I trust Ray."

"And you don't trust the detectives on the case?"

"It's more a matter of not knowing them. I know Ray."

"You look worn out, Jimmy. You've had a rough few days."

"I have a feeling it's going to get rougher, Meg. I feel as if I need to keep moving on this before it slips away from me."

"Do you have time for another cup of coffee?"

"Sure, I'd love another cup of coffee."

Meg rose from the kitchen table and moved for the coffee pot.

"Jimmy," she said.

"Yes?"

"It would be okay if you slipped your shoes off."

It was a welcome invitation.

Pigeon slipped off his shoes and put them back on his feet the following morning.

Jimmy was planted in the chair at his desk before nine on Wednesday morning. He surveyed the office, wall-to-wall, floor to ceiling. Looking for anything he might have missed or the police might have missed. Anything Lenny might have left to help explain the cryptic postcard.

He was rewarded with a stabbing headache and decided to try his luck with phone calls. Pigeon pulled Detective Raft's card from his wallet and reached for the telephone. Before he could get to the handset, the phone was ringing.

"Archer and Pigeon," Jimmy said. It was habit.

"This is Boyle. What the fuck is going on out there?"

Ray Boyle was an LAPD homicide detective. When Jimmy and Ray didn't dwell too much on their earlier professional encounters they got along fairly well.

"Good morning to you too, Ray."

"Your right-hand delinquent snagged me before I could get out of my office last night and he handed me a library book to check for fingerprints. I can only guess you chose not to employ the Santa Monica Police Department lab because you were afraid they would either laugh you out of town or simply stone you."

"Did you run it Ray?"

"Yes, I fucking ran it."

"No prints, right?"

"Not one," said Boyle. "So what the fuck is going on out there?"

"Lenny Archer was killed."

"I heard. I was sorry to hear it."

"Someone took that book from our office, Ray, wiped it clean and dropped it in a slot at the library the night Archer died. The author of the book coincidentally turned up dead the same night. Edward Richards."

"No shit. Who caught the case?"

"I don't know who caught the Richard's homicide, but LASD took Lenny. Since when does the LA County Sheriff's Department bother with our little beach town?"

"It happens; luck of the draw, the LASD gets around. Who are the primaries?"

"Raft and Tully. Know them?"

"Tully, no. Raft, unfortunately. Had to work with him once or twice. Dealing with Frank Raft is no picnic. Look, Jimmy. All due respect to Archer, I liked the man, but I don't have the time or the desire to butt heads with Raft or the Sheriff's Department; not to mention the LAPD brass would seriously hate me sticking my nose in."

"Are you saying you can't help me, Ray?"

"I'm saying I'd rather you didn't ask."

"Preference noted. Help me, Ray."

"Fuck," said Ray Boyle. "What the hell do you need me to do?"

"I'm not sure yet, I need to check in with Raft and hear the official line. Meanwhile, maybe you could just keep an ear to the ground."

"Don't mention my name, Pigeon."

"Wouldn't dream of it, Ray. I'll send Vinnie Strings over to collect the book."

"Tell him he can pick it up in the lobby. I really don't need to see him again so soon," Boyle said. "That kid makes me nervous."

"I'm sure the feeling is mutual, Ray. I'll be in touch."

"I can hardly wait," said Boyle, just before the line went dead.

Jimmy placed the headset in its cradle and took a deep breath before lifting it again and punching in Raft's phone number at the LA County Sheriff's Department Malibu Station in Agoura. He was politely informed that Detective Raft was out in the field and Tully was out for the day. Jimmy left his name with a request that Raft return his call. Then he dialed directory assistance with the hope of finding a lead to information on the subject of United States Navy veteran burial services.

* * *

Ricardo Diaz sat at the counter of Armando's Diner in Woodland Hills trying to remove a strand of hair from his sausage and egg omelet without giving it too much thought.

He nearly had it locked between his thumb and index finger when Frank Raft hopped onto the stool beside him.

"High protein breakfast, Diaz?"

Diaz looked up from his plate. Raft sat grinning and nodding like a bobble-head doll on amphetamines.

"Detective Graft, did I forget to feed the parking meter? Don't you have more important things to do?"

"What makes you think you're not important to me, Ricky?"

"Only my friends call me Ricky, Frank."

"What makes you think I'm not your friend?" Raft asked. "How is your court case looking, Ricky?"

"According to my lawyer, it's hopeless; he was shocked when they let me out on bail. How is that for confidence? If I didn't know he was right on, I would fire the useless bastard. Why the interest? Worried about where you'll cop your buzz after they put me away?"

"Actually, I stopped by to offer you a way out."

"It's beyond you, Frank. The DA has me cold. Three kilos of cocaine with intent to sell, two priors, fifteen to twenty, end of story. I've got nothing to bargain with. I only pray the food in Chino is fucking better than this," Diaz said, pushing his plate away.

"Mexico is just a hop, skip and a bail jump away."

"Very clever, Raft, kick a man when he's down. For some sick reason I gave you more credit. They took every fucking thing I had; I don't have a dime to my name. What am I supposed to do in Mexico without bread? Pick bananas until some bounty hunter finds my fucking tree? Where the fuck was your helping hand when I got busted?"

"One step over the line, Ricky. I told you a hundred times not to do business here in the hills. I warned you if the LAPD dropped you my hands were tied."

"So, you stopped by to say I told you so."

"Like I said, Diaz, I stopped by to offer you a way out," said Raft. "Two hundred thousand cash and the bail bondsman doesn't send a headhunter after you."

"What the fuck do I have to do for that, Detective? Kill someone for you."

"Do you want to hear about it or would you rather fish hair out of your eggs?"

"I'm listening," said Ricardo Diaz.

It took nearly two hours and telephone calls to Los Angeles, Sacramento, Washington DC and San Diego before Jimmy finally reached the desk of a U.S. Navy bureaucrat who could offer useful information. It was almost too much information.

"According to our records, 1st Petty Officer Leonard Archer was honorably discharged and is therefore eligible for burial benefits. There are a number of options. His body can be laid to rest at Los Angeles National Cemetery or Fort Rosencrans National Cemetery here in San Diego. The government will provide the transfer of the remains to either location and will provide a military graveside service and headstone. This service will be open to friends and family members. If preferred, 1st Petty Officer Archer can be buried at sea from a ship out of Long Beach harbor. Burials at sea, however, are never open to civilians. Is there a surviving widow or dependent children?"

"None."

"In that case, all we will need to process the request, once you decide, are faxed copies of Petty Officer Archer's death certificate and DD214."

"DD214?"

"Enlisted Record of Separation or discharge papers."

Jimmy jotted down the fax number and ended the call. He phoned Meg Kelly at home with the update.

"I'll go back to Archer's apartment and look for the papers, then I'll try to find out about obtaining a death certificate," Jimmy said. "I wonder if Lenny would have wanted to be buried at sea."

"Lenny would probably prefer sitting in an urn above the wine rack at Angelo's restaurant," said Meg. "We can talk about options later. Meanwhile, could his brother's name be Nathan?"

"Could be."

"I found a Nathan Archer down in San Diego," Meg said. "A licensed private investigator. I left a message on his answering machine."

"What kind of message?"

"That if he had a brother Leonard, he should get in touch with you. I left your home and office numbers. I need to get to work, drop by when you can."

"Will do. Thanks for the help, Meg."

"Anytime. I have to run."

As soon as Jimmy replaced the receiver, there was a tapping on the office door.

"Come in," Pigeon called.

John Barnum opened the door, took a long look at the newly replaced window, stepped into the office and closed the door behind him.

"Could I have a few words with you, Pigeon?"

"Sure, Detective. Have a seat."

John Barnum was Santa Monica Police, Robbery/Homicide Division. Jimmy was not delighted to see him.

"I was sorry to hear about Archer," Barnum said, walking over to Jimmy's desk.

"I was under the impression you didn't care much for Lenny."

"It doesn't mean I like what happened to him," Barnum said, sinking into the client chair.

"If you're here about Lenny, the LASD beat you to it."

"We were out on another call and the Sheriff's Department helped us out as a courtesy, but the Archer case is ours as soon as LASD completes their preliminary report. How well did you know Edward Richards?"

"Never met the man," said Pigeon.

"Talk on the phone?"

"No."

"According to Richards' phone records, he called here three times in the past few weeks."

"Never spoke with him. I've been out of town."

"But you've heard of him."

"The newspaper reported he was killed during a house burglary."

"And the fact he was killed less than two hours after your partner was killed and had called here doesn't peak your interest?" asked Barnum. "I'm sorry if this is boring you, Pigeon, but I'd like to know what was going on between Archer and Richards."

"I have no idea, Barnum. What are you driving at? Are you suggesting their deaths were related? Do you have anything to go on beside a few phone calls?"

"Thanks for your help, Pigeon," Barnum said, refusing to bite and rising from his seat. "I'll be in touch."

Jimmy sat and watched Barnum leave the office.

Pigeon counted to ten and phoned Detective Ray Boyle at Parker Center.

"What now, Pigeon?"

"I just had a visit from John Barnum. SMPD has the Richards case and they're going to take over the Archer case. Barnum is thinking about putting the two together."

"What's he going on?"

"All he gave me was phone calls from Richards to the office here. Can you find out what he's not telling?"

"Jesus, Pigeon, I've got a stack of open cases on my fucking desk. What did you give Barnum?"

"The same. Nothing. We danced around, stepping on each other's toes."

"If you have something, give it up. Barnum is a smart cop and he can get really ugly if he discovers you're holding out."

"I need a leg up first, Ray. Help me."

"I'll try. Don't call me, I'll call you," Boyle said and killed the connection.

Jimmy called Vinnie Strings. Vinnie's mother had to wake him.

"Vinnie, pick up the book at Parker. It's waiting for you in the lobby. I want you to check it out front to back, see if anything grabs you that may have got Lenny going. What do you know about Charlie Chan?"

"What do you want to know?" asked Vinnie. "Six novels, forty-five films in less than twenty years, three different actors playing Chan, a television series."

"Okay, save it for later, Vinnie," Jimmy cut him off. "Grab the book, look it over and meet me at Meg's Café at seven. I'll buy dinner."

"I'll be there. And Jimmy."

"Yes?"

"I forgot to return what was left of the two hundred yesterday."

"What did the rug set us back?"

"Eighty bucks."

"Keep the change, Vinnie. I'll see you at seven."

Jimmy put down the phone, grabbed his suit jacket and quickly left the office before the phone could ring again.

Jimmy picked up a club sandwich and a soft drink from a deli on Third Street, walked them down to a bench on the pier and called it lunch. A seagull greedily eyed the last of Pigeon's turkey club from its perch atop a bicycle rack. A teenage girl flew by on roller blades, sending the large bird into the air. A young mom pushed a stroller, stopping every few yards to retrieve the juice bottle her small passenger continually tossed overboard. An old man stood at a rail opposite Pigeon, dangling a fishing line into the ocean, speaking aloud to no one there, scolding a loved one for leaving him alone. A bearded man in an ancient Boston Red Sox ball cap held a paper cup out to Jimmy and politely asked for change.

"Change would do us all some good," Pigeon said, putting a dollar into the cup, tossing the sandwich wrapping and the empty soda can into a trash barrel and walking off the pier toward Lenny Archer's apartment building.

The gray haired landlady of the building stooped over a stone flower planter at the front entrance, picking out cigarette butts from around the stems of the tulips.

"There's no respect for beauty or personal property," she mumbled, turning to the sound of Jimmy's footsteps.

"How are you, Mrs. Epstein," Jimmy asked.

"There is no consideration, no grace," she sadly said. "It's horrible about Mr. Archer; he was a wonderful man, a wonderful tenant. He would help me with the garbage cans every Wednesday morning. This morning I had to pay a boy five dollars. Can you imagine such a thing, taking advantage of a helpless old woman? I miss my dear husband. It is terrible to lose your life's partner. What will become of Mr. Archer's possessions? I'll need to rent the rooms."

Jimmy hadn't thought at all about the contents of Lenny's apartment.

"I'll see it's taken care of before the end of the month, Mrs. Epstein," he offered.

"God bless you, Mr. Pigeon. There's a police officer up there now, I let him in," said the old lady.

"Okay."

"He is no gentleman," the woman added and turned back to her work.

Pigeon walked up to the second story, his enthusiasm considerably diminished. Jimmy found the door to Archer's apartment wide open. He looked in to find Detective Raft standing in the front room.

"Pigeon," Raft said. "I was just about to return your phone call. Come in. What brings you around?"

"I need to locate some papers the Navy needs to arrange for Archer's funeral. What brings you here?"

"Just taking a quick look around before I complete my report and hand it over to the SMPD. Did you happen to know Ed Richards, the reporter who was killed?"

"No."

"And Archer never mentioned Richards to you?"

"No. Are you thinking the deaths are connected?"

"We've established that Ed Richards phoned your office several times. Both your office and his home were searched by the perpetrators. Both Archer and Richards were shot in the head, execution style. Drug execution style."

"I never knew Archer to go anywhere near drugs."

"Isn't it possible Ed Richards was looking into the drug trade for a newspaper story and had employed your partner to help investigate?"

"Seems far-fetched," said Pigeon.

"Maybe, but it's all we have to go on at the moment."

"Who's handling ballistics?"

"We are. The bullet that killed Ed Richards will be picked up from Santa Monica. As soon as we get it to our lab we should be able to determine if both men were shot with the same weapon and present our results to SMPD."

"So you're suggesting Archer and Richards were silenced over an investigation into drug traffic?" Jimmy asked, finding the suggestion absurd.

"I'm saying SMPD will be looking into the possibility, yes. Once we send them our ballistics and medical reports the investigation will be in their hands."

"Who do I see about obtaining a copy of Lenny Archer's death certificate," asked Jimmy, changing the subject, "and to find out when his body will be released for burial?"

"We are sending Archer's body over to the Santa Monica Coroner late this afternoon; they should be able to provide that information. I'll leave you to look for what you need here," said Raft. "By the way, how were you planning to get into this apartment?"

"The same way you did, I suppose."

"So, you haven't been here before?" asked Raft. "I mean, since Archer's death?"

"No," said Jimmy.

"Feel free to call if there's anything I can do."

Jimmy watched Raft leave the apartment. When he heard Raft start down the stairs, he closed the door, sat on the sofa and considered the drug angle.

He considered it bullshit.

After leaving Archer's apartment, Detective Raft drove out to Tully's house in Sherman Oaks. He found his partner in the large back yard, trying to assemble a gas grill.

"You should have waited for this," Raft said, handing Tully a fistful of fifty-dollar bills. "You could have paid your kid to do that."

"My son couldn't unfold a card table," said Detective Tully, stuffing the bills into his pocket. "How did Masters react to the course of events?"

"He's not happy, he wants this cleared up and quick."

"So?"

"So, I have an idea," said Raft. "I need both weapons. The gun you used to kill Archer and the one you used on Richards."

"What makes you think I didn't get rid of them?"

"I know what a compulsive junk collector you are, Bob. I'm sure you have a few old charcoal grills in the garage."

"Three, actually. I've got both thirty-eights stashed over at my cabin," said Tully.

"Can you tell which gun is which?"

"Yes, Frank, I know which is which."

"Thank God, because I also need a bullet fired from the one you used on Archer," said Raft. "And it needs to appear as if it went into flesh and bone."

"There are a few stray dogs out there, I could pop one in the head and remove the slug."

"Good. Do it. I need both guns and the spent bullet by three. I'll meet you back here."

"Do you want to tell me about your *idea?*"

"Later," said Raft, leaving Tully to the chaotic heap of metal parts, bolts and tools on the lawn.

Pigeon dropped Archer's discharge papers back at his own apartment and grabbed the keys to his car. He drove a 1988 Chrysler LeBaron convertible. Power steering, brakes and windows, wood-trimmed, leather interior, seventy-seven thousand easy miles, showroom clean. He pulled out of the parking area behind his apartment building and headed out on Santa Monica Boulevard to Los Angeles.

Downtown, Jimmy miraculously found a parking space on South San Pedro near the corner of East 1st. He locked the car door and gave the ragtop a few gentle pats.

"Stick around," he said and then walked the two short blocks to Parker Center.

Jimmy had thought about calling ahead, but didn't want to give Detective Boyle the opportunity to tell him not to bother. He would have loved to surprise Boyle, but he knew that getting up to the Robbery Homicide Division Offices on the 3rd Floor without being announced and permitted through security was as good as impossible. Jimmy was hoping Boyle would give him a break and grant audience simply because he had made the trek, but he wouldn't bet on it. And then, as fate would have it, Jimmy entered the lobby of LAPD central headquarters and bumped into Sam Stephens heading out.

"Jimmy Pigeon," said Detective Stephens. "What brings you into our nightmare?"

"I need to see your partner."

"Is Ray expecting you?"

"No."

"Great. The cheap son of a bitch stuck me with the lunch check today. Allow me to escort you up; it'll serve the bastard right. No offense, Jimmy."

"None taken, Sam."

Pigeon followed Stephens through security and up the stairs to the door of the office Sam shared with Ray Boyle. Sam opened the door and poked his head in.

"I've got a surprise for you, Ray," he said.

"I don't like surprises," said Boyle from his desk.

"All the better," said Stephens as he ushered Jimmy into the room.

"Jimmy Pigeon, glad to see you," said Boyle. "I've been trying to reach you at your office."

"It figures," said Stephens. "Son of a bitch."

"Thanks for taking the time to bring Jimmy up," said Boyle. "I know you were in a rush to get somewhere."

"Don't mention it," said Stephens, stomping out.

"Trying to reach me at my office about what?"

"Your protégé, Vinnie Strings, picked up your library book about an hour ago. The kid walked out of the building and stepped into the path of a moving taxi cab on Los Angeles Street," said Ray. "An ambulance took him to Good Samaritan Hospital. Come on, I'll take you over there."

At three, Raft found his partner back behind the house swearing aloud as he fumbled through a toolbox for a half-inch socket.

"Fucking piece of shit."

"Calm down, Bobby, your face is going purple."

"Fuck," said Tully, throwing the ratchet wrench into the disorganized pile of designer outdoor gas grill parts.

"Did you get what I asked for?"

"In the bag," said Tully, pointing to a small cloth satchel sitting on a picnic bench.

Raft walked over to the bench and grabbed the bag.

"I have to fly," Raft said.

"Aren't you going to fill me in, Frank?"

"No time now. We'll talk later or in the morning. Have fun."

"Fucking piece of shit," Tully said again as Raft walked away.

When Raft reached the front of the house, he ran into Tully's son on his way in.

"Hey, Champ, how's my favorite centerfielder?"

"I thought Brett Butler was your favorite centerfielder, Uncle Frank."

"Not since you went three-for-four with six RBIs last Saturday. Your father is out back and he's in serious need of some help, Kevin."

"I need to get to practice, I just have time to drop off these school things and get changed."

"What do you have there?" asked Raft, finally noticing what the boy carried under his left arm.

"Check it out, it's really cool," Kevin said, dropping his school bag to the lawn and proudly displaying his prize to the detective. "It's a laptop computer; Dad gave it to me."

"It's very nice, Kevin. You're lucky to have such a generous father. I have to run, have a good practice."

Tully, you fucking fool, Raft thought as he climbed into his car for the drive to the SMPD crime lab.

At the lab, Raft signed-out the bullet removed from the skull of Edward Richards. Back in his car, Raft dug into the satchel for the spent bullet supplied by Tully. Using plastic gloves, he swapped the slugs. Raft placed the original evidence into the satchel and threw the bag behind the driver's seat. He took the substitute slug to the LASD evidence lab, where it would be compared with the slugs removed from Lenny Archer's head and stomach. With that business completed, Raft drove out to Woodland Hills to deliver the weapon that killed Archer into the hands of Ricky Diaz.

* * *

Pigeon sat quietly while Ray Boyle drove from Parker Center to Good Samaritan.

Jimmy was so anxious about Vinnie's condition he almost forgot the reason he had come out to see Ray in the first place. When it finally came back to mind, they were at the Emergency Room entrance and Pigeon decided it could wait.

They found Frances Stradivarius pacing in the hallway outside the recovery room.

"How is he, Fran?" Jimmy asked.

"He had a mild concussion, the x-rays were negative," she said. "His left leg was fractured badly; the surgeons set it in plaster and traction. A nurse just told me he's awake and they'll be moving him into a room shortly."

"Let us buy you a coffee, Fran," Jimmy said. "We'll let them know where we'll be and they'll let us know when we can see Vinnie. Have you met Detective Boyle?"

"Yes, the kind detective has helped my son out of a jam or two."

"The *kind* detective, well how about that," Jimmy said, smiling ironically.

"Don't spread it around," said Boyle.

Jimmy exchanged a few words with the nurse before he, Fran and Ray walked down to the hospital cafeteria. Less than twenty minutes later an orderly came to their table to tell them they could see the patient.

"I'll wait for you down here, Pigeon," Ray said. "I'm sure Vinnie will be fine, Fran, the kid is resilient."

They found Vinnie in bed, a bandage wrapped around his forehead, his leg suspended by pulley and cable. He looked as if he was having trouble keeping his eyes opened.

Vinnie was glad to see his mother and surprised to see Jimmy. Pigeon allowed Fran some time to fuss over her son before asking Strings how he felt.

"Like I was run over by a cab," said Vinnie. "I'm sorry, Jimmy."

"Sorry for what?"

"I think I lost the library book when the car hit me."

"Don't worry about it, Vinnie. Maybe one of the EMTs grabbed it off the street. I'm sure it will turn up or we can find another copy."

"I'll have lots of time to give it a good going over for you now," Vinnie said. "And I wanted to tell you all the stuff I know about Charlie Chan, but I'm very groggy. They gave me drugs and I can hardly stay awake."

"Relax, Vinnie, get some rest. I'll check on you in the morning."

Before leaving the room, Jimmy told Frances she should not hesitate to call him if she needed anything at all.

Boyle was waiting for Jimmy outside the cafeteria.

"I suppose you had something to bother me about before this distraction," Boyle said.

"Yes."

"Let's do it over dinner, I'm famished. I'll buy you a sandwich at Philippe's."

"I had a sandwich for lunch."

"But it wasn't a lamb French dip," said Boyle.

"No."

"With a cup of the Wednesday soup du jour."

"Oh?"

"Corn chowder."

"Lead the way," Pigeon said.

"So, all I need to do is stash this piece here in my place?" asked Ricardo Diaz, taking the .38 from Raft.

"Simple as that."

"Where's my cash?"

"I should have it in a day or two, I'll let you know," said the detective. "Meanwhile, do what you need to do to prepare for the move to sunny Guadalajara."

"If you're fucking with me, Frank, it would be a big mistake."

"Don't make threats, Ricky, it upsets me. Just get ready to disappear. I'll call you."

Diaz watched Raft walk out and then he looked down at the gun in his hand. Diaz thought about the high times he could have with two hundred grand below the border. Ricky Diaz wondered, just for a moment, why he deserved to be so fucking lucky.

BEAM AND BEETHOVAN

It is generally accepted as a historical fact that the French dip was originally created at Philippe's in downtown Los Angeles in 1918.

According to legend, Philippe Mathieu, the French-born proprietor, accidentally dropped a sliced French roll into the pan of hot juices while preparing a sandwich.

The patron, a Los Angeles policeman named French, told Philippe to use the bread as it was. The next day, Officer French returned with a group of fellow lawmen, each asking for their bread to be juice-dipped.

"So," asked Jimmy, between spoonfuls of corn chowder. "Was the sandwich named after the Frenchman, the bread or the cop?"

"Who cares?" said Ray Boyle. "So, what's on your mind?"

"I bumped into Raft. He insinuated Lenny and the newspaperman could have been murdered for snooping into the drug trade."

"And?"

"And it doesn't wash, Ray. Lenny Archer wouldn't have touched it. And there's the book. Someone thought it was important enough to bury back at the library and as far as I could see the book had nothing to do with drugs."

"Maybe you just didn't look close enough," said Boyle. "Where is the book now?"

"Vinnie lost it when he got hit by the taxi. It's probably being dragged to Ventura. But I don't buy it, Ray. Raft said they were working on a tip from an informant. Could you look into it?"

"I *did* some looking, and this whole business is a fucking circus sideshow. No one is sure who is doing what. The Sheriff's Department somehow got the ballistics and Santa Monica has the bodies. And anytime I ask a simple question I get told to mind my own fucking business."

"Damn," Jimmy said, "that reminds me. I was going to check into getting a copy of Lenny's death certificate for the government paper pushers. Raft told me LASD was sending Archer's body back to Santa Monica."

"That's exactly what I mean. The whole fucking business is like a Chinese fire drill. And the bottom line is this, Pigeon. However it shakes down, whoever is handling whatever evidence, the whole mess is out of my jurisdiction."

"I don't like it, Boyle."

"There's nothing to like about it. And admit it, if there was anything likable about it I doubt you would be here sharing it with me."

"Will you at least try finding out why they're trying to sell this drug angle, Ray?"

"And what will *you* be doing while I'm hanging my ass out in the wind?"

"I guess I'll try to find out if there's anyone at the newspaper who has any idea about what Richards was sticking his nose into."

"I'll say it once more, Pigeon. I'll see what I can do, no promises," said Boyle. "Now please, I beg you, let me eat this cold chowder before the fucking lamb gets here."

"I thought I asked you not to call me, Frank."

"We need to talk," said Raft. "We may have a problem."

"I don't like problems, Frank," Jackson Masters said, regretting he had answered the phone. "That is why I have you, Detective, so problems get solved before I need to hear about them."

"I have an idea for cleaning up the mess we made with Richards and the private dick. I want to run it by you before I go ahead. And then I need some advice, about Tully."

Masters listened patiently while Frank Raft laid out his plans for Ricardo Diaz.

"Fine, go ahead. Don't screw this up, Frank."

"Don't worry."

"It's in my nature to worry. Now, what about Tully?"

"He never took care of Richards' computer. He gave the fucking thing to his son."

"You assured me Tully could be trusted, Frank. Did he tell you that he destroyed the laptop?"

"Yes."

"So, he lied to you."

"Well, yes."

"Don't play with me, Frank. Tully told you he took care of it when he hadn't. He lied to you. There is no confusion here. The man cannot be trusted. You brought him in on this, Frank. Tully is your liability. You do what needs to be done."

"Jesus, Masters, do you know what you're asking?"

"I want you to tell me that you will take care of it, Frank. Can I trust *you*?"

"Yes, you can trust me. I'll take care of it."

"How old is Tully's son? What is the boy like?"

"Sixteen, he's a great kid, so?" said Raft.

And the boy calls me Uncle Frank, Raft wanted to say but couldn't.

"So, get the kid a new laptop, Frank," Masters said before hanging up the telephone.

Before leaving Philippe's, Jimmy made a telephone call to the *Santa Monica Outlook* hoping to reach someone working late who might help him get a line on Edward Richards' most recent news interests. His call was ultimately transferred to the desk of the City Editor.

"Look," said Hank Fellows. "I'm extremely busy at the moment. I have a morning edition to get to press. And I've already been through everything I know with both the Santa Monica Police and the LA County Sheriff's Department. So, who the hell are you and why should I care?"

"My partner was brutally murdered Sunday night, less than two hours before your reporter was killed. I believe the homicides are related."

"That's old news. We're running a story in tomorrow's paper," said Fellows. "Speculating your partner and Ed were working on an investigation that made some drug dealer nervous."

"And how does that sit with you, knowing Richards?"

"It surprises me."

"It more than surprises me, knowing Lenny Archer. I thought you might like to share our doubts."

"The paper goes down to the Press Room at nine. Meet me at my office, I'll give you fifteen minutes and then I'm going to get the hell out of this place. Nine sharp."

Jimmy arrived back in Santa Monica at eight and went directly to Meg's Café. He found Meg at the counter, her face buried in the newspaper.

"Are you hungry?" she asked, coming up for air.

"No, thanks. Ray Boyle treated me to dinner in LA. I just got back, Vinnie is in the hospital."

"Hospital? What happened?"

"He walked in front of a cab while it was moving. He'll be laid up for a while, but he'll be all right. What are you reading?"

"Oh, just an article about Edward Richards. A condensed life story. He had been a society writer for more than twenty years; he reported on the rich and famous, wrote half a dozen books. He had no family to speak of, a few ex-wives, no children. The funeral service is tomorrow morning. What about the arrangements for Lenny's funeral?"

"I'm waiting for a death certificate, so the Navy can get the ball rolling," Jimmy said. "I'll try to run it down in the morning."

"I have free time in the morning, if I can help."

"Maybe you can."

"Shoot."

"Maybe you could attend Richards' funeral and have a look at who shows up. I thought about going myself, but I want to downplay my interest. Just in case the SMPD or the LASD are there to pay their respects. My presence might be taken as a lack of confidence in the police investigation."

"A genuine lack of confidence?"

"A growing lack of confidence."

"Sure, I can do that," said Meg.

"Great."

"Speaking of great, Jimmy, did you have as much fun as I did last night?"

"At least."

"Up for a rematch?"

"I can't tonight, Meg. I need to run over to the newspaper office at nine and I'm really wasted. I wouldn't be much of a challenge, but I do appreciate the offer and I hope it won't be the last."

"You have enough time for a cup of coffee," Meg said, leaving it at that. "Interested?"

"Very interested."

"Start packing, Diaz, we're on for tomorrow night."

"I'm good to go, Raft, as long as you can cover your end," Diaz spoke calmly into the phone.

"Two hundred grand and a free pass to your favorite hacienda, Ricky, but I need something else from you."

"Oh?"

"Do you remember asking if you would have to kill someone for me as part of the deal?"

"I think I was joking, Raft."

"Well, start thinking more seriously."

"I don't know."

"What's not to know, Ricky? Twenty years in Chino or a nice little chicken ranch on the Rio Bolaños. Are you still on the line, Diaz?"

"I'm here."

"Good. So shut up and listen."

Pigeon found Hank Fellows standing at his desk, preparing to leave for the day. Fellows stopped what he was doing and sat, inviting Jimmy to do the same.

"I appreciate your time," Jimmy said, taking a seat in a chair opposite the City Editor.

"You have only fifteen minutes, use it judiciously."

"I read your piece on Richards in today's paper. It was nicely done."

"Flattery will not buy you more time, Mr. Pigeon."

"Then I'll get to the point."

"Please do."

"I'm interested in hearing anything you can tell me about what Ed Richards may have been investigating prior to his death. If your short biography of the man is any indication, crime reporting would seem to be way out of his field of expertise."

"I would have to agree with you there. Richards was a fine writer, very good at what he did. But what he did was human interest, not hard news. He reported Hollywood, entertainment, it was rarely front page. I told the police what I will tell you. If Ed Richards was taking a stab at crime reporting, I knew nothing about it. And to be quite honest, it would surprise me."

"Would it be possible to take a look around his desk?"

"You said the private investigator who was killed that night was your partner."

"Yes."

"I can understand your zeal, but that would be out of the question even if Ed Richards had a desk here. Richards was a contributor, Mr. Pigeon, he was not on staff. He did his work at home. On occasion, he would bring his computer down here and I would find him a place to sit where he could write or print out copy. If there's anything that may help, you would most likely locate it at his house or on the hard drive of his laptop."

Suddenly, the roar of the printing presses below shook the room.

"For what it's worth," Fellows said, raising his voice to compete with the din, "Ed did mention he was researching a new book, but he neglected to mention the subject."

"How can you handle that racket?" asked Jimmy.

"I can't handle it, that's why I try my best to be gone before it begins. I really need to go."

Fellows rose from his seat and Jimmy followed suit.

"I'm sorry I couldn't be more help," Fellows said as he collected a few files from his desk. "If you discover anything concrete concerning Richards' death, please let me know. I liked Ed Richards and I would like to know who is responsible."

"Not to mention the news value," said Jimmy.

"Please do not underestimate my sincerity, Mr. Pigeon. In some cases selling the newspaper is not my major concern."

"I'm sorry, I was out of line."

"Again, I appreciate the commitment to your late partner. If there is something I can do to help, please trust that I will make every attempt."

"Thank you," said Pigeon. "I'll keep that in mind."

They came out of Maria's Italian Kitchen on Mulholland Drive and crossed the parking lot to the red Camaro.

At the car, Carlos Valdez took Angel by the elbows and kissed her once on each cheek.

"Be well, *amiga,*" Carlos said. "And if you get tired of this fool, you know where to find me."

"It might be sooner than you think," Angel Rivas said, laughing as she opened the car door.

"Very cute," said Ricardo Diaz, suppressing a smile. "Two comedians, fucking Lucy and Desi."

Angel started the Chevy engine and the two men turned to each other. Carlos took Ricardo into his arms and they shared a strong embrace.

"Will you be good?" asked Carlos.

"I don't know how to be good, *compañero,*" said Diaz.

"I mean, will you be all right?"

"Better than all right, bro. Free and flush."

"*Buena fortuna, hermano,*" Carlos said. "Be sure to let me know where you roost."

"You'll be the first to know and there will always be a place for you wherever we land."

They embraced once again before Ricky climbed into the passenger seat of the Camaro. Valdez looked on silently as the car moved away.

"Drive to my place," said Diaz as Angel pulled out of the lot.

Ten minutes later, they sat in the Chevy outside of Ricky's sub-let condo in Woodland Hills.

"Why can't I stay tonight?" asked Angel.

"Because I have too much to do before we leave. And so do you. We've been through this. Go home, get packed and tomorrow make sure you get everything you need to take with you. I don't want to hear you whine about not being able to find the right shade of nail polish once we get into Mexico."

"You're cruel, Diaz," Angel pouted.

"Give me a break, Rivas. Be here tomorrow evening at eight. Don't be late. Park in back. Wait for me in the car. Got it?"

"Yes, I got it. So get out if you're getting out."

"I promise you, *bonita*," Ricky said, kissing Angel's forehead, "I will treat you like a queen."

"Or else," Angel teased. "Go."

Diaz climbed out of the car and stood watching as the Camaro drove off.

Free and flush, he thought.

The drive over to his apartment from the *Santa Monica Outlook* brought Pigeon past his work place. He slowed the LeBaron as he made the turn onto Fourth Street, rolled to a stop opposite the building and briefly considered going up to check the telephone answering machine. He realized if there were any recorded messages, they would most likely be for Lenny Archer. The thought of screening phone calls for the dead was not inviting. He looked up to the second story of the building and decided it could wait until morning. Pigeon stepped heavily on the accelerator and continued home. Had he lingered for only a minute longer, Jimmy would have noticed the movement of a flashlight beam in the windows of his office facing Fourth Street.

Ten minutes later, Jimmy stood at his kitchen counter. He poured bourbon over the ice cubes in a large tumbler and carried the glass to his bedroom, gulping half its contents on the way. Jimmy placed the glass on top of a dresser and opened the bottom drawer. He pulled a 9x19mm Smith and Wesson 669 from under a stack of folded dress shirts and placed it beside the bourbon. Jimmy grabbed the shoulder holster off a hook on the closet door, slipped the weapon into the rig, retrieved the glass and moved back to the kitchen. He set the holstered handgun on the kitchen table and drained his drink. He found two magazines in a cabinet above the sink, each one holding fourteen rounds of ammunition, and he placed both on the table beside the weapon. He refreshed his drink and carried it, with the bottle, into the living room.

Jimmy settled into his armchair, placed the bourbon on the side table and lit a cigarette. A well-worn paperback copy of *Les Misérables* sat on the table beside the ashtray. He lifted the book and opened it to the place where he had left off reading, the spot marked by a business card which read *Archer and Pigeon, Private Investigation.*

Jimmy lost the impulse to escape into literature.

He chose instead to lose himself in Beethoven's Ninth and the fifth of Jim Beam.

PETER QUINCE

Pigeon had a very rough time dragging himself out of bed the next morning. Thursday. He eventually found his way to the bathroom, plugged the drain in the tub and ran the hot water.

Jimmy walked to the kitchen, started a pot of coffee brewing, grabbed a full quart bottle of orange juice from the refrigerator, carried it back to the bath, chewed two aspirin, washed them down with juice and placed the bottle on the floor within reach of the bathtub.

Pigeon eased himself into the steaming bathwater. He could feel the alcohol seeping from his pores. He soaked for thirty minutes and emptied the juice bottle.

Back in the kitchen he fried a few eggs, slapped them between two pieces of wheat toast, poured coffee and took his breakfast at the kitchen table. The Smith and Wesson, the shoulder holster and the two ammo magazines sat where he had placed them the night before.

Today, Jimmy would be carrying.

Over his second cup of coffee, Pigeon scribbled a list of the things he needed to achieve. The itinerary was daunting. His initial challenges would be managing to look presentable and making his way to the office.

A shave, two more aspirin, a cold shower just for good measure and Jimmy was ready to tackle getting dressed. He slipped on a pair of dark slacks, a dress shirt and a blue necktie. Deciding to make a few phone calls before leaving the apartment, he draped his suit jacket across the back of the living room sofa and returned to the kitchen.

The telephone in Vinnie's hospital room was picked up by Vinnie's mother. Frances told Jimmy her son was asleep. No surprise. Strings had been complaining about the pain. Complaining loudly. His doctor had recommended medication to keep the patient silent. Pigeon reminded Fran she should call him if they needed anything.

Jimmy phoned the Santa Monica Police Department to see about obtaining a death certificate and was curtly informed he would need to come down to fill out a form.

Finally, Pigeon rang the Los Angeles County Sheriff's Department to inquire if ballistics tests had come up with a match on the bullets that had killed Archer and Richards. He was told he would have to speak with Detective Raft for the results. Raft was unavailable, Jimmy left a message.

Pigeon marveled at his lack of progress.

Jimmy strapped on the shoulder holster, scooped up the ammunition and dropped it into his pocket, slipped into his suit jacket and headed for the office.

Armed and irritable.

There was no hiding the fact that someone had broken in. The office door was wide open. The Oriental rug had been carefully rolled up and moved aside, the faded blood stains revealed. Both desks had also been moved and all the drawers of Lenny Archer's desk pulled out. The metal grill that concealed the hidden audio recorder sat on the floor against the wall, the recorder beside it. The tape recording of Lenny's final minutes gone. All Jimmy could think to do was rearrange the furniture.

His desk back in place, Jimmy reluctantly checked the phone answering machine for messages.

If the machine's built-in date and time stamp could be trusted, the first message was recorded the previous afternoon just after Pigeon left the office following the visit from Detective Barnum. A call to remind Lenny he was scheduled for a dental check-up on Friday morning. It was followed by a call from a woman, phoning Lenny to check if dinner was still on for Friday night. These were the sort of calls Jimmy had expected and dreaded having to deal with. Appointments Archer would never meet; notifications and cancellations Jimmy would have to see to.

Next, around the time Jimmy had been talking with Raft at Lenny's apartment, a message from Ray Boyle with news of

Vinnie's accident. It was followed by a call from Vinnie's mother, reporting the same.

Around the time Jimmy was driving back from LA, a call from Meg to ask if he was planning to come over to the café for dinner. When he'd been at Meg's, there had been a call from the Los Angeles Public Library. A book checked out of the Santa Monica Public Library by James Pigeon, and picked up off the street near Parker Center, was returned to LAPL. The library was calling to notify Pigeon the book was being sent overnight to SMPL. Next, there was a phone call from a man wanting to employ a private investigator to find out if his wife was having an affair.

While Pigeon had been at the newspaper office, there had been two hang-ups. Calls made; no messages left.

The final message, recorded just before he had arrived that morning, was Meg again. She was leaving for Richards' funeral and would report back later.

The entire ordeal only served to remind Jimmy that he disliked telephone answering machines nearly as much as he disliked telephones. He had learned next to nothing. The rescued library book, a suspicious husband and a couple of disconnected calls, most likely from last night's intruder, was how it added up.

That, and the phone calls Jimmy would have to make.

Return calls to let it be known that Lenny had no more need for dental x-rays, no more time for wining and dining.

Jimmy Pigeon, bearer of bad tidings, a leather holster pressing uncomfortably against his rib cage.

He made the calls, erased the telephone messages, and headed out of the office to fill out a form.

Peter Quince sat at his worktable in the far corner of the high school Computer Sciences Lab, installing a compact disc drive into a desktop CPU.

"Mr. Quince."

The teacher looked up from his project to find Kevin Tully holding a laptop.

"Shouldn't you be in class, Kevin?"

"It's my free period. I was hoping you could help me."

"What can I do for you?"

"It's this computer," Kevin said

"What seems to be the problem?"

"I've been trying to install game programs and I get an error message saying there's not enough memory."

"There should be. Let me have a look."

Quince booted the laptop and checked the hard drive for available space.

"Is this your notebook?" he asked.

"My dad gave it to me."

"Do you know where he got it? It's not new."

"At one of the police auctions, I think."

"Well, there are a lot of programs and files here that were left by whoever used it before. I could delete nearly all of it and leave you with an operating system and a word processing program. That would afford you more than enough space for loading games," suggested Quince.

"Could you?"

"The question is, would we be losing information that someone still needs? It would be best to find out exactly where the computer came from just to be certain."

"I guess we could wait until I ask my father," Kevin said, clearly disappointed.

"Tell you what I can do. I can copy the files onto a disc before I delete them from the hard drive. That way we'll have them saved in case they are important. I'll have some time this afternoon. You can pick up the notebook before you leave school today."

"Great. Thanks, Mr. Quince."

"No problem, Kevin, I'll see you around three."

The boy left happy. Quince went back to his work.

Jimmy stood in a line to pick up a Request for Death Certificate form, filled in the blanks, waited in another line to turn in the completed form, stood in a third line to pay the six dollar processing fee and sat to wait for his name to be called. He could have had a roll of film developed in less time.

The document finally in hand, Jimmy found his way to the Medical Examiner's office to see about the release of Lenny's body. At the office door he bumped into Solomon Meyers walking out.

"Jimmy."

"Doc."

"I saw you talking with the detectives Monday morning and I thought you would be coming back up to your office," said Meyers. "I wanted to say I was sorry about what happened to Archer. It was terrible."

"Yes, it was. Did Lenny's body arrive here?"

"Late yesterday afternoon, along with the LASD Coroner's report."

"Official cause of death?"

"The shot to the head. Their findings suggest Lenny was still alive, but barely. He suffered considerable blood loss. The stomach wound alone would have been fatal if left untreated."

"Is there any solid evidence connecting the deaths of Lenny Archer and Edward Richards?"

"We're still waiting for the ballistics report. All we know at this point is that the executions were similar, both victims shot in the head while lying in the prone position, both shot with a .38 caliber weapon."

"Why are the victims here and the bullets with the LA Sheriff's Department?"

"The homicides are tangled up; we're trying to sort it out. Since both were killed in Santa Monica, we took on the bodies. LASD has a better equipped ballistics lab."

"Tangled homicides, a Southern California tradition. I need to find out when the Navy can pick up Lenny's body. Lenny has a military funeral coming to him; they're waiting for the body to be released."

"It has been released. His brother was here, picked up a copy of the Coroner's report and moved the body."

"Lenny's brother. Moved it where?"

"I really couldn't tell you."

Pigeon calmly slipped the hard-earned six-dollar death certificate into his suit jacket pocket. *Terrific.*

Jimmy thanked Solomon Meyers, left the building and decided to revisit the Santa Monica Public Library.

It was no secret that most visitors to Tony's Barber Shop in Malibu were not looking for a haircut. More often than not, Anthony Gravano would be sitting alone in one of the two barber chairs studying the *Daily Racing Form*. The bell above the shop door jingled, interrupting his careful consideration of the Daily Double at Santa Anita.

"Tony."

"Frank. Need a trim?"

"I need a laptop computer," said Raft.

"I think you're in luck."

Tony locked the front door and hung a sign in the window. *Back in 15 Minutes.*

"*Andiamo*, let's see what we've got," Gravano said, leading Raft to the basement stairs.

The large room below the shop was filled wall to wall with boxed electronics. Televisions, VCRs, video cameras, stereo equipment, car radios, computer monitors. Gravano pulled a flat box down from a metal shelf unit and handed it to Raft.

"Brand new, top of the line. Retails for three grand."

"And?" said Raft, setting the box down and reaching into his jacket pocket.

"Six hundred."

Raft peeled off four one hundred dollar bills and he slapped them into Gravano's open hand.

"That'll work."

"It's always good doing business with you, Anthony," Raft said as Tony removed the sign and unlocked the door.

"Likewise, Frank."

Jimmy found the kid shelving books.

"Whitman."

"Yes?" said Donaldson, looking up from the cart.

"Remember me?"

"I do."

"I need another favor, or two."

"Oh?"

"The book I checked out the other day. It was misplaced and I understand it was sent back here. I'd like to retrieve it."

"I put it back on the shelf," said Donaldson. "You're lucky it was returned, it's an expensive book."

"Yeah, I'm a lucky guy."

"Follow me."

Whitman pulled the book off the shelf and handed it to Jimmy.

"You should be more careful," he suggested.

"I will," said Jimmy. "I could use something else."

"What's that?"

"Are you aware that the author of this book recently passed away?"

Donaldson glanced down at the book cover.

"Wow, yes, I read about it. That's the guy who was killed, a robbery they said."

"Yes, well I'm looking into it."

"Assisting the police?"

"Exactly. And you can help."

"Oh?"

"I was curious about any books Ed Richards may have checked out lately; let's say the last few weeks."

"You know I'm not allowed to do that. It would take a court order."

"I was hoping you and I could get around that roadblock, Whitman," said Jimmy. "For old time's sake."

"I could get into a lot of trouble."

"How much trouble?" asked Jimmy, reaching for his wallet.

"Forty bucks worth?"

"How about fifty?" Pigeon said, pulling out a bill, "and you throw in a printout."

Peter Quince began exploring Kevin Tully's computer. From the start menu, he opened the control panel and went to *Programs.* He discovered a number of professional writing and graphics programs loaded onto the hard drive, software he felt Kevin could live without. Quince uninstalled them.

Next, Quince explored the saved files. He found word documents and photographs.

Quince connected the CD-writer to the parallel port on the laptop. He had purchased the external CD burner on the trip to Japan during his spring break, they were difficult to come by in the States and very expensive. He copied all of the files to a CD and deleted them from the hard drive.

In the process, a word document title caught his eye. *Interview with Tom Hanks.* Hanks had recently won the Best Actor Oscar for *Philadelphia.* Quince opened the document and went to *Properties* from the file menu. The file had been created in late March, soon after the Academy Awards' ceremony. The author of the document was Edward Richards. Quince thought he had heard the name before, but couldn't recall the occasion.

Quince finished deleting the files. He picked up a marking pen and wrote the names Tully and Richards on the face of the CD. He slipped the disc into a plastic jewel case and threw it into his desk drawer.

Pigeon tried calling Raft from a phone booth outside the library. He was told the detective was expected at three. Jimmy walked over to Meg's Café.

He took a seat at the counter and was greeted by Meg's assistant manager, Pam Walker.

"Jimmy," she said. "I'm really sorry about Lenny."

Though he had heard it a number of times now, Pigeon still didn't know how to respond to condolences. What do you say to sincere expressions of regret? *Thank you?*

"So am I, Pam," he said. "Did Meg get in yet?"

"A few minutes ago, she's getting changed. Coffee?"

"Okay."

"Having lunch?" Pam asked as she poured.

"Sure."

"The special?"

"Why not," said Jimmy.

Pam went to the kitchen. Jimmy set the book on the counter. He took the computer printout from his pocket and looked again at the titles Ed Richards had borrowed from the library a week before he died.

The Birth of Las Vegas and *Hollywood Meets the Mob.*
So what?

"Food is on the way. What have you got there?"

Jimmy looked up to find Meg tying her apron.

"Ed Richards' reading list."

"Catchy titles," said Meg, glancing at the printout. "What does it tell you?"

"Absolutely nothing. Did you come across anything worth mentioning at the funeral?"

"I'm not sure. Possibly, but it will have to wait. I need to take care of the dinner prep work and I have a few errands to run in LA. I thought I'd drop by the hospital to see how

Vinnie is doing. I should be back here by five and then I'll be around until closing."

"Can you do me a favor?"

"Sure," said Meg, warming his coffee.

"Take this book to Vinnie; it'll give him something to keep from going stir crazy. He already knows what I'd like him to do. Tell Strings it would be a great help, he loves hearing that."

"Will do," said Meg, taking the book. "I've got to get going. Stop back this evening."

Meg hustled back to the kitchen as Pam came out with Jimmy's lunch.

Pigeon reached for the knife and fork.

Salvatore Bando and Nathan Archer stood together at the long stainless steel table looking down at the body.

They had transported the corpse from the Santa Monica morgue to Bando's Funeral Home on Main Street and moved it down to the large basement workspace where the remains of the dearly departed were made ready for public viewing. A task which often required great artistry.

"Jesus, Nate," said Bando, "they hurt Lenny bad."

"Yes they did, Sal," said Archer.

Bando and the Archer brothers went back a long time. The three ran around town together when Nathan and Lenny shared the PI office on Fourth Street. Though Salvatore had not heard from Nate in more than a year, when his old friend called for help, Bando came running. It had been nearly four years since Nathan had seen Lenny. Nate had tried many times to patch things up with his brother, to work it out, but Lenny wouldn't have it. Nate had always held on to hopes for a reunion. But not this, never this.

Lenny, I hardly know you.

"Nate, are you okay?"

"Yes, Sal. Thank you for your help."

"Anytime, Nate, anything at all, you know that."

"I know, Sal."

"I'll be upstairs," Bando said, sensing that Archer wanted to be alone with his brother. "You need something, just yell."

"I will."

When Bando was gone, Nate slipped on a pair of latex gloves and picked up the Coroner's report. He stood over Lenny's body, going through the report, comparing what he read with what he saw on the stainless steel table.

Words could not describe it.

At three, Frank Raft climbed out of his car and walked over to the phone booth. From where he stood, the entrance to Sherman Oaks High School was in clear view. Raft called the LASD Malibu Station and asked to speak with Bob Tully.

"Detectives' Division, Tully."

"Hey partner."

"Frank, where are you?"

"I'm running late, hold the fort, I'll be in no later than four," said Raft. "Don't forget we have business in Woodland Hills later today, and keep it under your hat."

"The PI has been trying to reach you. Jimmy Pigeon. He was told you would be in by three."

"Fuck Pigeon."

"What if he calls?"

"Just deal with him, Bob. Be very helpful and polite. Give him anything he needs within reason," said Raft. "And pay attention to what he's asking."

Raft looked across to the high school and spotted the boy walking out through the front doors.

"I have to run, Bob, see you in an hour."

Raft went back to his vehicle. The detective watched from the driver's seat as Kevin Tully broke away from a group of students and started up the street alone. Raft drove away from the curb and he followed the boy at a close distance. Two blocks from the school he pulled up alongside the boy.

"Kevin."

The boy stopped and looked over to the car. When he realized who it was he moved to the passenger window.

"Uncle Frank," he said.

"Hop in champ. I'll give you a ride home."

Kevin climbed into the passenger seat. The laptop from the basement of Tony's Barber Shop sat on the seat between them.

"What's this?" asked Kevin.

"It's a spanking new notebook computer to replace that prehistoric laptop your father gave you," said Frank. "It became available today. We wanted to get it to you before you got too attached to the dinosaur."

"Where's my dad?"

"He got tied up at the station, so he asked me to drop this off to you on my way over there."

"Wow, this is great," Kevin said as they pulled up in front of the house. "I'm going to call Dad and thank him as soon as I get in."

"Let it wait, champ, your father is very busy right now. I'll let him know how pleased you are. Take it in and check it out. Your dad will call you up later and you can tell him all about it."

"Thanks, Uncle Frank," Kevin said, picking up the box.

"Leave the other one, Kevin," Raft said.

Kevin placed the old notebook on the seat and climbed out of the car with the new one. He moved toward the front door of the house, floating on air. Raft couldn't help but smile over the boy's excitement.

When Kevin reached the door, he remembered the compact disc Peter Quince had made, the backup copy of all the files on the computer. Quince had told Kevin he would hold onto the disc. Kevin realized Raft might want to know about it.

"Oh, Uncle Frank, wait," Kevin called, turning back.

Detective Raft had already driven off.

After lunch, Jimmy had gone to his office. The *new message* indicator was blinking on the telephone answering machine. He sat at his desk, lost in thought, hypnotized by the steady flashing of the small red light. Just past three, he telephoned Raft again at the Los Angeles County Sheriff's Station and was put through to Tully.

According to Detective Tully, the bullets removed from the bodies of Lenny Archer and Edward Richards were clearly fired from the same weapon. The results had been passed on to the Santa Monica Police Department. SMPD was now fully in charge of the ongoing investigation. The suspicion that the homicides had been drug related was still on the top of the list. Tully recommended Pigeon direct any further inquiries to Detective Barnum at SMPD. After he passed the buck, Tully apologized for needing to get off the telephone to take another call.

Jimmy placed the handset down and saw the flashing red light beckoning. He decided to get it over with and he hit the play button on the answering machine.

Frank Raft ran over to his house in Malibu. Down in the basement he placed the reporter's laptop into a large metal basin and he beat it to death with a framing hammer.

He dumped the small pieces into a heavy black plastic bag.

Then he phoned Jackson Masters.

"Give me some good news, Frank," Masters said. "The old man will be back Saturday."

"It should be over by tomorrow, all of the loose ends should be tied up tonight."

"You used the word *should* twice in the same sentence, Frank. I'm not pleased with your vocabulary."

"It's fucking Jimmy Pigeon. He's been nosing into the reporter's business. He's been to the newspaper and might have dug something up at the library."

"I warned you about Pigeon, Frank."

"I'm watching him and I've got help. If he keeps sniffing around he's going to lose his nose."

"I need guarantees, Raft, not fucking movie clichés."

"He won't be a problem."

"I sincerely hope not," said Masters before he hung up the telephone.

* * *

Nathan Archer moved the stainless steel table into the walk-in cooler. He dropped the plastic gloves into a waste can and walked upstairs. He found Sal Bando at the kitchen table, drinking coffee and reading the newspaper.

"There's roast beef in the refrigerator, if you want to make a sandwich," Sal said.

"I think I'll just have some of that coffee," Archer said. He poured a cup and joined Sal at the table.

"So?" asked Sal. "Did you find anything?"

"The Coroner's report seems pretty thorough. But I may have found something missing."

"Oh?"

Archer pulled a sheet of paper from his inside jacket pocket.

"I picked up Lenny's personal belongings at the police station early this morning. His wallet, wristwatch, a few other things. I was also given a list of everything being held back as evidence. His clothing, his handgun and two teeth."

"I'd love to get my hands on the cocksucker who did that to Lenny," said Bando.

"You and me both, Sal. Here's the thing. According to the medical report and what I could see as I examined the body, there were three teeth missing. Where is the third tooth?"

"Could Lenny have lost it earlier?"

"I don't think so. If you look into his mouth I think you would agree they were all knocked out at the same time."

"He could have swallowed the tooth."

"Could have, but didn't. It doesn't show up in the autopsy report."

"And you didn't find it in Lenny's office?"

"No. I found a few other things that may answer some questions, but no teeth."

"Where are you staying?" asked Sal. "There's plenty of room here."

"Thanks, I'm going to stay at Lenny's apartment. I saw his landlady yesterday when I got into town. I told her I was Lenny's brother and she asked to see ID. The old lady is quite a character. I told her I planned to use the place for a while and that I would take care of moving his things. She seemed okay with it, but said she would need to start showing the place after the middle of the month, to make certain she could have it rented by the beginning of July. If I'm still down here next week, I'll give her the rent for July to keep her from bringing people in. I'm not leaving until I find out who murdered my brother."

"Have you found anything at Lenny's apartment?"

"I haven't had much time to look. It's been at least four years since I was in the place, I'd have no idea if anything was missing. The old lady said a police detective had been up there and Lenny's partner, Jimmy."

"Have you spoken with Pigeon?"

"Not yet," said Archer, "but I think it may be time to meet him."

Nate rose from the table and went for the coffee pot. He refilled Sal's cup and his own.

"Have you seen today's paper?" Sal asked.

"No," said Archer, taking a seat.

"The night Lenny was murdered a local reporter was killed also. According to this article, the police have reason to believe the two deaths could be related. They suspect the reporter, Ed Richards, was investigating illegal drug trade and your brother was working with him."

"Based on what?"

"Not much. The way they were both executed."

"No. Unless Lenny had changed drastically in the past four years, he wouldn't go near it," said Archer. "Do you know where Richards lived?"

"We could find out. Why?"

"I'd like to take a look around his place."

"I'm sure you would have no trouble breaking in," Sal Bando said.

BOB TULLY

Raft drove around to the row of trash dumpsters behind a large shopping center on Wilshire Boulevard. He dropped the black plastic bag containing the shattered remnants of the dead reporter's laptop into one of the large bins.

On his way to the Malibu Station, Raft stopped again to call Ricky Diaz from a street corner public phone.

"We'll be there at eight," Raft said.

"I'm all set," said Diaz. "Don't forget the cash."

"Are you sure you've got it straight, Ricky?"

"I'm a felon, Raft, not a fucking moron."

"Humor me, Diaz."

"I open the door, pull the trigger, drop the gun, take the money and disappear into the bowels of Old Mexico."

"Very good, Ricky. I'm proud of you."

"Save the flattery, Frankie. Don't be late."

When Raft walked into the Detectives' Division office at the Malibu Station, Tully was touting his son's hitting abilities to Detectives Landers and Mallory.

"The kid is batting .348 with fourteen homeruns, best in the county. He hasn't made an error all season. Stanford and UCLA are courting him for a baseball scholarship and Kevin is still a Junior."

"Not to mention the six runs batted-in last Saturday at the semi-finals," Raft added. "Sherman Oaks is a lock to take the State Championship this weekend."

"What's the line on the championship game?" asked Bill Landers.

"You would gamble on a high school baseball game?" said Tully.

"Bill would bet on a fourth grade dodge ball game if he liked the spread," said Mallory. "You're a lucky guy, Tully. You should be very proud and you should let the boy know about it every chance you get."

"You know, you're right for a change, Mallory," Tully said. "I should call him right now and do just that."

"Save it, Bobby, I need you right now," said Raft.

Raft headed out of the office and Tully followed.

"Later, gents," Tully said as he left.

"You're a lucky son of a bitch, Bob," Mallory called after him.

Ray Boyle was just about to leave for the day when his Captain stopped him in the hall.

"Ray, I need you to stick around for a while."

"Are you kidding? It's fucking half past six; I've been in this fucking asylum since eight this morning."

"I appreciate your enthusiasm, Ray, but it can't be helped. Where's Stephens?"

"Sam ran out at six, when I should have."

"You missed the boat, Ray."

"Where the fuck is everyone else? Who has the four to midnight?"

"Vannater and Lange."

"So?"

"They caught an armed robbery in Century City, liquor store. It looks like they'll be tied up there for a couple of hours. And I have two detectives out sick. I need you here in case we catch a call, Ray. I'll cut you loose the minute Phil and Ron get back. I'll owe you one."

"Don't forget it."

"I won't. Thanks, Ray."

"You're fucking welcome, Captain, sir."

Jimmy had intended to see Meg, to learn what she might have picked up at Richards' funeral while he grabbed dinner at the café.

He changed his mind.

Instead, Jimmy decided on Angelo's Ristorante. He sat alone at a small table in the far corner of the dining room over a large kettle of steamed mussels in marinara.

"How was the *cozzi a zuppo?*"

Jimmy dropped the last empty shell into a side bowl and looked up at his host.

"Perfect as always, Angelo."

"Mind if I sit for a minute?"

"Not at all," Jimmy said.

"Lenny loved that dish," said Angelo, taking a seat.

"Yes he did," said Jimmy, grateful that Angelo Ricci had allowed him to finish his meal and had kindly forgone voicing his sympathy over Lenny's death. Jimmy pushed his plate aside and looked at Angelo. Ricci sat uncomfortably, as if trying to decide how to begin.

"What's on your mind, Angelo?" said Jimmy, hoping to help.

"Stop me anytime," Angelo said.

"Go ahead."

"Look, Jimmy. I don't know what's happening with the murder investigation, it's really none of my business. But if anyone was interested in my opinion, I would have to say the police are barking up the wrong tree. I knew Lenny a long time, *and* his brother. If there was one thing Lenny and Nathan agreed on, it was to steer clear of any case dealing with drugs; and if they found that a case in progress was pointed that way, they dropped it cold."

"Thanks, Angelo."

"For what?"

"For letting me know I'm not the only one who believes the police investigation is way off base."

"I'm sure of it, Jimmy. One more thing and I'll be out of your hair. I have certain acquaintances I can reach out to, I won't name names. I just want you to know if you're not happy with how it plays out, I will see what I can do to get you some satisfaction."

Angelo Ricci waited for a response. Jimmy could think of nothing to say.

"*Finito,*" Ricci said, rising from the table.

"Angelo?"

"Yes?"

"What can you tell me about Lenny's brother?"

"A brilliant investigator. He studied forensic sciences. He could tell you when a victim had his last haircut. And there isn't a lock Nate couldn't pick."

"What happened between the brothers?"

"I wouldn't feel right talking about it," Ricci said. "I need to get back to work, Jimmy. Should I send over an espresso?"

"Sure, Angelo. An espresso would be good."

"Why are we stopping?" Tully asked as Raft pulled the car into the parking area of a small convenience store.

"I need smokes. Can I get you anything?"

"Diet Coke," said Tully.

"Sit tight."

Ricardo Diaz sat in his kitchen, drumming his fingers on the tabletop, staring at the thirty-eight. He looked up at the wall clock. Seven forty-five. His suitcase was packed and ready at the foot of the sliding glass door that opened out to the fenced patio. Ricky rose and he slid the door open. The tall cedar patio gate out to the parking lot behind his condo was latched from the inside. He paced nervously, his eyes darting back and forth between the clock and the gun.

Raft called the Malibu Station from a pay phone in the convenience store and asked for Commander Jefferson.

"Yes, Frank?"

"Tully got a tip on someone who may help us on those two homicides last Sunday; we're going to check it out."

"That's Santa Monica's headache now, Frank."

"We're right here, Chief. And this cat isn't going to hang around. He could be gone by the time SMPD can get out here."

"Where?"

"Woodland Hills."

"That's the city, Frank. Maybe you should call LAPD."

"Jesus, you know the fucking wait time, I just want to get to this guy before he vanishes, a few simple questions. I think we can handle it without the fucking marines."

"What's the address? I'll send a unit."

Raft gave Jefferson the location of the condo, grabbed a pack of cigarettes and a Diet Coke and went back out to the car.

"Remind me again why we're going to see Diaz," Tully said as they pulled away from the parking lot. "Isn't he supposed to blow town?"

"Ricky called, said that he wanted to see us before he leaves. Maybe he wants to kiss us goodbye."

Diaz nearly jumped out of his skin when the doorbell rang. He picked up the .38 and moved to the front door.

"Yes?" he said.

"Ricky, open up."

Diaz pointed the weapon to the floor and opened the door.

"Jesus, Ricky, what's the gun all about?"

"What the fuck are you doing? I told you to wait in the car."

"I have to use the bathroom, Ricky, stop yelling."

Diaz let her pass and shut the door behind her.

"Why didn't you use the back entrance?"

"Because the gate is locked," Angel said. "If I stand here answering twenty questions I'm going to wet my pants."

"Fuck. Make it fast and then go out the back way and wait in the fucking car."

"You don't have to be such a fucking asshole," Angel complained as she rushed off to the toilet.

Diaz jumped when Angel slammed the bathroom door and jumped again a moment later when the doorbell rang.

Fuck.

"Yes," Diaz called.

"It's your favorite law enforcers, Ricky," Raft said from the hall. "Come to wish you bon voyage."

"The door's unlocked," Diaz said, raising the weapon.

"After you, Bobby," Raft said to Tully.

Tully turned the doorknob and pushed the door open. He took a step in and Diaz shot him in the chest. Tully went down hard.

The silenced .38 made a popping sound that Angel Rivas heard just as she was about to flush the toilet. Then she heard the body fall. She came out of the bathroom and she moved silently up the hallway.

Angel stopped across from the kitchen entrance and took a quick look into the front room.

Diaz and Raft stood side-by-side looking down at Bob Tully, their backs to Angel. Tully looked only at Raft.

"Finish it," Raft said.

"Frank?" Tully said.

Diaz put a bullet into Tully's head.

Angel stifled a scream and slipped into the kitchen.

"Is he dead enough for you?" Diaz said.

"Just drop the fucking gun and get the fuck out of here," said Raft.

Diaz let the .38 fall to the floor.

"How do you justify killing your own partner, Frank?"

"Just business, Ricky, nothing personal," said Raft. "It's all about money."

"Speaking of which, where's mine?"

"I've got it right here, pal."

Raft pulled out his service revolver and shot Ricardo Diaz twice.

Angel screamed and ran through the sliding glass door. She fumbled with the gate latch and ran across the parking lot, leaving the Camaro behind. Raft raced out after her. By the time he made it through the patio, Angel was out of sight.

Fuck.

Raft walked back to the front room and he stared down at the two bodies. He took a few minutes to get his story straight. He went to the phone and called it in.

"Jesus Christ, Frank, how the hell could this happen?" Commander Jefferson asked when Raft told him that Detective Tully was dead.

"The guy was supposed to be a harmless snitch, Chief. He invites us in like we were his long lost cousins. And then the maniac starts blasting and he put two into Bobby before I could take him down."

"I sent a unit over to you when you called me earlier, they should arrive any minute," said Jefferson. "Keep the uniforms out of the place, Raft. Its Woodland Hills, I'll fucking need to call Parker Center. Wait there until LAPD takes over."

"I'm not going anywhere," said Raft. "I'm staying right here with my partner."

DINNER BREAK

"Are you hungry, Jake," Jimmy asked, interrupting his story without ceremony.

"I could eat," I said.

"Let me buy you dinner, we can talk about baseball or the weather. We'll get back to Raft, Tully and Diaz later."

Jimmy Pigeon could talk sports for hours, and he loved to talk cases, but in all the time I knew him he never had much to say about himself personally. What I did learn about Jimmy's life, I had put together from bits and pieces picked up here and there.

A patchwork biography.

Jimmy had been raised in West Los Angeles, a half mile from where Vinnie Strings grew up. If the two had anything else in common, it was that both were teenagers when their fathers died. Nicolas Pigeon had been a Los Angeles police officer, killed on the job. Nick and his partner responded to a call, a robbery in progress at a neighborhood grocery. When they arrived the perpetrator was holding the clerk at gunpoint, threatening to shoot the man if the police didn't back off. Nick asked his partner to call for backup and he slowly approached the store entrance.

At the door, Pigeon called to the gunman, asking for permission to come in and talk. He said he would come in unarmed. The gunman told him to come ahead. Nick placed his service weapon on the ground near the door.

Nick Pigeon had talked criminals down dozens of times before. He had a way of calming them, appealing to better judgment, controlling a potentially volatile situation.

All it took for Nick was a few compelling words, some sensible advice, an empathetic appeal. *Give it up, before someone gets hurt. Don't turn an ill-fated hold-up into a capital crime. Let's work this out together.*

It had never failed.

It was the late fifties. When the heat had you cold, you gave it up and cut your losses.

Pigeon walked into the grocery store, arms held above his head, smiling, unthreatening, just about to speak when the perp turned the weapon on Nick and pulled the trigger. Four times. Then he killed the clerk and ran out the rear door as Pigeon's partner was coming in the front.

The gunman was never caught.

Jimmy was fifteen years old.

After losing his father, Jimmy couldn't stay out of trouble. His mother had her hands full with Jimmy's two younger sisters and the boy was often left on his own.

His father's partner, LAPD Officer Charles Lake, tried reaching out to the boy. Jimmy was unreceptive; he blamed Lake for letting his father go into the grocery store alone and refused to listen to reason.

It was Nick Pigeon's commanding officer, Captain Roger Rollins, who ultimately managed to get through to Jimmy and provide a substitute father figure and positive role model, in much the same way as Jimmy would for Vinnie Strings many years later. Under Rollins' influence, Jimmy settled down and began to excel in school; waiting for the day he would be old enough to join the police department. It was Roger Rollins who convinced Jimmy he could look forward to a much more successful career in law enforcement if he had a college education. Jimmy graduated high school with honors and began studies at the University of California at Santa Barbara in the fall, majoring in Criminology.

During his last year at UCSB, two events occurred that would change the course of Jimmy's life.

A serious viral infection left Jimmy deaf in one ear. It spared him from Vietnam. Then Jimmy met Hannah Sims, a fellow UCSB Senior from northern Colorado. The two became inseparable. Sims was active in the anti-war movement and Pigeon tagged along. In the middle of their last semester, they were both arrested at a campus peace rally.

After graduation, Hannah was determined to return home to teach school. Realizing his hearing impediment and arrest record had ended his hopes for a career with the Los Angeles Police Department, Jimmy followed Hannah Sims back to Colorado. They were married in July, at a small chapel in the foothills of the Rockies. What happened in Colorado was something no one seemed to know about, or cared to talk about. What I did eventually discover was that three years later, at the age of twenty-five, Jimmy had quit the marriage and was back on the streets of Los Angeles.

When Jimmy had knocked around aimlessly, for far too long, he decided to look up Roger Rollins. Rollins had retired from the LAPD and gone private. Jimmy found Rollins in a one-man PI office on Wilshire Boulevard. Rollins said he would be glad to give Jimmy some work, Jimmy jumped at it. To celebrate the reunion, Rollins took Pigeon for a drink at the saloon where Roger had often shared a shot of whiskey with Jimmy's father.

It was there at the bar that they ran into former LAPD Officer Charlie Lake. Lake was in sad shape. That was the night Jimmy Pigeon learned the identity of the man who had murdered his father.

"They let him go, Jimmy," Lake moaned. "He killed the best friend I ever had and they let him walk."

"What are you talking about, Charlie?"

"Cady. Will Cady," said Lake, tripping on every word. "They let him walk out of San Quentin two weeks ago."

"Who is Will Cady?" Jimmy asked.

It took a while to make sense of what Charlie Lake was trying to say. The man was very drunk and looked as if he had been that way for weeks.

Then, finally, Rollins and Jimmy understood.

On the night Nicolas Pigeon was killed, Al Linger and Steve Gold were arrested for the armed robbery of a jewelry store in Santa Clara; a third man got away. The perps were masked and couldn't be identified by shop employees but the two in custody had been caught with the goods when they ran from the scene. The next day, William Cady turned himself in to the SCPD claiming he was the third man on the jewelry job. Linger and Gold concurred. The three were convicted and sentenced to a dozen years each at San Quentin and all were granted early release, eleven years later.

Charlie Lake saw the TV news report.

"They were all lying, Jimmy," Lake cried. "I swear on my mother's grave. I watched Cady walk out of prison and I swear he was nowhere near Santa Clara that night, because I saw him that same night in Los Angeles. Saw Will Cady kill your father in cold blood."

"I believe you, Charlie," Jimmy said.

Jimmy wanted to talk to the others before approaching Will Cady. With Rollins' help, Pigeon found Al Linger and Steve Gold in Oakland. He visited them separately. Jimmy surprised Linger at the door to his flophouse room. With a .357 magnum pressed to his ear, Linger quickly confessed to Pigeon that the third man on the jewelry heist was Will Cady's brother. Cady had told his younger brother he needed an alibi and would take the rap for the robbery in Santa Clara; the brother didn't argue. And when Will Cady turned himself in the next day, Linger and Gold went along. Using similar methods of persuasion, Pigeon heard the same story from Steve Gold. As a bonus, Gold told Pigeon where in Los Angeles he could find Cady.

A week later, Will Cady's body was found in an orange orchard east of the city. Cady had been shot in the chest four times. The homicide was never solved.

Jimmy worked with Roger Rollins for seven years, up until the day Rollins called it quits. Pigeon kept the office and worked investigation in Los Angeles for another fifteen years before taking up Archer's offer to join him in Santa Monica. Three years later, Pigeon was hunting for Lenny Archer's killer.

We had dinner at a Mexican joint on Main Street.

I was a little disappointed Jimmy didn't take me to Meg's Café. I found myself wanting to meet Meg Kelly. But the food was red hot and the Mexican beer was ice cold. Pigeon paid the tab and we hit the street. It was a cool, clear night and the sky was sunset red.

"Mind walking to the Pier, Jake?" Jimmy asked. "The office is beginning to feel too small."

"Sure," I said.

We found an empty bench and sat looking out at Santa Monica Bay and the Pacific Ocean beyond.

"Where was I?" Jimmy asked.

"The condo in Woodland Hills. Raft, Tully and Diaz."

"And then Ray Boyle got pulled into it."

"I'll bet he loved that," I said.

"The funny thing is, Ray wound up thanking me," Jimmy said. "It spared him that mess over in Brentwood three days later."

Part Two

HARD BOYLE

> "If you do the deed in my back yard,
> you're going to be dealing with me.
> And trust me, it is definitely not
> Mister Rogers' neighborhood."
> —*Ray Boyle*

RAY BOYLE

Ray Boyle sat at his desk, praying the telephone wouldn't ring, trying to forget the three files sitting on the desktop, three open homicide cases getting absolutely nowhere.

"Ray."

Boyle looked up to find Captain Tanner wearing his *no nonsense* demeanor. Ray tried to think only good thoughts.

"Phil and Ron are back and I can finally get out of here," Boyle said, just to hear the sound of it.

"Phil and Ron are still on the liquor store shooting and we've got two dead bodies out in Woodland Hills."

"And I'm one unlucky son of a bitch."

"Here's the address," said Tanner.

Boyle stood up, threw his jacket over his arm, moved to Captain Tanner and snatched the address slip.

"I fucking knew this would happen," Boyle nearly shouted. "Woodland Fucking Hills."

"Take a few deep breaths, Ray," said the Captain, "and then do us both a favor and go do your job."

Boyle arrived at the scene thirty minutes later. He surveyed the landscape before leaving his vehicle.

A marked unit in front of the building, two uniforms standing at the building entrance, an LA County Sheriff's patrol car parked across the street, two uniforms sitting in it. Ray walked up to the two officers at the entrance, chose the older of the two and took him aside.

"Detective Boyle, LAPD," he said. "Were you first on the scene?"

"Yes, sir. Officer John Billings, sir. West Valley Station."

"Drop the *sir*, Billings. What's with the car across the street?"

"They were here when we arrived, but they haven't been inside."

"I'll be right back," Boyle said.

Boyle walked over to the LASD cruiser and he tapped on the driver's window. The patrolman behind the wheel rolled the window down.

"LAPD Homicide," Ray said, showing his shield. "We're not going to need you this evening. I'm anticipating more than enough support; it would be better if you took off."

Boyle headed back to the building without waiting for a response. When he reached Billings, the LASD patrol car was already gone.

"Who's in there now, John?"

"Two detectives from our station, Cole and Williamson, a County Sheriff's Detective and two males DOA," Billings said. "One of the victims was also a detective, LASD."

"Okay, John," said Boyle. "I want you and your partner glued to this door. No one gets in except the Crime Scene Unit and the Medical Examiner. No one. Got it?"

"Yes."

"I want you to call for two more uniforms, whoever is nearest to our location, LAPD only. I would like the four of you to keep all civilians and reporters away. At least a hundred feet away."

"Got it."

"Good," Boyle said. "Which way am I going?"

"When you get in turn right, it's at the end of the hallway on the left."

Boyle entered the building. When he reached the end of the hall he found the door to the condo open. He went in. The two West Valley detectives stood in the middle of the room, hands in pockets to control any urge to touch a thing. They knew better, but Boyle had to ask anyway.

"Touch anything?"

"No," they said in harmony.

Ray ushered the detectives into the kitchen, ignoring Raft and the two bodies for the moment.

Boyle turned to the two men and got right to it. This was homicide; these guys would only get in his way. Having Sam

Stephens along would have been preferable, but the ball bounced the other way. It was his back yard, he would deal with it.

"I don't want to offend anyone," Boyle said, not even asking their names. "I'd like you to leave. I'll take it from here. We could use you outside; do some door-to-door canvassing. Someone may have seen or heard something."

"Sure," said one.

"Glad to help," said the other.

They walked back through the front room and out of the condo. Boyle watched them leave and then went over to talk with Frank Raft.

Detective Raft was sitting in a stuffed chair close to Bob Tully's body.

"Tough break, Frank."

"Yeah."

"Are you okay?"

"I'm not even close to being okay, Boyle."

"Can you tell me how it happened?"

"How it happened?" Raft said. "It happened too fast."

"Let's take a walk, Frank. Get some air."

"I don't want to leave him alone."

"We'll put a uniform on the door, Frank. The ME is on the way. We need to talk," Boyle said. "We have an officer down and you shot and killed a civilian. Internal Affairs is going to be all over this, Frank, and I need to hear it from you first. For your own protection. Come on."

Raft stood and moved to the door. As Boyle followed, he finally stole a quick look down at the two victims. He knew the dead detective was Bob Tully, though he had never met Tully before. It was the other victim that took Boyle by surprise. Ray recognized the dead man instantly. Detective Boyle had known Ricardo Diaz very well.

Boyle and Raft stood leaning against Ray's car. Raft lit another cigarette and offered the pack to Boyle. Ray reminded Raft again that he was trying to quit.

Boyle had put Billings on the front door of the condo and had sent Billings' partner out back to the patio gate. A second LAPD unit had arrived; two uniforms were keeping rubbernecks from crossing over the police line. The West Valley detectives were questioning bystanders and jotting notes. Crime scene investigators and the Medical Examiner had finally arrived and were beginning their work inside.

"Where did this tip come from, Frank?" asked Boyle, trying to make sense of what he had heard so far.

"I don't fucking know," said Raft, losing patience. "Tully picked it up, he didn't say where. He asked me to come along for the ride."

"It looks as if Tully never got his weapon out," said Boyle.

"He said we were going to talk to a guy, that the guy was harmless. I asked if we needed backup and Tully said no. We go to the place, the guy invites us in and then he starts blasting. By the time I pulled my piece, Tully was down. How many ways do you need to fucking hear it?"

"Calm down, Frank. I'm just trying to understand it. Why would the guy start shooting?"

"How the fuck should I know?"

"Did you know him?"

"Know who?"

"The man you shot, Frank."

"What do you mean did I fucking know him?"

"Take it easy, Frank, I'm just asking a question. Did Tully say who it was you were going to see? Did he mention the guy's name?"

"Tully said that we were going to talk to a harmless snitch, I don't remember if he mentioned a name."

"Do you know who you shot, Frank," asked Boyle. "I mean *after* you shot him, did you know who he was?"

"I don't know, maybe he looked familiar," said Raft. "I may have seen him around Malibu a few times."

"Does the name Ricardo Diaz ring a bell, Frank?"

"That's Diaz in there?"

"Yes, Frank," said Boyle. "The same Ricardo Diaz who was out on bail, awaiting trial for cocaine possession with intent to sell and looking at some very hard prison time. Don't you get mug shots out in Agoura?"

"Get off my back, Boyle."

"So you have heard of Ricky Diaz and you think the face inside looked a little familiar. So what is it, Frank? Do all Hispanic drug dealers look alike to you?"

"Fuck you, Boyle; you're way out of line. I'm through talking with you. I'm going back inside."

"No."

"What do you fucking mean, no?"

"The crime scene is closed, Raft. Strictly LAPD from here on. Something is very wrong here, Frank. You walked in on a twice-convicted drug felon with your hands in your pockets. You say you didn't know it was going to be Diaz, fine. But what about Bob Tully? It was his lead, he must have known. What was he thinking when he walked into that room? It looks like an ambush to me, Raft. I'm trying to work out why Diaz would want you and your partner dead."

"Tully said it had to do with those homicides over in Santa Monica late Sunday night, Monday morning," Raft said. "Maybe Diaz was mixed up in it somehow and panicked when we landed on his doorstep."

"Diaz was mixed up in it? That's your theory, Frank? *Mixed up* is putting it mildly. The way those two homicides have been handled is a running joke at Parker Center. And now here it comes stumbling into my neighborhood and there you are, Raft, not much help at all."

"That's all I fucking know."

"Well then, if that's all you know, I guess I'll go do my job. You can leave, I'll catch you later."

The two men locked stares for a moment, Raft broke eye contact first. An ambulance turned onto the street.

"I'll be in touch, Raft. I'm sorry about Tully. Good luck with IAD."

Raft had nothing to add.

Boyle turned away and walked back into the building.

* * *

Back in the condo, Boyle found Victor Jackson kneeling over Tully's body. Ray knelt beside the Medical Examiner.

"Find anything worthy of rash speculation, Jax?"

"Who did you piss off to deserve this one, Ray?"

"It had to be God," Boyle said.

"All I can find are these two gunshot wounds," Jackson said, pointing to Tully's chest and forehead. "I'm thinking he took the one between the eyes when he was already down."

"Plane geometry?"

"Something like that," said Jackson, "but don't quote me. I may know more when we get to the lab, maybe not."

"What about the weapon?"

"I'm guessing it was the silenced .38 found near the shooter's body. It's been bagged and tagged."

"How about the shooter?"

"What are we calling him, John Doe or John Doer?"

"Ricardo Diaz."

"Your Ricardo Diaz, the mope you busted toting three kilos of cocaine?"

"The very one."

"What was he doing out on the street?"

"Something called bail, Jax. Don't ask me to commend its virtues."

"Diaz took two in the chest," Jackson said, "and *that* weapon should be with Detective Raft. Unless you took his gun away from him. As evidence."

"It never crossed my mind, Jax." said Boyle. "I just spent thirty minutes with Raft, trying to make him believe he doesn't scare the shit out of me. What's that?"

"What do you see?" asked Jackson.

"Take a look at this, stuck in the sole of Tully's shoe," said Boyle. "Is that a fucking tooth?"

"It sure is," said Jackson.

"What's that blue stuff?" asked Boyle.

"Harriman, let me see your magnifying glass," Jackson called to one of the two evidence technicians who had been quietly working the room.

Harriman came over and handed Jackson the glass.

"I don't know," said Jackson. "Little blue pebbles?"

"Let me have a look," said Harriman. "Looks like the small gravel you'd find on the floor of a fish tank."

"Harriman, bag the shoe before we lose any of it," said Boyle.

"The ambulance guys are itching to get in," said Sam Stephens at the condo door.

"I thought your son had a soccer game," said Boyle.

"It's nighttime, Ray. The game was over more than two hours ago. Tanner finally called me. We thought you might like company, but I don't have to stay."

"You can stay."

"Thank you, Ray," Stephens said. "It's nice to feel welcomed. How are you doing, Doc?"

"Just dandy, Sam, thanks for asking."

"So, Ray."

"Yes, Sam?"

"This is quite a mess."

"You can't imagine."

"I'm certainly willing to try," Stephens offered. "How about you start by telling me what the fuck you *think* happened here."

ANGEL

Angel Rivas had dressed for comfort, anticipating the long drive down to Mexico. White tennis shoes, a two-piece designer sweat suit and a Los Angeles Dodgers baseball cap. To the casual observer, she was a very fashionable jogger. Angel had run madly through two residential subdivisions, too frightened to look back even briefly to see if she was being followed. She didn't stop racing until she reached a shopping center more than three miles from Ricardo's condo and dashed into the interior mall. A huge wall clock told her it was close to nine. The mall was quiet, almost empty, store clerks preparing to close shop. She spotted a movie theater at the far end of the mall and quickly headed that way. She opened the change purse attached to her key chain, praying she would find some cash. All of her things were back in the Camaro. Clothing, credit cards, money, ID. Angel pulled a crumpled ten-dollar bill from the purse and nearly cried out for joy. She ran up to the ticket booth.

"Which movie?" asked the cashier.

"I don't care, the longest one, the most crowded one, any one," Angel said, gasping for breath. "Just hurry."

She grabbed the ticket and she ran into the theater.

"Motherfucker," Frank Raft yelled.

He was flying up Ventura Boulevard after being told to leave Tully and Diaz in the hands of the Los Angeles Police Department. Exiled. Fucking LAPD. Fucking Boyle. Mother fucking high and mighty Joseph Wambaugh paperback thumping wannabe movie hero motherfucker. He stomped on the brakes as the traffic light went red at Topanga Canyon Boulevard.

"Motherfucker," he shouted.

He turned to the sound of two teenage girls in a green BMW convertible stopped at the light beside him. They were staring at Raft, visibly amused by his outburst.

"What the fuck is so fucking funny?" he screamed.

The girls went silent and turned away, faces forward. When the light changed, the BMW didn't budge. Raft made a right turn and headed over to Burbank Boulevard. The last place he wanted to be was at the Malibu Sheriff's Station, sitting in Commander Jefferson's office, going through the whole fucking thing again. What he needed to be doing was hunting for the girl who had run from the condo. But Raft knew if he didn't report in, Jefferson would send the troops out looking for him.

Raft merged onto Route 101, floored the gas pedal and drove north to Agoura.

After Jimmy left Angelo's Ristorante, he dropped in to see Meg at the café.

"I ran into Al Hall at Richards' funeral, he's a staff writer for the *Santa Monica Outlook*," Meg told Jimmy. "Hall spoke with Richards at the newspaper about two weeks ago."

"Oh?"

"Richards was banging keys on his laptop computer and Hall asked him what he was working on. Richards said it was research for a new book, a Hollywood biography, but wasn't more specific."

"Richards' editor said more or less the same thing."

"But how about this?" asked Meg. "Richards tells Hall his research had led him to a story guaranteed to make national news."

"But he didn't tell Hall what it was."

"No," said Meg, "but I'd bet it's in that laptop."

Jimmy was tempted to offer Meg an evening on the town; instead he thanked her for her help and said goodnight.

He was not in the best frame of mind and didn't think he would succeed at being good company.

What Jimmy *was* in the mood for was a drink or two.

He walked from Meg's over to Murphy's Saloon, where he had knocked down quite a few.

Ray Boyle was leaning against his car again, this time with his partner.

They had sent the ambulance team inside to collect the bodies and had sent the second unit away. Officer Billings remained posted at the building entrance; Billings' partner remained out back. The two West Valley detectives were out ringing doorbells. The crowd on the street had thinned, as neighbors lost interest and returned to their homes; opting for Thursday's Must See TV.

Sam Stephens waited for Boyle to begin. He pulled out a pack of cigarettes and was just about to light one before having second thoughts; unable to decide whether he should offer Boyle a smoke or if he should put the Marlboros back into his pocket.

"What the fuck are you doing, Sam?"

"Trying to be sensitive. I know you've been trying to quit."

"You are a considerate man, and a good partner. Light the fucking thing already. I've had so much smoke blown in my face since I got here, a little more won't hurt."

"Raft?" asked Sam, flicking his Zippo.

"Try this on for size," Boyle said. "Tully gets a tip. Raft has no idea who they're off to see, only that it might have something to do with the two homicides in Santa Monica Jimmy Pigeon has been busting my balls about. I know Frank Raft. He's a crazy bastard but he's not stupid. So here he is, going in blind, twiddling his thumbs like he's dropping in to visit his Aunt Tillie, and all hell breaks loose. And then, when I ask Raft why he thinks Ricky Diaz greeted them so inhospitably he says something like: *Golly, Ray, I really don't know, maybe Diaz thought we had him made for the Santa Monica murders and he lost his head.* How does that sound to you, Sam?"

"Perfect, except maybe for Tully. Raft takes down a cop killer; probably gets a commendation which would make the grieving process easier. It will clear the homicides in Santa

Monica, which should make SMPD happy. These two tonight would only be a matter of paperwork, which will make Captain Tanner happy. Not to mention the State of California saves the expense of putting Ricky on trial for the cocaine bust, which will make the taxpayers happy. Everybody is happy, Ray. So why aren't you happy?"

"Because it's *too* fucking perfect, Sam."

"There is that," Stephens agreed.

"Let me have one of those fucking cigarettes," Ray Boyle said.

Angel had walked into a dark, crowded auditorium; the movie had just begun. She took a seat in the back row, not wanting to create a distraction or attract attention. She tried watching the screen. Her eyes burned. They had been tearing since she ran out of Ricky's condo. She closed her eyes instead, hoping to erase visions of what she had seen; trying to come up with the slightest idea about what to do.

When Angel opened her eyes again, the end credits were rolling across the screen and the crowd was quickly leaving the auditorium. She didn't move. She was gripping the key chain in her hand; she needed to get to the Camaro.

After a few minutes the house lights came up, leaving Angel exposed and alone. A young man in a red jacket, the Assistant Theater Manager, was telling Angel she would have to go. When he noticed she had been crying he asked her if there was anything he could do.

"I could use a ride to my car," Angel said, holding up her keys. "It's only a few miles from here. I came with a boyfriend, we had an argument and he left. I thought maybe he would come back for me. Guess not."

"It'll be another twenty or thirty minutes before I can get out of here."

"I don't mind waiting," she said, with a *Gracias a Dios* under her breath. "My name is Angel."

"Jason," he said.

"Can I sit here while I wait, Jason?"

"Sure. I'll be as quick as I can."

***

Ray Boyle lit another cigarette. He and Stephens had watched as the bodies were loaded into the ambulance. The ambulance drove off and the coroner joined them at Boyle's car.

"The evidence team will be in there for a while," said Jackson. "I'm following the bodies, I'll do them tonight."

"Call me as soon as you know if Tully was down when he took the second bullet," Boyle said. "If you can tell."

"Sure," said Jackson, moving to his car.

The two West Valley detectives walked up to Boyle and Stephens.

"Get anything?" Boyle asked.

"A few neighbors heard shots," said Detective Cole. "No one counted more than two."

"A guy next door says he saw a woman running across the parking lot out back, just after the gunshots," said Williamson.

"Description?"

"Not much of one. Young, mid to late twenties, ball cap, sweat suit. Maybe Hispanic."

"Probably a jogger," said Stephens.

"Did he say how soon after the shots?" asked Boyle.

"Immediately, he looked out his back window the moment he heard the shooting."

"And she was running?"

"Full throttle the guy said."

"Away from the building?"

"Yes," said Williamson, checking his notes.

"Go back, ask this guy if he can remember seeing head-phones," said Boyle, "and try to get a better description."

The two detectives walked off.

"What are you thinking?" asked Stephens.

"I'm just wondering why she didn't hear the gunshots, react, stop or slow down," said Boyle. "I need coffee."

"There's a donut shop just up the street. Let's go."

***

Shortly after Boyle and Stephens left the scene, a blue Mustang convertible turned onto the street.

"It's up here, on the right," Angel said.

Jason slowed the car as they approached the building. From the passenger seat, Angel quickly spotted the police officer standing at the entrance.

"Keep driving," she said. "Turn right into the alley and go to the rear parking area."

Jason followed her instructions and they came into the parking lot. Angel was directing him to the Camaro when she saw a second officer standing at the gate to Ricky's patio.

"Let's get out of here," she said with urgency.

"What's wrong?" Jason asked, as he passed through the lot and headed back out to the street.

"This is his place, the guy who left me at the movie theater," Angel said. "I saw him up in his window and I don't want to deal with him right now."

Officer Billings had noticed the Mustang when it had passed and turned into the alley. Now, moments later, the car exited and passed again. Billings instinctively took down the license plate number.

"Where to now?" Jason asked.

"Can you drive me over to Santa Monica?"

"What about your car?"

"I have a friend in Santa Monica I can stay with tonight. She can bring me back for my car in the morning."

Jason headed out to Santa Monica Boulevard.

Angel asked him to drop her in front of a large white house. She had been fighting to control her emotions since they left Woodland Hills.

"I don't know how to thank you," Angel said, as she opened the passenger door.

"I'd like to see you again sometime."

"I'm kind of unsettled right now, why don't you give me your telephone number and I can call when I get things straightened out."

Jason gave her the number, without much optimism.

She stood watching as he drove off. Then she crossed the street to a small green house and pounded on the front door.

As she waited, she lost her composure. When Carlos Valdez finally opened the door he found Angel sobbing and trembling.

"Angel, my God, what it is?"

Angel brushed past him into the house and dropped onto the sofa. Carlos closed the door and went to her. She was shaking violently.

"Tell me what happened? Where is Ricardo?"

"I think he's dead."

"What are you talking about?"

"I can't breathe," she said.

Carlos went quickly to the kitchen and filled a tall glass with water. He came back, handed it to her and sat beside her on the sofa. He waited. He watched her as she emptied the glass and took a few deep breaths. When Angel appeared able to speak, Carlos asked again.

"What happened?"

"There were two of them. One was on the floor, on his back, hurt bad, Ricardo and the other man were looking down at him. Ricky leaned over and he shot the man in the head. And then the other man shot Ricky, twice. I ran."

"Have you called the police?"

"No."

"We have to call, Angel, and tell them what you saw," said Carlos, moving to the telephone.

"No," she screamed.

He turned back to her, she was trembling again.

"It *was* the police," Angel said, choking on the words. "The man Ricky shot and the man who shot Ricky. They *were* the police."

When Jimmy came into Murphy's Saloon, the first thing he had done was order a double shot of Jim Beam. He drank it quickly, called for another and asked Murphy for the bar telephone. He phoned Good Samaritan Hospital to check with Vinnie Strings.

"Meg came by," Vinnie said, "and brought the book. I started reading it, but I'm fading. It's the painkillers. They want to keep me another day and stop the drugs, to see if I can handle it. So I should be able to get through the book with a clear head tomorrow, I'll have plenty of time."

"Do what you can, Vinnie," Jimmy had said. "I'll call back tomorrow."

Two hours later, Jimmy was still at the bar, calling for another drink.

"You may have had enough, Jimmy," Murphy said. "That stuff will cook your brain. You know what they say, about the reason God created whiskey."

"What do they say, Murphy?"

"God didn't want the Irish to rule the world."

"I'm not Irish and I'm not interested in ruling the world," Jimmy said. "So let me have one more for the road. Make it a double."

It was nearly midnight when Jimmy Pigeon stumbled up the stairs to his apartment. When he reached the door he found it unlocked and he could see the light spilling out from the front room. He pulled the gun from his shoulder holster and he pushed the door open.

ARCHER AND PIGEON

Jimmy stepped slowly into his apartment, leading with his handgun. The intruder sat in the easy chair facing the door. Jimmy quickly checked the man's hands and saw he was unarmed, unless he planned to use the Victor Hugo paperback as a weapon. Jimmy looked up to the stranger's face and he clearly saw the resemblance.

"Good reading," the visitor said, indicating the worn copy of *Les Misérables*.

"What's the proper greeting for someone who breaks into your home?" asked Jimmy.

"Well, you could shake my hand or not. Either way, I wish you wouldn't point the Smith and Wesson at me."

Jimmy lowered his arm.

"How did you get in?" Pigeon asked.

"It's my specialty."

"So I've heard."

"Have you?"

"Angelo Ricci praised your skills."

"How is Angelo?"

"Colorful. Angelo got me thinking it was you who went through the office last night," Jimmy said.

"We need to talk about what happened to Lenny."

"You look a lot like your brother."

"Not anymore," Nate Archer said.

Jimmy placed the gun on the sofa, took off his jacket and shoulder holster and laid them down over the weapon.

"Let's move to the kitchen," Jimmy said. "If I don't get coffee into me, I won't be able to stay conscious long enough to talk."

Archer rose from the chair and extended his arm. Jimmy accepted the handshake.

With further introductions unnecessary, Nathan Archer followed Jimmy Pigeon to the kitchen.

* * *

Boyle and Stephens brought coffee back for everyone. Billings and his partner, Randall, Detectives Williamson and Cole, Harriman and the second evidence investigator.

It was after midnight. Boyle had been on the job since eight that morning. He gathered them all together in front of the building.

"Cole, Williamson, why don't you call it a night, it's late. Pick it up again in the morning where you left off. If you're not available, ask your captain to find a couple of replacements from your station to continue the canvassing and bring them up to speed."

"We can be here," said Cole.

"Good. And I want all of your notes from this evening. Make photocopies and send them over to me at Parker Center in the morning."

"By the way, the woman who was seen running out back wasn't wearing headphones," Williamson said.

"Did you get a better description?" asked Boyle.

"Not really."

"Put whatever you have into the report. And when you get here tomorrow, go out in the direction she was running. Maybe someone saw her, saw which way she was going. Follow it as far as you can. Harriman, where are you guys at?"

"Just about done. We think there may have been someone else in the condo tonight."

"Oh?"

"The toilet," he said. "The seat was down and someone had urinated and not flushed. And there was toilet tissue in the bowl. It suggests a woman used it last. And there were fresh scuffmarks on the kitchen floor, near the door out to the patio. Rubber sole, probably running or tennis shoes, small. The marks didn't come from any of the shoes worn by Raft, Tully or Diaz."

"Our jogger?" said Stephens.

"Put it in your report, Harriman," said Boyle. "And speaking of shoes, I want to know about Tully's shoe, the tooth and the blue gravel, anything you can tell me. Also, get with the SMPD and LASD, find out who has the slugs that killed Edward Richards and Lenny Archer and have them sent over to you. I want them compared to the ones that killed Detective Tully. While you're at it, I want copies of everything they have on both those cases; evidence reports, medical reports, testimony, everything, all sent over to me at Parker as soon as possible. What about the suitcase at the kitchen door?"

"Packed and ready to go," said Cole. "I would say Diaz was planning to travel."

"Randall," Boyle said, turning to Billings' partner.

"Yes?"

"I want you to list all the vehicles parked back there in the lot. Makes, models, tag numbers. Billings."

"Yes?"

"I need you and your partner to remain here until the evidence team is done. Front and back. I want to know if anyone comes by, anything even slightly suspicious."

"There was a car that passed through here, drove in back and came out only a minute later," said Billings.

"The blue Mustang?" asked Randall.

"Yes," Billings said. "Male driver, female passenger."

"I saw it also. It rolled by me and didn't stop."

"I have the license plate number," said Billings.

"Have the tags run," said Boyle, "and put it into your report. I want all of your reports on my desk, first thing in the morning. Harriman, Cole, let me know what you find as you find it. Detective Stephens and I are leaving now. I'll be at Parker Center by eight."

"So?" said Stephens as he walked Boyle to his car.

"So, we may have an eyewitness, if we can find her."

"If our jogger was Hispanic," said Stephens, "and if she was in the condo, she may be a girlfriend of Ricky's. I'll check into it tomorrow. Unless you're looking to get in a little more overtime tonight."

"I'm looking to get in bed," said Boyle. "Thanks for coming down, I won't forget it. See you in the morning."

***

Archer and Jimmy sat at the kitchen table each working on a second cup of coffee.

The two men agreed it was very doubtful Lenny's death had something to do with a narcotics investigation; but neither man had the faintest idea about how his death could have anything at all to do with Charlie Chan.

"What was it you said you found in the office?" Jimmy asked.

"Fine blue gravel, like aquarium bedding," Nate said.

"And you found this near Lenny's desk?"

"Yes."

"There were two crime scene investigators working the room, why didn't they find it?"

"I can think of three possibilities. They missed it or they found traces and only collected what they needed. If they did get a sample, it will show up in the evidence report. If we could get our hands on it."

"And the third possibility?" Jimmy asked.

"The gravel may have been left after the investigators were done with that area of the room," said Archer. "Who else has been in the office between the time Lenny was discovered and the time I went in last night?"

"Only me, my associate Vinnie and the building super. As far as I know."

"Have you stepped into a fish tank lately?"

"No. Not lately."

"And if we could eliminate Vinnie and the super?"

"What you found could have been there before Lenny was killed," said Jimmy. "It could be in the report."

"That's true," Archer agreed. "I would still like to know who left it there. Who else was in the office Monday morning, with the evidence team?"

"Two LASD detectives, Raft and Tully."

"It's possible it came from one of them and it's nothing, but I would sleep much better if we could confirm it somehow; particularly if the police missed it entirely. Can we get hold of their evidence report?"

"Maybe, but it won't be easy."

"So we'll try hard. And I want to get into Richards' place."

"So do I. There may be a laptop there that could tell us something."

"How about tomorrow night, after dark?"

"Sure, why not. I was wondering what you did with Lenny's body."

"Bando's Funeral Home on Main Street, Sal Bando is an old friend."

"I spoke to the Navy. They'll give Lenny a military funeral."

"I'll take care of it. Lenny hated the Navy. All the Navy ever gave him was a drinking problem. We talked about it once, back when we were talking. Lenny wanted to be cremated. Sal Bando is making preparations."

"What happened between you and your brother?" Jimmy asked.

"Is that important?"

"I don't know. Is it?"

"Do you have anything to drink stronger than this coffee?"

"Sure."

Jimmy walked to the kitchen cabinet for the bottle of Jim Beam and two glasses.

Jimmy poured. Nate knocked his drink down in one shot and began his story as Jimmy poured him another.

It happened four years earlier. Lenny was drinking a lot. He had gone through bad periods on and off since his Navy service.

Lenny entered the Navy in 1968 and he was schooled in surveillance. He was shipped to the Tonkin Gulf, off South Vietnam, six months later. He was assigned to a cargo boat carrying mail, food, medical and military supplies up river to Dong Ha, near the demilitarized zone. He returned home a year later with a Navy Cross and an addiction to opium.

Lenny eventually kicked the drug habit, using liquor as a cure. Staying off the alcohol was a constant battle, a battle Lenny was losing badly when he and Nathan parted ways.

At the time, he was drinking heavily after three sober years. He had been living with a woman named Annie for two years and she didn't know him drunk. Nathan never learned why his brother fell off the wagon, but Lenny fell hard.

Late one night, Nathan's sleep was interrupted by loud pounding at his apartment door. He found Annie standing in the hall. She was trembling and the left side of her face was battered and swollen.

It was a chilling vision for Nate. He had seen his mother this way, when he and Lenny were boys, before she found the courage to take her two sons and flee from her husband's alcoholic violence.

Nate took Annie's elbow, gently guided her into the apartment and sat her on the couch. He gave her a moment or two to calm down before asking.

"Was it Lenny?"

"He's like a stranger, Nathan," Annie said, trying to slow her breathing. "The past four days he's been drinking every night and not coming home until two or three in the morning."

"I wondered why Lenny didn't show up at the office today. Why didn't you call me?"

"I was confused. I didn't know what was happening. I thought it was something I'd done, but he wouldn't tell me what was wrong. Things had been going so well between us. We had been talking about taking a trip together, maybe a honeymoon trip. He came home drunk again tonight. I told him it had to stop, that he had to talk to me or else seek outside help. Then he hit me. He hit me hard, Nate, and he left me there hurt. I didn't want to be there when he gets back. I can't believe I would ever feel this way, but I'm afraid of him. He really scared me tonight. I'm not sure if I can ever feel safe with Lenny again."

"You'll be safe here, Annie," Nate said. "I'll get you something cold to drink and some ice for the swelling. The sofa opens into a bed. There are sheets and a pillow in the hall closet. I'll see Lenny in the morning and try to find out what happened to set him off."

Annie was awake when Nate came out of his bedroom in the morning. She had closed the sofa bed and had cleared the sheets and pillow. The swelling on her face was still evident and her eye was ringed in purple and black.

"How did you sleep?" Nate asked.

"Not very well," she admitted.

Nathan felt compelled to call Lenny. Despite Lenny's actions the night before, Nate knew his brother loved Annie and would be worried about her being gone over night. Seeing Annie's bruised eye changed his mind. He decided he needed to see Lenny face to face.

"Can I use your shower?" Annie asked.

"Sure. There are clean towels in the hall closet," Nate said. "I'll make coffee."

Fifteen minutes later someone was rapping at the door. Nate moved from the kitchen to answer it. Lenny rushed in, extremely agitated.

"Annie's gone," he said. "I waited up all night and she never came home."

Nate could see Lenny had been up all night with a bottle; he was still very drunk. Before Nathan could say a word, Annie was calling from the bedroom.

"Nathan, do you have sweat pants and a t-shirt that I can borrow," Annie said as she walked into the front room wearing Nate's robe.

Nathan saw the terror in Annie's eyes as she spotted Lenny. He turned to Lenny and opened his mouth to explain, but before he could speak Lenny hit him in the face and he went down. And then Lenny was on top of him, punching him once, and then again, and Nate blacked out.

When Nate came to, Annie had his head in her lap and a wet towel across his forehead. Lenny was on the floor near them, a broken table lamp lying at his shoulder.

Lenny began to regain consciousness.

"I hit him, I thought he was going to kill you," Annie said. "I called the police."

Nate moved quickly to his brother. There was blood on the back of Lenny's head. Nate tried to help Lenny up, but Lenny shoved him away and tried to hit him again. A moment later, two uniformed officers came in from the hall. Lenny fought as they pulled him to his feet. One of them, Nolan, cuffed Lenny's hands behind his back. They each took hold of an arm and began to lead Lenny out.

"Where are you taking him?" Nate asked.

"We'll have a doctor look at him and then we need to take him to the station. You might want to see a doctor also, both of you," said Nolan.

"Leave him. I'll take care of him. I'm not pressing charges."

"It doesn't matter, we have to take him in and we need to write up an incident report," Nolan said. "You'll both need to come down to the police station to give statements. At that time, we can talk about charges."

Nate looked at Lenny; all he could see was hate in his brother's eyes.

And then the uniforms took Lenny away.

"That was the last time I saw my brother," Nate said. He poured another shot of Beam and he held the bottle out to Jimmy.

"I'm good," Jimmy said.

"When we arrived at the police station, they wouldn't let us see Lenny, so I asked to see Detective Barnum. John is an old friend of mine."

"I know Barnum," Jimmy said.

"We told John we weren't pressing charges, it was a misunderstanding and we didn't want to jeopardize Lenny's investigator's license. John said my brother was out of control. They had to sedate him at the hospital before they could patch up his head. John told us he would clear the arrest record only if Lenny went into an alcohol detox program. Thirty days, minimum. John said if Lenny wouldn't comply, I could commit him as next of kin. So, that's what I did. Lenny was in for sixty days. I tried to visit him a number of times the first month. He refused to see me. Finally I gave up. I thought it would be best for his recovery if I wasn't around when he got out. So, I packed up the apartment, and what I had in our office, and I moved down to San Diego. I started up my own business and I've been down there ever since. I tried more than a few times to reach out to my brother over the years, but he never responded. I guess Lenny got back on his feet and must have had the PI concern going well, at least well enough to take on a new partner."

"If it's any consolation, in the three years I worked with Lenny, I never knew him to take a drink," Jimmy said.

"The last thing I remember is that look of hate in his eyes. Consolation *might* come if I find out who did this to him. I have to go. I need to phone my wife, tell her I'll be up here a while longer," Nate said, finishing his drink. "I'll be staying at Lenny's place if you need me. Otherwise meet me at the office, nine tomorrow evening. We'll try to get into Richard's place without earning a B&E arrest."

Jimmy walked Nate to the door.

"What happened to Annie?" Jimmy asked.

"Annie wound up in San Diego also. Before Lenny was released from the rehab clinic she went down to stay with her sister."

"Did you ever run into her again?"

"She found out I was working there and she popped into my office one afternoon. We had lunch together. Five months later we were married," Archer said. "And I have to get out of here and telephone her. I'll see you tomorrow at nine. Thanks for the hospitality, next time I'll wait for you to invite me in. And, Jimmy."

"Yes?"

"For the time being," Nate said as he left, "I would prefer it if not too many people know I'm around."

Soon after the crime scene investigators had finished their work inside and left the scene, Officer Billings went to the back of the building to help his partner collect the information Boyle had requested on every parked vehicle.

When Billings and Randall were done, they locked and taped the back door of the condo and walked around to do the same in front.

After one last look around, the two officers climbed into their cruiser and drove off.

A few minutes later, a car that had been parked at the end of the street rolled up to the building and back to the parking area.

The car slipped into an open parking space and Frank Raft stepped out of the vehicle.

Raft quietly moved from car to car. Before long he came across a red Camaro with two large suitcases in the rear seat and a woman's handbag on the passenger seat.

A blinking red light on the dashboard told him he couldn't get to the bag without waking the neighborhood; he would have to settle for the registration.

Raft pulled out his notepad and copied the license plate number.

SIX-TEN-NINETY-FOUR

Peter Quince was at Sherman Oaks High School early on Friday morning, grading the Thursday afternoon tests from one of his Computer Sciences classes. He opened his desk drawer to look for a red pencil and spotted the disc, the files he copied from Kevin Tully's laptop and forgot about after Kevin came to pick up the computer. He placed the CD on the desktop as a reminder to get it to Kevin, found the pencil and went back to the test papers. Fifteen minutes later, one of his colleagues walked into the computer lab holding the *LA Times*.

"Good morning, Kathleen," Quince said.

"Peter, have you seen this?" she asked. She came over and placed the newspaper on the desk in front of him.

"What is it?" Quince asked.

"Here," she said, pointing out a short article on the bottom of page three. "Kevin Tully's father was killed."

"My God," said Quince. "That's horrible. Do you mind if I read this?"

"I'll leave it, I have to run to class," she said. "I feel so terrible. Kevin is such a great kid. And the state championship game is tomorrow. I'll talk with you later."

When she was gone, Peter read the article.

Bob Tully had been fatally shot by Ricardo Diaz at a Woodland Hills condominium. Diaz, a twice-convicted felon, was subsequently shot and killed by Tully's partner. Diaz was thought to have information about the deaths of Edward Richards, a freelance news reporter, and Leonard Archer, a Santa Monica private investigator.

Quince turned from the *Times* to the compact disc on his desk. The previous day, he had written the names Tully and Richards on the face of the CD. Peter Quince added the name Archer and returned the disc to the desk drawer.

* * *

Raft pulled up to the front of a small house in South Central LA. After a torturous hour with his commander the night before, trying to explain the fiasco out in Woodland Hills, Raft had run the plates of the Camaro. Angel Rivas. Twenty-four years old. Five-six. One hundred twenty-nine pounds. Bingo. Before leaving his car, Raft examined his face in the rear view mirror. Knit cap, dark thick-framed glasses, bushy stage mustache. It would do.

It was just before eight in the morning when Raft rang the doorbell. He flashed his detective shield to the woman who answered and then and he quickly put it away.

"Detective Johnson, LAPD," he said. "I'm looking for Angel Rivas."

"I'm her mother. Is there something wrong?"

"Is she here?"

"No. What is this about, Detective?"

"Can you tell me where she is?"

"Not if you can't tell me what it's about."

"A man named Ricardo Diaz was killed last night. We have reason to believe your daughter may have known Diaz. We need to speak with her."

"*Dios mio*, Angel was supposed to be with Ricardo last night. They were taking a trip. She was all packed to go."

"We found her car behind Ricardo's condo, there was no sign of your daughter," Raft said. "Would you have any idea where she may be?"

"No."

"Please think, *señora*. Someone she may have gone to if she was frightened or in trouble?"

"Ricardo has a close friend, Carlos, the three were often together. Angel liked Carlos very much."

"What's his last name? Where does he live?"

"Santa Monica, I think. I don't know his last name."

"Please, *señora*. Your daughter may be in danger."

"My God. How was Ricardo killed?"

"I can't talk about the investigation, *señora*. We will do all we can to see that Angel is safe."

"I will call Angel's friends; maybe one of the girls has heard from her or knows how to find Carlos. Is there a phone number where I can reach you, Detective...?"

"Johnson. It would be best if I call you. I'll check back with you this afternoon, sooner if we learn anything." Raft thanked the woman and he returned to his car. He pulled off the cap and eyeglasses, peeled the mustache from his upper lip, and dropped them all on the passenger seat.

Carlos from Santa Monica. Great fucking help.

Raft looked at his wristwatch. Eight-fifteen. He had to meet with Commander Jefferson and two investigators from IAD at nine. *Go over the same fucking thing again for the third fucking time fucking Boyle fucking Jefferson fucking Internal Affairs.* And then he would have to think of what the fuck he was going to say to Jackson Masters.

Carlos had made up the sofa for Angel and finally she had settled down enough to get to sleep. At eight-fifteen Friday morning, Angel was pacing the kitchen like a caged animal as Carlos prepared breakfast.

"What am I going to do?" she said.

"You need to call your mother," said Carlos. "If she hears about Ricardo, she'll be worried sick."

Ray Boyle had told everyone he would be back at Parker Center by eight in the morning; had urged them to send over everything they had, first thing. At eight-thirty he was having breakfast at a favorite greasy spoon. Boyle had decided to get in at nine, with faint hopes that at least a few of the reports would show up *only* an hour late. It was well after ten before an LAPD mailroom clerk arrived with a large brown envelope sent over from the LA County Sheriff's Department. The envelope held copies of LASD reports, all of the information they had collected regarding the Archer homicide before turning it over to SMPD.

Lenny Archer was still alive at midnight Sunday. An attorney working late in an adjoining office saw Archer come in. The lawyer left his office a few minutes later, exiting through the rear of the building. The building super discovered Archer's body at seven Monday morning and phoned 9-1-1.

Detectives Raft and Tully were available and closest to the scene. They responded to the all-points radio call. The Santa Monica medical examiner, Solomon Meyers, arrived around ten. Meyers had determined from examination at the scene that Archer had been dead no fewer than eight hours. He estimated the time of death fell between midnight and two; an estimate later supported by lab tests and the attorney's eyewitness account.

Lenny Archer had been shot twice and had fired his own weapon. He had also been brutally beaten around the mouth, probably kicked. There had been extensive bleeding from an abdominal wound and a bullet wound to the left temple. By all indications the head wound was suffered after the wound to the stomach, but not immediately. Archer bled profusely and had been physically punished before the fatal bullet to the head.

Boyle had been trying his best to avoid involvement in the Archer case from the moment Jimmy Pigeon had brought it to him. Now, after seeing the details of the homicide, Ray found himself hoping the Diaz investigation might lead to the identification of the sick fuck that had ended Lenny Archer's life so coldheartedly.

Also among the papers in the brown manila envelope was an LASD ballistics report, indicating that Archer and Richards were killed with the same weapon, making the connection between the homicides official. Boyle had a strong feeling the weapon in question was the .38 that had killed Bob Tully, but Ray wasn't sure about how pleased the revelation would make him. *Too fucking perfect.*

Boyle moved on to the next report, listing all of the evidence collected at Archer's office by the investigators. An entry on the list caught Boyle's eye. Two loose teeth.

Boyle was reaching for the phone to make a call when it rang loudly.

"Boyle, Robbery Homicide," he answered.

"Detective Boyle, this is Officer Billings."

"I don't see your report on my desk, John."

"We were hoping to locate Jason Reed before we sent it over," Billings said.

"And who would that be?"

"We ran the license plates on the blue Mustang. The vehicle Randall and I both saw at the condo last night. The car is registered to Jason Reed, a twenty-two-year old kid from Woodland Hills."

Boyle couldn't help liking John Billings. A twenty-three-year old kid who referred to a twenty-two-year old kid as a kid.

"We went to the kid's house," Billings continued. "He wasn't in. His roommate said we would find Reed at his job around noon, he works at the movie theater in the Woodland Hills Mall."

"Probably dropped over to visit someone, didn't find the person's vehicle in the lot and drove on," said Boyle. "Check it out anyway. While you're waiting, head back to the scene and see how Cole and Williamson are doing. You and Randall can help them follow the girl's tracks."

Boyle ended the call and was waiting for a dial tone when Sam Stephens walked in. Boyle cradled the receiver.

"So?" Boyle said.

"So, I've been out all morning looking into Ricardo's love life," Stephens said. "Seems Diaz was running around with a girl from South Central. Angel."

"Angel what?"

"Angel something, that's all I got. This just came in from SMPD," Stephens said, holding up a thick folder. "It's the case file on the Richards homicide."

"I've got the Archer file here. We can take a look at them together and do what we do best."

"Wild guessing?"

"Precisely, have a seat," Boyle said, "and let's see what you've got there."

According to the SMPD Coroner's Office, Ed Richards died sometime between two and four on Monday morning; an estimate based on testing at the scene and then later in the laboratory.

A neighbor testified she heard loud voices coming from the Richards home at around two-thirty. She thought it was a TV at top volume and she tried ignoring it. Not long afterward she heard what sounded like a gunshot followed by a loud crashing sound. She dialed 9-1-1 at two-forty-nine.

"So Richards was killed after Archer," Stephens said.

"Looks that way, for what it's worth."

"And are we fairly certain these two homicides were connected?"

"According to LASD ballistics, the same weapon. How long does it take to get from Archer's office to Richards' place?"

"At that hour, on a Sunday night, ten minutes, fifteen tops."

"And what does that tell us?" asked Boyle.

"Not a hell of a lot."

The telephone on Boyle's desk rang.

"Boyle."

"Billings."

"Where are you, Billings?"

"We caught up with Detectives Williamson and Cole in Woodland Hills. They moved out from the rear of the Diaz condominium, in the same direction the girl was seen heading out. There's a road just off the parking lot that cuts through two subdivisions. A young woman fitting the description was seen running on that road at approximately eight-thirty yesterday evening and seen by another witness a mile further down."

"Get to the point, John."

"That road comes out directly in front of the Woodland Hills Mall," Billings said.

"And the movie theater."

"Yes."

"Go over there and find that kid, Jason Reed. Didn't you tell me the kid had a female passenger with him in the Mustang?"

"Yes."

"Get there, Billings. Wait for him if he hasn't shown up yet. Phone me as soon as you know what the kid was doing at the condo last night and who he was with."

Boyle hung up the phone.

"We may have caught a break," Boyle said to Stephens. "Our jogger may have been in the blue Mustang that did the drive-by last night and we've found the driver. He might be able to ID the girl."

"Makes me wonder," said Stephens.

"What?"

"If she was in such a hurry to get out of there, why would she want a ride back?"

"Good question."

Before they could come up with a good answer, they got word that the ME wanted them down at the Coroner's Office.

SURVIVORS

Jimmy Pigeon had a hard time getting to sleep Thursday night and consequently slept in late Friday morning.

Jimmy had not been entirely truthful with Nate Archer. He wasn't sure why. There *had* been an incident, about a year earlier, when Lenny Archer had hit the bottle hard. Jimmy got a call from Murphy at the saloon. Lenny had been drinking for hours and was out of control. Jimmy ran down and somehow managed to get Lenny away from the bar and back to his apartment. Pigeon sat with his partner for two days before he felt it was safe to leave Lenny alone.

In 1968, Archer was assigned to a cargo boat in South Vietnam. Running up river to Dong Ha, the small craft was fiercely shelled by enemy mortar fire. All but three crew members were killed. The survivors, Lenny Archer, Bernie Silver and Ted Anders, made it to shore and, after a fierce firefight, retreated into the jungle. It took thirty-six hours for a Marine patrol from Dong Ha to get close enough to pull them out. The three survivors remained very tight through the years following what Lenny could only describe to Jimmy as *a horrible, dehumanizing, living nightmare.*

In 1990, Ted Anders and Lenny Archer received notice that Bernie Silver had passed away. Lung cancer. The two men met in Los Angeles and embarked on a marathon drinking binge. Afterwards, Archer continued drinking heavily over the next four days.

After hearing about Lenny and Annie from Nate Archer, Jimmy realized the events that had torn the brothers apart coincided with Bernie Silver's death back in 1990.

The night Pigeon dragged Lenny out of Murphy's Saloon three years later, Lenny was clutching a telegram; holding the news that Ted Anders had taken his own life.

What Jimmy couldn't decide was whether that knowledge would benefit Nate Archer in any way. The inner debate had kept him up half the night and remained unresolved Friday morning.

Finally up and ready to face the day at eleven-thirty, Jimmy made his way over to Meg's Café.

Ninety minutes in with Internal Affairs investigators had Frank Raft about to go postal.

After the IAD scumbags finally got off his back, Raft told Commander Jefferson he was calling it quits for the rest of the day. His impulse was to go back to Woodland Hills and ask around, try to find out who the fuck Carlos was. Raft decided it wasn't a great idea. Had risked enough by going out to visit Angel's mother, false identity or not.

With no excuse to put it off any longer, Raft headed out for Sherman Oaks to offer condolences to Tully's wife and son; knowing it would prove to be much more difficult than bumping heads with fucking IAD.

When Boyle and Stephens reached the Coroner's Office they found Harriman in with Dr. Jackson.

"Harriman. Just the man I wanted to see," Boyle said.

"I'm short on time, Ray," Jackson said. "Let me give you what I have, so I can get out of here."

"Go on."

"Tully was definitely down when he took the bullet to the head. Makes me wonder what Frank Raft was doing while Diaz was taking the time to move in for the kill."

"He says Tully went in first and was shot immediately. Raft pulled his weapon before following and heard a second shot," said Boyle. "He rushed in and fired at Diaz twice."

"I suppose it's possible," said Jackson. "There isn't much more I can tell you and I really have to run."

With that Jackson was gone and Boyle shifted attention to Harriman from SID, Scientific Investigations Division.

"The tooth wedged in Tully's sole was an adult molar," Harriman said. "I still believe the blue gravel is exactly what I thought it was last night."

"Fish tank bedding."

"Yes. And we're sure the tooth was picked up first."

"If you looked at two other teeth, could you tell if they came from the same mouth?" Boyle asked.

"DNA, dental records, but it would be much faster if I had the mouth."

"I know we can get the teeth. There were two of them collected at the scene and according to the medical report Archer lost three neighboring teeth that night. The third tooth was never found. The ME checked Archer's stomach and determined Archer hadn't swallowed it."

"Tully was at the scene investigating the homicide," said Stephens. "Tully may have picked it up on his shoe before the evidence guys arrived."

"Sure, but I want to know if that's the errant molar; missing evidence bugs me. Try locating the body if it's still around. Otherwise, have the two other teeth sent over from whoever the fuck has them; see what you can come up with. Did we get the .38 slugs we asked for?"

"They're down in ballistics with the gun and the bullets that killed Tully. We should have word in a few hours."

"Keep me informed," said Boyle.

Harriman left just as a uniformed officer came to the door of the Coroner's Office.

"Telephone call for you, Detective Boyle," he said. "You can take it at Dr. Jackson's desk."

"Thanks," Boyle said. He picked up the receiver and hit the blinking hold button. "This is Boyle."

"This is Billings."

"What?"

"We found the kid. He met a girl at the movie theater last night, called herself Angel."

"Son of a bitch. Did he get a last name?"

"No. She asked to be driven to the condo, to pick up her car."

"What kind of car?"

"He doesn't know. When they got back to the parking lot she told him to keep driving and leave," Billings said. "Maybe seeing Randall there scared her off. In any event, she told him to drive her out to Santa Monica. He claims he dropped her there and then he went home."

"Have him take you over to where he dropped her, take Randall. Go back to the condo first. Tell Williamson and Cole we need to locate her car, need to look for cars that shouldn't be there, don't belong to any of the tenants."

"Okay."

"Tell them to look in the windows of all of the vehicles. If Diaz was ready to leave town, maybe she was there to give him a ride. Have them look for baggage, whatever, and have them call me if they find something. And you call me as soon as you and the kid get to Santa Monica. I'm going back to my desk at Parker Center. I don't want you to go in anywhere before you call me. Understood?"

"Yes."

"Good work, John."

"Thank you," said Billings before signing off.

"Well?" asked Stephens.

"We'll see," said Boyle.

"What's the thing that most peaks your interest, Ray, I mean beside who did what to who?"

"Peaks my interest?"

"Stimulates your imagination."

"I guess it would be blue fish tank gravel, Sam."

Jimmy grabbed an *LA Times* from the counter at Meg's. He ordered a late breakfast from Pam Walker and carried the newspaper and coffee to a booth to wait for his food.

Pigeon put the front section aside and went to Sports. The Dodgers had miraculously held onto first place since overtaking the Giants four weeks earlier. After a 5-4 loss to the Marlins on Wednesday and a travel day Thursday, they were set for a weekend series against the Cubs at Wrigley.

Pigeon wondered how much this would all really matter if the players decided to go out on strike. He moved on to the Weekend section to check out the new movie releases.

A few minutes later Meg came over to the booth with his bacon, eggs and toast.

"Hey," Jimmy said. "Can you get off this afternoon?"

"Probably, what's up?" she asked, taking a seat.

"There's a new movie opening today that I'd like to see, I thought we might catch a matinee."

"Why not tonight?"

"Too many teenagers on Friday night," Jimmy said. "And I was planning to watch the Dodger game."

"What time this afternoon?"

"There's a showing at two-thirty, over at the Woodland Hills Mall. We could grab a quick bite after the show."

"You're on. What's the film?"

"*Speed.*"

"What's it about, amphetamines?"

"It's an action, suspense movie."

"What's the attraction?"

"According to this review here, it's a heart-thumping, non-stop roller coaster ride," said Jimmy. "And more than that, I make it my business to never miss a Dennis Hopper flick."

"Well, Jimmy, I can't argue with you there," Meg said. "And by the way?"

"Yes?"

"What's going on with plans for Lenny's funeral?"

"Seems his brother turned up and collected his body. I guess he's making his own plans."

"That's it?"

"That's it," Jimmy said, hoping Meg wouldn't ask him if he'd run into Nathan Archer. She didn't.

"Okay, I need to get back to work," Meg said, hopping to her feet. "I'll be ready at two."

Nate Archer had decided what he would like to do just before calling his wife the night before. Nate would have more than enough time to go down there and be back to meet Jimmy Pigeon by nine. When Nate told Annie what he had in mind, she quickly agreed.

Friday afternoon at one, Nathan was on the road down to San Diego. Lenny's ashes were resting on the passenger seat in a plain brown cardboard box.

***

Boyle was back at his desk at Parker with Stephens when the telephone rang.

"Boyle."

"It's Billings."

"Where are you?"

"In front of the house where the kid dropped the girl last night. Santa Monica, Ninth Street off Washington."

"Okay, John. Listen carefully. The kid stays in the car. Send Randall to the back of the house, you go to the front. Ring a bell, knock on a door, find out if the girl is there. Call me the minute you get anything."

"Got it," said Billings.

"Stay alert, John," Boyle said before hanging up.

"What's up?" asked Stephens.

"Waiting," said Boyle.

Five minutes later the phone rang, Boyle lunged at it.

"Billings?"

"It's Detective Williamson."

"Go ahead."

"We found a car, a red Camaro, suitcases in the back seat," Williamson said. "We ran the plates. Angel Rivas, South Central address."

"Let me have it."

"Want the phone number also?"

"Sure," said Boyle. He jotted down the information. "Call for an evidence team and stay with the vehicle."

Angel Rivas spotted the squad car from a window in the front room. She watched two uniformed officers move toward the white house across Ninth and then she recognized Jason in the back seat of the cruiser.

"Shit, shit, shit."

"What is it?" asked Carlos.

"Cops. Across the street. The kid from last night brought them."

"Get away from the window, Angel. I don't think they'll be checking every house. If they do show up here, I'll play dumb. Stay cool. Did you phone your mother?"

"No."

"Call her," Carlos said.

Maria Rivas hurried to answer the telephone.

"Angel?"

"This is Detective Johnson, *señora*," said Frank Raft. "I spoke with you earlier. I'm calling to find out if you heard anything from or about your daughter."

"I spoke to one of her girlfriends," Mrs. Rivas said. "Ricardo's friend, the boy I mentioned, his name is Valdez. Carlos Valdez. And he does live in Santa Monica. That's all I can tell you."

"That's a great help, we should be able to locate an address and send someone right over there. Your daughter is going to be all right."

"And you'll call me if you find Angel?"

"Without fail, *señora*," Raft said.

He put the telephone down and began his search for an address on Carlos Valdez in Santa Monica.

Boyle and Stephens were almost out of the office when the phone rang.

"Boyle."

"This is Billings. The woman in the house never heard of the girl and didn't notice anyone getting dropped off in front last night."

"We found an address on her, in South Central. We're heading over there," Boyle said. "Her name is Angel Rivas. Check some of the neighboring houses."

"Should we check both sides of the street?" Billings asked.

"Use your own judgment," Boyle said. "Call dispatch if you get anything, they'll find us."

He put down the phone and turned to Stephens.

"Let's roll to South Central," Boyle said.

Raft checked the *Santa Monica White Pages*. He found three possibles. CJ Valdez, Carlos Valdez, Carlos Miguel Valdez. He moved to Tully's desk and found Tully's login password taped to the bottom of the keyboard. Raft logged on and punched up DMV data for all three names.

Carlos Miguel Valdez fit the bill. Close to the same age as Diaz, Valdez looked vaguely familiar. Raft thought he may have seen Carlos once or twice, running around with Ricardo. Then again, to Raft they all looked alike.

Valdez lived on Ninth Street. Raft pulled up a Santa Monica city map to find the cross streets; the address was between Washington and Idaho Avenues.

Raft took one last look at the driver's license photo. He decided he *had* seen Carlos before. It was time to see Carlos again.

Billings and Randall separated to canvass residences on both sides of the home they had visited, deciding they would check three houses in each direction. In less than ten minutes both officers were back at the squad car with nothing.

"Well?" asked Randall.

The kid in the back seat was complaining loudly that he had to get back to work.

"Let's try the two houses directly across the street," Billings said. "Then we can take him back to the Mall and check in with Detective Boyle. I'll take the green one on the left."

The two officers crossed Ninth Street.

Angel tried to phone her mother but the line had been busy. Now she was back at the window watching as a police officer crossed Ninth and came toward the house.

"Carlos, one of the cops is out here," Angel called. "Carlos, he's walking up the front steps."

"Calm down," Carlos said, coming out from the kitchen. "Go stand at the back door. I'll take care of it."

Angel moved quickly through the kitchen and hid out of sight at the rear exit of the house. A moment later, there was a rapping on the front door.

Carlos put on his poker face.

"Sorry to bother you, sir," Billings said when Carlos opened the door.

"No bother, Officer. Can I help you?"

"We're looking for a young woman who was dropped off here last night, just across the street. I was wondering if you saw or heard anything."

"We get a lot of traffic here at night. It can get annoying, I try to ignore it."

"This would have been around midnight."

"Sorry, nothing," Carlos said.

"Do you know a woman named Angel Rivas?"

Valdez paused for a moment, trying to quickly decide if the officer already knew the answer to the question.

"No," Carlos finally said, calling the bluff.

"You don't?" Billings said. He waited for a moment, Carlos stood mute. "Well, again, sorry for intruding."

Carlos watched Billings walk down the front steps and he closed the door.

"He left. I told you there was nothing to sweat about," he called, walking to the kitchen. "Angel? Did you hear me? The cop split."

His wallet was on the kitchen table, emptied.

The back door was wide open.

Angel was gone.

"Anything?" Billings asked, back at the patrol car.

"Nothing," Randall said. "Let's go before this kid has a nervous breakdown and then maybe we can get lunch before I pass out."

The officers climbed into the cruiser and drove away.

* * *

He had turned onto Ninth from Wilshire heading north and saw the LAPD cruiser before reaching the intersection at Washington. He parked close to the corner and watched. He spotted two officers returning to the patrol car and a few moments later they climbed in and drove away toward Idaho Avenue. He threw on the eyeglasses and knit cap.

He couldn't find the mustache.

"Fuck it," Frank Raft said.

He got out of the car, crossed Washington, and walked up Ninth toward the Valdez address.

"Hold on," Billings said after they turned the corner onto Idaho. "Pull over."

"What?" asked Randall, stopping the car.

"I want to stick around. Something at the last house bothered me, drop the kid at the Mall and come back. Call Boyle and tell him I'm still here."

"I shouldn't let you stay here alone. Detective Boyle won't like it."

"It's okay. I'm just going to watch the house. Bring back some food."

Billings got out of the cruiser and walked back toward Ninth Street.

Angel had moved quickly up the alley between Ninth and Tenth to Wilshire, over to Twelfth and down to Broadway.

She found a pay phone at Broadway and Sixteenth. She had taken four twenty-dollar bills from Carlos' wallet and had grabbed some change from a bowl on his kitchen counter. She called her mother.

"*Hola.*"

"Mama."

"Angel. *Dios mio, novia,* where are you?"

"Mama, please listen. Don't talk. I need money and a car. And clothing. I'll call you later and tell you where to meet me."

"Angel, the police are searching for you, a detective came. He told me Ricardo is dead and you could be in danger."

"I know about Ricardo, Mama. Don't talk to anyone."

"Angel, whatever it is, the police can help you."

"No, Mama. No police. I don't know who we can trust. If they come again don't say a word. You haven't spoken to me. Promise me, Mama, no police."

"Yes. I promise."

"I'll call you later, Mama. I love you."

Angel hung up and glanced up and down Broadway. She saw a motel sign three blocks east on Nineteenth.

Angel quickly headed that way, hoping the motel accepted cash.

A few moments after Mrs. Rivas had spoken to Angel on the telephone, Detectives Boyle and Stephens were knocking on her front door.

Raft had his shield out when Carlos opened the door.

"SMPD," Raft said. "Are you Carlos Miguel Valdez?"

"Yes, is there a problem?"

"We're looking for Angel Rivas and we have reason to believe she may have come here."

"I don't know an Angel Rivas," Carlos said.

"It's a bad mistake to lie to a police detective," said Raft. "I spoke with Angel's mother."

"All right, I do know Angel. She was here, but she's gone," Carlos said, hoping to cut his losses.

"Then you won't mind if I come inside and take a look around."

"Yes, I would mind."

"Well that's too fucking bad because I insist."

Raft stiff-armed Carlos and sent Valdez halfway into the front room on his back. The detective stepped inside, shut the door and pulled out his throwaway weapon.

"Jesus, I know you, you're Raft," Carlos said, looking up from the floor.

"And you're fucked," Raft said. "Now, where is she?"

When Billings turned onto Ninth, he saw a man stepping through the door of the green house. He considered calling for backup. He didn't call.

Instead, he walked back down to the house, climbed the front steps and rapped on the door.

Raft had Carlos up on his feet and was holding the gun to his head.

He shoved Carlos to the front door.

"See who's out there," Raft said.

Carlos glanced through the window.

"It's a cop, he was here before," Carlos said. "That's why Angel ran. I swear she's gone and I have no idea where she went."

Billings rapped on the door again.

"Shut the fuck up and open the door," said Raft. "And if you say a single word, I will kill you both."

"Well, do you think she was holding out on us?" asked Stephens. They were heading back to the car after talking with Angel's mother.

"I don't know, my Spanish is rusty," Boyle said. "We told her six different ways that her kid was in danger and the goon with the ski cap and mustache was no fucking LAPD detective. If that didn't persuade the woman to open up to us, maybe she's honestly in the dark."

"So, what now?" Stephens asked.

"We pick up a pizza and head back over to Parker. We hope for a break. Maybe we find out something about teeth or .38 slugs or blue fucking gravel or Billings calls to tell us he bumped into an Angel on the Boulevard."

"What if this is exactly what it looks like? Ricky Diaz shoots Archer and Richards to stop their snooping, Tully and

Raft stumble on it, Ricky shoots Tully, Raft shoots Ricky and Angel is running scared."

"Then who the fuck came to visit Angel's mother saying he was LAPD? Who else is looking for the girl and why? We can only hope her mother *doesn't* know where she is; if she gave the mustache more than she gave to us we could all be fucked."

"Maybe Ricky wasn't alone when he went after Richards and Archer," said Stephens. "What if there's an accomplice out there and Angel knows something about it? It could be why she's running and why she's avoiding the police. She's afraid she might be implicated."

"Or afraid she might be eliminated," said Boyle as they got into the car. "What do you want on the pizza?"

It was two-thirty Friday afternoon.

Raft had exited the green house through the back door, walked the alley to Washington and crossed over to his car on Ninth. He slipped behind the wheel and drove off.

Randall dropped Jason at Woodland Hills Mall. He was reluctant to tell Boyle he'd left Billings behind, so he never called Boyle. Instead, he picked up two take-out burritos and headed straight back to Santa Monica.

Jimmy Pigeon and Meg Kelly were sitting in one of the movie theater auditoriums at Woodland Hills Mall patiently waiting for the Dennis Hopper flick to begin.

Angel had checked into the motel on Broadway, having sweet-talked the check-in clerk into taking sixty dollars to cover the cost of the room and a twenty-dollar deposit for phone calls. In the motel room, she threw herself on the bed and lay there crying.

Peter Quince was preparing to leave the high school, looking forward to the weekend. Before he rose from his desk, he remembered the CD. He opened the drawer and took the CD out. He had been thinking about Kevin Tully all day and about the files he'd copied from the laptop. Files authored by Edward Richards. He didn't know what to do with the disc, who to turn it over to. However, he did know he was very curious about the contents of the files.

Quince placed the CD into his briefcase, thinking it wouldn't hurt to look it over at home for few days while he decided where it should go from there.

Boyle and Stephens were back at Parker Center. The ballistics report confirmed the weapon used to kill Richards and Archer was the gun that killed Tully. They were waiting for Lenny's dental records to arrive at the lab, where they would try to determine if the tooth from Tully's shoe came from Archer's mouth.

Nate and Annie Archer had driven across the Route 75 bridge from San Diego to Coronado and then traveled south on Silver Strand Boulevard toward the U.S. Naval Amphibious Base. They stopped along the east shore and moved to the water's edge, the downtown skyline rising across the way. Nate opened the cardboard box and very gently spilled his brother's ashes into the San Diego Bay; he placed the box on the ground at his feet, stood behind Annie and reached his arms around her waist.

"I can barely bring my fingertips together," Nathan said.

"And whose fault is that?" Annie said.

"Annie?"

"Yes?"

"If it's a boy?"

"Sure, but only if it's a boy," Annie said, turning to face him. "Will you stay down here with me tonight? We can think about girl's names, just in case."

When Randall turned onto Ninth, he immediately saw the two police cars. He drove up as close as he could, double-parked, threw the burrito onto the passenger seat and jumped out of the car. He rushed over to the green house, but was stopped at the door by two Santa Monica police officers.

"I'm sorry, we can't let you in," one of the officers said.

"My partner may be in there," Randall pleaded.

"Wait here, I'll get Detective Barnum."

Randall waited, the second officer blocking his way.

Fifteen minutes passed, during which time an ambulance had arrived. And then twenty minutes more, spent answering questions for Barnum once the detective appeared. And then another forty minutes passed before Officer Randall learned anything about the scene inside.

An hour later, Ray Boyle finally got the call.

It took them less than twenty minutes to make it from Parker Center to Santa Monica. Siren screaming, dome light flashing, Stephens speeding as fast as the car would travel because Boyle was ticking like a time bomb ready to blow.

Boyle jumped out of the car before it stopped rolling and ran to the house. Stephens stomped on the brake pedal, threw the car into Park and chased after Boyle holding his detective shield high above his head yelling *"LAPD"* at the two SMPD uniforms stationed at the door, knowing Ray Boyle was not in a mind to deal with formalities; although the look in Ray's eyes as he ran up the steps was enough to inspire the officers to make way.

Stephens stopped on the front porch to exchange a few words with the two uniforms before following Boyle into the house.

Stephens found Boyle, fists clenched, looking down at the dead body of John Billings. He quietly came up behind Ray and placed his hand on his partner's shoulder.

"Goddamnit," Boyle said. "Goddamn-this-fucking-goddamned job."

"The fucking job," Stephens said. "You are absolutely right, Ray, now loosen up before you burst a blood vessel."

"Twenty-three years old, Sam."

"I know, Ray, it's bad news. But it is what it is, and now we need to figure out what the fuck it is."

"Find out where his partner is, Sam," Boyle said.

"Officer Randall is at West Valley station, trying to explain to his captain how this thing went so wrong," said SMPD Detective Barnum, approaching Stephens and Boyle. "I talked with Randall for twenty minutes, but it didn't tell me much. I was trying to understand what the two officers were doing here in Santa Monica in the first place."

"They were following a lead," said Stephens. "Putting one foot in front of the other."

"So I heard, but it led here and we like to know when someone is shaking a tree in our neck of the woods."

"It's not a real good time for a lecture," Boyle said. "True, we should have reached out to you. I apologize, get over it and help us now. What do you *think* happened here?"

"By the looks of it, they shot each other."

"And how does that play?" asked Boyle. "They each take five paces, turn and draw."

"Neighbors from three separate houses reported hearing two gunshots, coming out to the street, seeing no one leave this house and calling it in. I'm only telling you how it appears; two weapons found, two gunshots fired and two men down. It'll take more time before we can determine if it's any fancier than that."

"Who's the other DOA?" Boyle asked.

"Driver's license says Carlos Miguel Valdez. And then we found this," Barnum said, scooping up a plastic evidence bag from the sofa, "between the cushions."

Boyle took the bag. It held a set of keys attached to a small purse inscribed with the name *Angel*. He passed the bag to Stephens and headed outside. Stephens looked at the purse and handed the plastic bag back to Barnum.

"Thanks," Stephens said, hurrying after Boyle.

Barnum called after them, something about quid pro quo but no one was listening. Boyle was in the car, behind the wheel, engine running. Stephens jumped in.

"Call dispatch," Boyle said. "Send two unmarked cars to South Central. We want one in front and one behind the Rivas house; two plainclothes in each car watching for the girl and the girl's mother goes nowhere without a tail."

Boyle shifted into Drive and punched the accelerator.

After speaking with Angel and stonewalling Detectives Boyle and Stephens, Maria Rivas rushed to the bank and she withdrew a thousand dollars in cash from a savings account. Returning home, Maria went through the clothing Angel had left behind. She packed undergarments and casual wear into a large suitcase. In a top drawer of Angel's dresser, she found Angel's passport; thankful for a change that her daughter's habitual lack of sensible planning had resulted in her forgetting it in the first place. She put the passport, cash and a bank debit card into a small hand purse.

Maria's car was parked in the drive, closer to the back of the house. She threw the suitcase into her trunk.

Now she sat nervously near the telephone, waiting for her daughter to call.

Before making it back over to Parker Center, Stephens and Boyle were called to an apartment complex in Westwood. Domestic disturbance, shots fired.

"Motherfucker," Boyle said.

"What can you do, Ray," Stephens said. "It's like a shooting gallery out here."

"Call Tanner, tell him we're in the middle of something."

"You know what the captain will say, Ray. *We've got to be able to keep more than one ball in the air.*"

"Fucking circus sideshow jugglers."

"There you go."

"Tanner and his clever fucking analogies."

"He's got a way with words."

"And I've got his *balls in the air* swinging. Call him and make sure the two cars are planted outside the Rivas house," Boyle said. "And tell Ringmaster Tanner no one better fuck up. Son of a bitch, what's the fucking address in Westwood?"

Jimmy and Meg had dinner in a Vietnamese restaurant in Woodland Hills after the movie and then went to Meg's Café for coffee and dessert.

When Jimmy left the café he drove out to Ed Richards' house, wanting to look over the lay of the land while there was still daylight.

The reporter's home, a large bungalow southwest of the intersection of Appian Way and Vincente Terrace, was fairly secluded with only one residence close enough to cause any concern. The rear of the bungalow was concealed by foliage and trees, which ultimately ended at the beach. Jimmy felt confident they could get up to Richards' place without attracting much attention if they parked their car on Ocean Avenue or Pico Boulevard and approached on foot.

After the short reconnaissance mission, Jimmy went to his office to check phone messages. He found thirteen and he hoped it wasn't an omen. Four telemarketing junk calls, three callers who thought Lenny Archer was still alive and four others trying to contact any private investigator who *was* alive. The other two messages were from Nathan Archer and Vinnie Strings.

Vinnie had called to remind Jimmy he would be out of the hospital and back home the next day. Vinnie said he had been going through the library book and he'd discovered a few things Pigeon should find interesting. The call from Archer was a notice of postponement. Archer had decided to remain overnight in San Diego with his wife. He apologized and said he would call in the morning, hoping they could go into the Richards place on Saturday night. Nate also asked if Pigeon happened to see the article on the bottom of page three of the Friday *LA Times*. Jimmy had only looked at the Sports and Weekend sections. He would pick up a copy of the *Times* on his way home.

Pigeon made seven return phone calls. All seven calls were picked up by machine. He didn't mind at all. He broke the news of Lenny's passing to three machines and told four machines the business would be on hiatus until further notice. He decided to wait until morning to call Vinnie.

Jimmy left the office and walked down to his car, all dressed up with no place to go, and he stopped at a liquor store on Main Street for a six-pack of beer. He picked up an *LA Times* from the counter and opened it to page three.

Jimmy found the short piece on the bottom of the page. LASD Detective Bob Tully had been killed in Woodland Hills. The shooter, Ricardo Diaz, was subsequently shot and killed by Detective Frank Raft. Diaz, a drug dealer, was believed to have information concerning the murders of journalist Ed Richards and private investigator Lenny Archer earlier that week.

Jimmy closed the *Times* and returned it to the counter. He grabbed the six-pack and his change and went back out to his car. He sat a while, trying to evaluate what he'd just read. He decided it was not enough information and he would do better to put it temporarily out of mind.

He went home to his apartment, popped open a bottle of Heineken and tuned in to the Dodgers and Cubs at Wrigley.

Angel decided to wait until eight to call her mother. She turned down the volume of the baseball game on the TV in the motel room.

"Hello?" Maria Rivas answered.

"It's me, Mama."

"Angel, I've been worried to death."

"I'm okay, Mama. Did you get money?"

"Yes, I have cash for you and a bank card," her mother said. "And I found your passport."

"Thank God, I have no identification at all. I left everything in my car."

"I packed clothes for you. I can let you have my car, but what will you do for a driver's license?"

"I'll have to take my chances," Angel said.

"Where will you go?"

"I don't know yet. Listen, I'm at the Best Western in Santa Monica at Nineteenth and Broadway, Room 210. Meet me here as soon as possible."

"I'll come right now," said Maria Rivas.

"And, Mama."

"*Si, novia?*"

"Bring food. I haven't eaten a thing all day."

Maria took her keys, the cash, passport and bank card and slipped out back. From the porch, she spotted the car in the alley behind the house. Black Ford, two men aboard. She lifted a house plant off the porch rail and carried it inside for effect. From the window in the front room, she saw a second car across the street. She went to the phone and called directory assistance for Santa Monica.

Maria got the number for the motel and spoke with the front desk clerk. She put the charges for Angel's room on her credit card, for that night and for Saturday, and then asked to be connected to her daughter's room.

When the phone rang, Angel jumped. She picked up the receiver and squeaked out a hello.

"Angel, there are cars in front and back of the house. I'm sure they are police. I cannot come to you now. They will follow me. I paid for your room, today and tomorrow. The front desk clerk will return your cash."

"Mama."

"It's all right, baby. I will figure it out somehow. Just stay there. Get something to eat. I promise I will call you and get you out of there as soon as I can."

"Please hurry, Mama."

"I will, baby. I love you."

Maria put the receiver down, placed her hands together on her lap and prayed.

Boyle and Stephens were back at Parker Center after a three-hour ordeal, coaxing a handgun away from a woman who had put two bullets through her bathroom door; her husband locked in the bathroom screaming out the window for help.

"The job," Stephens had said as they went up.

Two hours outside the apartment door pleading with the woman to let them in so they could work it out face-to-face. Forty minutes face-to-face, the .357 pointed at *them* now, telling the wife that no matter how much of a low down cheating son of a bitch he might be it wasn't worth twenty-five years to life in prison to teach the no good bastard a lesson he would never forget.

Finally, the woman agreed to give up the weapon; after putting two more bullets through the door for emphasis.

Balls in the air.

Back at Parker, Boyle got word that Maria Rivas was at her house. She had stepped out once, apparently to take in a house plant. Boyle radioed both of the stakeout cars and told them to stay put until replacements arrived at eleven. He wanted the house covered through the night. He asked to be paged if the woman moved or someone else arrived.

At last, Boyle and Stephens left Parker. Stephens off to family and late dinner; Boyle headed to the local saloon for a few drinks and a bar seat for the Dodgers ballgame.

"Well, we're still in first place," said the bartender when Boyle called for another Scotch.

"The way things are going, it only increases the odds of a fucking players' strike," Boyle said.

Angel went down to the front desk to pick up her cash.

"You owe me eighty dollars," she said to the check-in clerk. "My mother called and paid for the room. Rivas."

"Do you have ID?"

"No, I don't have ID," Angel said. "I lost my wallet. I'm the woman who handed you eighty dollars this afternoon. Don't you remember me?"

"Yes."

"Then *you're* my ID. Didn't my mother's credit card cut the mustard?"

"Yes."

"Okay then, bro. Give it up," Angel said.

The clerk took four twenties from the cash drawer and counted them twice before handing them to Angel.

"How much did a swell motor hotel like this set you back?" Angel asked, snatching the four bills.

"I don't own the motel," he said.

"You sure act like you do," she said and walked out onto Broadway to look for food.

Angel was back in twenty minutes with Chinese takeout and a quart of Diet Coke.

"Remember me?" she teased the clerk.

"Yes," he said.

He turned away and tried looking busy.

Angel grabbed a complimentary *LA Times* from the lobby and went back up to her room.

After devouring the beef with broccoli and pork fried rice she browsed through the *Times* and saw the piece about Ricky's death.

Bullshit.

If there was one thing she was sure about after twenty-four hours on the run it was that Ricardo had nothing to do with the two killings in Santa Monica.

Angel found a pen on the bedside table and circled the names Raft, Richards and Archer in the article. She looked in the local phone book, searching for Archer under Private Investigators. She located a listing for Archer and Pigeon Investigation. She circled the phone number and turned her attention to the baseball game.

And waited for her mother to rescue her.

***

Frank Raft had been watching the Rivas house from the corner of the street for three hours and the pair of LAPD plainclothes in the car out front. At eleven, another car pulled up and the first car drove off. Raft imagined the same scene was playing out in back. *Fucking LAPD.* He drove home, planning to return early Saturday morning.

Maria called the motel to inform Angel that a second set of police cars had arrived to replace the first.

"It looks like they'll be here all night," she said.

"What are we going to do, Mama?"

"I'll work something out," Maria promised again. "I'll call you in the morning. Try to relax and get some rest."

"I will, thank you, Mama," Angel said.

Relax and get some rest. Fat chance, Angel thought.

The Dodgers beat the Cubs, 2-1. During the post-game wrap up, the two broadcast commentators expressed optimism that the salary dispute would be settled in time to thwart a players strike.

Fat chance, Pigeon thought.

Jimmy turned off the TV, grabbed another beer and opened the paperback copy of *Les Misérables* to the page marked with an *Archer and Pigeon Investigation* business card.

RUNNING WITH THE BULLS

At seven on Saturday morning, Maria Rivas watched from her kitchen as a second car replaced the one sitting in the alley behind the house. She ran to the living room in time to see the changing of the guard on the street out front.

Her initial impulse was to phone her daughter, to tell Angel she would have to wait. Maria decided to put off the bad news, hoping Angel was getting some sleep. If the police continued to survey the house much longer she would have to come up with an alternate plan.

Frank Raft had been watching the house since six. He caught the shift change at seven and wondered how the LAPD could justify the manpower. *Fucking LAPD.* Raft had taken a few days off for Tully's wake and burial. He would have to get to the funeral parlor in Sherman Oaks at one. Raft poured a cup of coffee from a thermos and he thought about Jackson Masters. The old man was coming back to town that night and Masters was still waiting to hear that Raft had the situation under control. Raft's only comfort was his fee was about to increase considerably. Frank Raft had his mind set on early retirement. He took a doughnut from a paper bag on the car seat and hoped for a fucking break.

Angel had been awake for hours; she hadn't slept much at all. She was lying on the motel bed, watching a really dreadful movie on cable, stomach queasy from worry and the Chinese food, praying for the telephone to bring word from her mother. Angel took a shower, disgusted that she would have to get into the grubby underclothing and jogging suit she had been sweating in since the night before last. By eight she was climbing the walls trying to resist the urge to telephone Maria, wanting to spare her mother additional grief. Finally, Angel had to get out. She needed air and thought a walk would calm her down. She gathered all the money she had left, went down to the lobby, walked out onto Broadway and headed southeast toward the ocean.

Ten minutes later, Maria Rivas phoned the motel. She left a message, asking Angel to call. The day clerk wrote down her name. After the call, the clerk went back to the newspaper article he'd been reading. A gun battle the day before had led to the death of a Santa Monica resident and a uniformed police officer. SMPD was searching for a young woman named Angel Rivas, wanted for questioning. The desk clerk telephoned the Santa Monica Police Department asking to speak to the detective in charge of the investigation.

Barnum made it over to the motel in eight minutes.

Ray Boyle woke up with a splitting headache. Much too much Scotch Friday night. Before dragging himself into the shower he called Parker Center to make sure the Rivas house was covered.

"We still have cars in front and back," Stephens told Boyle, "but probably not for long."

"What do you mean?"

"The captain is bitching and moaning about overtime. He's ready to call them in."

"Stall him, Sam," Boyle said. "I'll be there in less than an hour."

Jimmy was up early on Saturday. He waited until after nine to call Vinnie Strings. Vinnie was asleep. Jimmy told Fran he would come over to the house around one in the afternoon to visit her and her son.

At nine-thirty, Jimmy sat at a booth in Meg's Café. A headline in the *Santa Monica Outlook* had caught his eye the moment he walked in. *Shootout on Ninth Street.* He grabbed the newspaper and read the front-page story over coffee.

The shooting, which took the lives of a civilian and a police officer, was thought to be related to the two deaths in Woodland Hills on Thursday and the deaths of Ed Richards and Lenny Archer at the beginning of the week.

What the hell was going on?

It was the first time investigators in any of the three police departments entangled in the *related* incidents had suggested the possibility there may have been more than one man involved. Pigeon knew there were two men in the office when Archer was killed, but had kept it to himself. A hold card, in the event the police decided the death of Ricky Diaz wrapped up the case. So here comes Carlos Valdez. Two suspects, both dead, end of story, case closed; drugs and guns, villains and martyrs, crime doesn't pay and police work doesn't pay enough. Good triumphs over evil at a terrible cost and the curtain falls.

So who in the world was Angel Rivas and what the hell could she possibly have as an encore to this Shakespearean slam-dunk?

Jimmy threw the newspaper across the table, frustrated and bewildered. He waved to the waitress for a refill.

Angel had walked to the Santa Monica pier with a large cup of fresh squeezed orange juice and sat down on a bench, needing to clear her mind and hoping to settle her stomach. The soothing sound of the ocean succeeded in doing both. In fact she lost track of time and was rushing back to the motel for word from her mother when she saw the headline on the cover of the Santa Monica daily paper through the front pane of a corner vending machine. *Shootout on Ninth Street.*

She dropped two quarters into the coin slot, scooped up the newspaper and found an empty chair in the rear of a nearby coffee shop. *Oh, God. Carlos.* Angel soon noticed her own name in the article and she knew she would not be returning to the motel.

"Bad news," said Stephens when Boyle reached Parker.

"Why am I not surprised?"

"SMPD put the girl's name out there. It showed up in a front-page story in the Santa Monica rag and Barnum got word the girl had checked into the Best Western. She must have stepped out earlier, Barnum has been over at the motel for more than an hour and she's not back."

"If she reads the newspaper she's not coming back."

"According to the motel clerk, her mother paid for the room and left a message for the girl this morning. I guess the woman wasn't entirely forthcoming when we talked to her yesterday."

"Let's go back to see her mother, try to convince the woman the girl is scared shitless and we need to find out what the fuck she's afraid of before it is too fucking late," Boyle said.

"Tanner wants to see you," Stephens said.

"The captain will have to wait," said Boyle. "Let's get out of here."

"Tanner won't be happy, Ray."

"Well, Sam, who the fuck is?"

Angel tried calling her mother, but the line was busy. She went to the counter for coffee. When she reached into her pocket for cash she found the piece of the page she had torn from the motel phone book. The address and the phone number for Archer and Pigeon Investigation. Angel sat for a while before trying to call her mother again.

Maria had been on the phone, calling the motel. When she asked for Angel's room, a police detective came on the line. Maria could honestly say she had no idea where her daughter had gone. A few minutes after Barnum finally let her go, Boyle and Stephens were at her front door. By the time Angel called again, Boyle had Maria so frightened the woman was ready to cooperate. She told Angel she would meet her at the coffee shop in thirty minutes.

"All you need to do is bring her out to your car and we'll be there," said Boyle. "Please believe me, you are doing the right thing. You are protecting your girl from harm."

Boyle told the stakeout teams to remain watching the Rivas house. Boyle and Stephens jumped into their car and waited until Maria came out of the driveway. They started off to Santa Monica and Maria followed.

Frank Raft pulled out from the curb at the end of the street and headed out after the two cars.

Jimmy made a quick stop at his office to check phone messages and thankfully he found only one. Nathan Archer would be at Jimmy's apartment at nine that night with his lock picks ready.

As Jimmy left the office he decided to leave the door unlocked. If anyone wanted to get in they would get in, no use jeopardizing the new window.

Angel stood inside a small boutique across the street from the coffee shop waiting for her mother; wanting to be sure Maria hadn't been followed. Angel had purchased and changed into fresh undergarments, a pair of gym shorts and a T-shirt reading *Property of the Los Angeles Raiders.*

From the window of the boutique, she saw Maria's car pull into the parking lot beside the coffee shop, and a second car pull in alongside. She saw Maria say several words to the other driver and walk to the coffee shop entrance.

Oh, Mama. Why?

Angel waited until Maria was inside. The two men in the second car remained in their vehicle. Angel put down the bag that held her old clothing, quickly walked out of the boutique and up the street away from the parking lot. Boyle and Stephens didn't notice her and she was soon out of their line of sight.

Frank Raft, in his car at the far end of the street, saw the girl come out of the boutique and move away at a slow run. He took off after the girl. When Raft turned the corner, she was gone. He looked at his watch. There was just enough time for him to get home and changed and over to the funeral parlor by one. Raft could only hope the girl would continue to be unbelievably adept at avoiding the police.

He wished her luck and he drove off.

Maria returned to the parking lot.

"Where is she?" asked Boyle, jumping out of the car.

"Gone, God help us," Maria answered. She was holding the purse in her hand; passport, bank card and a thousand dollars in cash. "My baby is still out there, all alone."

Boyle and Stephens followed Maria back to her house in South Central. When they arrived, both stakeout cars were gone.

"Motherfucker," said Boyle.

"It's Tanner, Ray. He said he would pull them off."

"That girl knows something, Sam. She was there at the Diaz condo and she was there at the Valdez place and if she disappears you know what will happen."

"Six homicides will be cleared and a couple of mayors and the brass of SMPD, LASD and LAPD will rejoice."

"They can all slap each other on the back until their hands are raw and swing from the fucking rafters until the next election, but I will not let them forget Officer John Billings. This case is open until I am convinced beyond a shadow of a doubt that his killer is not still out there."

"So be it, Ray. I am with you one hundred percent," said Stephens. "Except for tomorrow."

"What's tomorrow?"

"Tomorrow is my wedding anniversary. Thirty years of marital bliss. And if I fail to show Linda the time of her life, it will be me swinging from a rafter."

"Thirty years."

"Three zero."

"Lovely Linda. What a woman."

"They broke the mold, Ray."

CHARLIE CHAN IN BEVERLY HILLS

Jimmy Pigeon sat in an overstuffed armchair, a library book on his knees. Vinnie sat beside him in a wheel chair, his broken limb propped up horizontally by the leg support.

"Page seventy-three," Vinnie said.

Jimmy flipped through the pages.

"I'm making lunch for Vinnie," Fran said, coming into the room. "Can I interest you in a tuna sandwich, Jimmy?"

"I don't know, Fran," Jimmy said. "I'm not really sure if I'm hungry."

"Chunk white on white toast, lettuce and tomato."

"Hellman's mayonnaise?"

"Of course," Fran said.

"Sure, sound's great."

"Coming right up," said Fran, heading for the kitchen.

"Okay, I got it," said Jimmy, opening to page seventy-three of *Homes of the Hollywood Stars, History and Mystery* by Edward Richards. "What I am looking at?"

"You're looking at a mansion built for Warner Oland in 1933 at a cost of two hundred thousand bucks, a hefty chunk of change at the time. Warner Oland also owned mansions in Boston and Santa Barbara and a very large horse ranch down in Mexico."

"So, now that I have a good handle on his real estate portfolio," said Jimmy. "Who the hell is Warner Oland?"

"Warner Oland *was* an actor who played Charlie Chan in sixteen movies between 1931 and 1937."

"Well, how do you like that. What else?"

"What else?"

"We know from phone records that Lenny and Ed Richards were talking with each other and could have been working an investigation together, an investigation which possibly got them both killed. Lenny drops the name Charlie Chan onto a postcard and here is a photograph of Charlie

Chan's crib in Richards' book. If there's nothing else, then their deaths go down as two drug related homicides and goodbye Charlie," Jimmy said. "So, what else?"

"How about this," Vinnie said. "In 1937, Charlie Chan vanished."

"Tuna sandwiches and cold milk," Frances Stradivarius announced, carrying a tray into the living room.

"Vanished?"

"Disappeared."

"You should eat the sandwiches before they get soggy," Fran suggested.

"Disappeared. Hold that thought, Vinnie," Jimmy said.

Ray Boyle and Sam Stephens sat side by side in chairs facing Captain Tanner's desk.

Tanner stood behind the desk like a preacher about to give a sermon, which was exactly what he was about to do. The detectives had been warned to remain silent until Tanner was done speaking. Boyle made a big deal of locking his fingers together and placing his hands on his lap like a kid in Sunday school.

"Don't get cute, Ray," Tanner said.

They waited.

"I'm catching holy hell from upstairs because you guys are running all over creation looking for this girl with no concern for jurisdictional protocol. Whether we like it or not, we rely on cooperation from the County Sheriff and the local municipalities and they expect the same. There is an APB out on Angel Rivas and that is that. If you hear she's in Malibu or El Segundo or anywhere outside of the city you will notify the local police department and let them handle it. Am I understood?"

"Yes," said Stephens before Boyle could say something he would be sorry for.

"Good. Now whatever this girl may or may not have to contribute, the evidence speaks for itself. Everything we have says Ricky Diaz shot Bob Tully with the same gun that killed the reporter and the PI in Santa Monica. Diaz was a known drug felon and it's been confirmed that Carlos Valdez was a known associate. And there is no evidence to contradict the assumption that Valdez and Officer Billings killed one another in an unfortunate confrontation."

"Unfortunate confrontation," said Boyle, rising from his chair. "This is fucking bullshit."

"Sit down, Ray," Tanner said.

"The girl was in both places. How can we make fucking assumptions before we talk with her?"

"We don't know if she witnessed anything, Ray, and we don't know if she would tell us a thing if she did. There are three police departments aching to get these homicides cleared. That's the track this train is racing down, it's out of control and I have no way to stop it. And you guys are off the case. Now, please sit down, Ray."

Boyle looked down at the chair as if he was ready to hurl it through the window onto North Los Angeles Street.

"Sit, Ray," Stephens urged. Boyle sat.

"Sam, you're off tomorrow," Tanner said.

"Yes."

"I want you to take the rest of the day off. Both of you. Ray, you are on tomorrow, seven to three, and I need you on call Sunday midnight until seven Monday morning."

Tanner waited for a response, there was none.

"Then I want you both back here ready to work Monday morning. You have open cases on your desks; find one that keeps you in the city."

The two detectives rose to leave the office.

"Happy Anniversary, Sam," Tanner said.

"Thank you, Captain."

"Don't fuck around, Ray."

Fuck you, Captain.

"Great lunch, Fran," Jimmy said.

"I'm glad you enjoyed it, there's more tuna salad."

"Thanks, that was perfect. We should get to work."

"Then I'll leave you two alone," said Fran. "Yell if you need anything."

"Mom really likes you," Vinnie said when she was gone.

"And I really like her and you are very lucky to have her. Don't ever forget that, Vinnie."

"I know how lucky I am. Don't worry, I won't forget."

"Okay, good," Jimmy said. "Now, tell me about Charlie Chan's disappearing act."

Vinnie told Jimmy all he'd learned from reading books about Charlie Chan while trapped in his hospital bed.

Earl Derr Biggers, while vacationing in Honolulu in 1919, read a newspaper article about the remarkable work of a Chinese police detective named Chang Apana.

In 1925, the *Saturday Evening Post* carried the first installment of *The House Without a Key*, featuring Charlie Chan of the Honolulu Police Department. The story was so well received, Bobbs-Merrill published it in hardback. Biggers followed with a second Chan book, *The Chinese Parrot* in 1926. Both Chan titles were soon brought to the silent screen. The overwhelming popularity of the Charlie Chan franchise earned Biggers twenty-five thousand dollars for a serialized version of *Behind That Curtain.* In 1929, Fox Film Corporation paid the writer generously for screen rights to the third Chan mystery. Biggers would pen three more Chan stories before his death in 1933.

With the Fox Films release of *Charlie Chan Carries On* in 1931 and *The Black Camel* four months later, the Chinese detective became a national sensation and soon an overseas phenomenon. Fortunes were made. The success of the films rested squarely on the shoulders of a classically trained, Swedish born actor who brought immortality to the Oriental sleuth. Warner Oland would portray Charlie Chan in a total of sixteen films in less than seven years.

Then in 1937, Warner Oland disappeared.

Oland arrived in America from Sweden in 1892, at age thirteen. In his twenties, he enjoyed great success as a stage actor. Oland married artist Edith Shearn and they co-authored the first English translation of the plays of August Strindberg. Oland alternated work on stage and in silent film.

In the movies he was often cast in Oriental parts because of his vaguely Asian features. In 1931, at the age of fifty-two, he landed the role of Charlie Chan.

By 1935, eight films starring Oland as the immensely popular detective had been released by Fox. The ninth in the series, *Charlie Chan in Shanghai*, marked the birth of Twentieth Century Fox. The studio, the producers and the distributors of the Chan films were sitting on a goldmine and Warner Oland knew he was a major contributor. He demanded a larger piece of the pie. In order to maintain a profitable budget, the studio robbed Peter to pay Paul; cutting the salary of Executive Producer Reginald Masters to accommodate Oland's demands. Masters was not pleased. At the same time he understood that if push came to shove, the studio would find it much more expedient to replace a fledgling producer than to replace the actor who laid the golden egg. Masters decided to grin and bear it. He was young and ambitious and he felt his time would come. He hoped to outlast both Warner Oland *and* Charlie Chan.

In 1937, preparations were being made for the filming of the seventeenth Chan movie. Warner Oland was beginning to be more a liability than an asset to the studio. He was demanding another salary increase and artistic control of the material. At the same time, the actor's personal life was in turmoil. His wife had left him, he was drinking to excess and he seemed on the verge of a nervous breakdown. The schedule was strenuous, the studio was knocking out at least three films each year to satisfy audience demand and Oland's condition and temperament was threatening to bring the Chan money machine to a grinding halt. The studio put it to Reginald Masters in no uncertain terms, either solve the problem or we will find someone who can. Halfway into the shooting of *Charlie Chan at Ringside*, Oland walked off the set. He never returned. *Charlie Chan in Honolulu* was released in 1938 with Sidney Toler in the lead role. The actor would go on to portray Chan in twenty-one additional films in nine years and Reginald Masters earned a handsome raise in status and income. A decrease in foreign markets caused by the war led Fox to terminate the series in 1942. Reginald

Masters brought Charlie Chan and Sidney Toler over to Monogram Pictures in exchange for a partnership in the small but growing film studio.

"So what happened to Warner Oland?" Jimmy asked.

"According to everything I've read, he went to Sweden and died in Stockholm," said Vinnie. "Bronchial pneumonia."

"So there is nothing to suggest he was knocked off," Jimmy said.

"No. But there's a lot to suggest he was locked out, strongly persuaded to take a hike," Strings said. "As in seriously threatened."

"Oh?"

"Here's where it gets interesting. About this time, a New York gangster came out to Hollywood when things got too hot for him back East. Apparently he had friends out here; guys he grew up with in New York. Actors and what not. He and a partner named Moe Sedway infiltrated the extras union and started making big bucks extorting money from producers who needed the extras they controlled. They were also used by studio brass as *problem solvers,* settling disputes among actors, directors and producers when all else failed. This cat from New York was one scary character; it's not hard to imagine he may have had something to do with Warner Oland's sudden departure. Particularly since he wound up living in Oland's Beverly Hills mansion after Oland split."

"This mansion?" Jimmy said, pointing to the photograph in *Homes of the Hollywood Stars.*

"Yes, that mansion. So then I got to thinking if the Charlie Chan trail ended in Stockholm, maybe what Richards and Lenny Archer were looking into was the mansion itself. Or what happened there in 1947."

"Which was?"

"The scary New York mobster was murdered in the living room, two shotgun blasts to the head."

"Ouch. Did this scary character have a name?"

"Benjamin Siegelbaum."

"As in Benjamin *Bugsy* Siegel?"

"That's the one."

"This can't be about who killed Bugsy Siegel, who the fuck cares. All this happened in the thirties and forties, everyone involved must be long dead. Who lives here now?" asked Pigeon, tapping his finger on the photo.

"I don't know, but it shouldn't be very difficult to find out," Vinnie said.

"This whole fucking thing leads nowhere," Jimmy said, tossing the book to the sofa in disgust. "Son of a bitch."

"What?"

"Look at this," Jimmy said, remembering the print-out from the library, pulling it out of his pocket and handing it to Vinnie.

"What is this?"

"Two books Richards recently checked out."

"*The Birth of Las Vegas* and *Hollywood Meets the Mob,*" Vinnie read. "There you go, Jimmy, this has Bugsy Siegel written all over it."

"Do you think you can get your hands on these books, Vinnie? Look them over and see if anything jumps out."

"Probably. Mom can go to the library or check a few of the large bookstores," Vinnie said. "Didn't you say you were going into Richards' place tonight?"

"So?"

"Maybe you'll get lucky and find the books there."

"Maybe I'll get real lucky and find his laptop."

Angel Rivas had meandered aimlessly through downtown Santa Monica for hours, doing whatever she could to avoid being out in the open. She stopped in a number of retail stores, loitering for as long as she could, until a sales clerk asked to be of service one too many times or looked at her suspiciously. She had come across an apparel shop and purchased a sweat shirt and a pair of long pants, the weatherman having predicted an unseasonably cool mid-June evening. She had stopped into a fast food restaurant for a hamburger and then wished she hadn't. She didn't phone Maria; she felt her mother had betrayed her.

Angel walked into yet another retail shop, prepared to try the patience of yet another saleswoman. She gazed at a pair of Italian leather shoes she knew she could never afford. And it suddenly dawned on her. Over the course of the traumatic day, her fear had gradually turned into anger. She thought of Ricardo and the nightmare he had dropped her into, without warning. Telling her nothing beyond the fact they were taking a trip to Mexico with lots of cash to burn. Angel knew Ricardo's money was dirty money, but she had no idea there were dirty cops involved and she would be running for her life from those entrusted to serve and protect. *Fucking Ricky. Fucking Detective Raft.* Angel decided she wanted those Italian shoes, and more.

She possessed knowledge that had to be worth something to someone, and someone was going to pay.

"Can I show those to you in your size?" asked a female sales clerk, coming up behind her.

"Maybe soon," Angel said, taking the address of Archer and Pigeon Investigation from her pocket and holding it out for the woman to see. "Can you tell me where this is?"

"It's very close. Fourth is the next street up; there you'll go right, a block and a half at most."

Angel thanked her and headed out to Fourth Street.

Frank Raft had run from the funeral parlor out to the Beverly Hills Country Club. He felt like a fool, standing outside of the dining room dressed in a black suit and tie as men and women golfers done up in their expensive little golf outfits passed him by as if he were a fucking busboy. Raft had arranged to meet Jackson Masters and Masters was making him wait. *Fuck this.*

Finally, Masters appeared. He tapped Raft on the back and signaled for the detective to follow. They moved into a small private room.

"What the hell is going on, Frank, bodies are dropping like flies."

"It's all under control," Raft said. "The whole mess will be cleaned up before the end of the weekend. All the loose ends are tied up."

"How about the loose end named Angel Rivas, Frank? I read the newspapers, too."

"She's long gone; she's running like a scared rabbit. Even if she turned up, the girl couldn't say anything that anyone would believe. Worst came to worst, she could only lead them to me."

"That's exactly what worries me, Frank."

"Well, then, I have a quick fix for your woes."

"Oh?"

"You get me three hundred thousand dollars and I will disappear," said Raft. "As in no one will ever find me."

"That's a lot of money, Frank."

"Depends on who you are, Jackson," Raft said. "I think the old man will consider it a small price to pay. What do you think?"

"I don't know."

"Well, I suggest you ask him when he gets in tonight," said Raft, "and let me know how it goes. Soon."

"It's not a smart idea to threaten him, Frank."

"I haven't had a smart idea in a long time, so I guess I'll take my chances."

"Where can I reach you?" asked Masters.

"I'll call, tomorrow afternoon," said Raft. "And don't try anything cute, Masters, it wouldn't pay. Three hundred grand is nothing compared to what it will cost if you tried crossing me."

"Call me tomorrow. Use a public phone."

"How about treating me to dinner in that classy mess hall across the corridor?"

"I can't, I need to get ready for the old man."

"Nice golf shorts, Jack," Raft said, turning to leave the room. "Give my best to your grandfather."

Jimmy had dropped Fran Stradivarius at the Main Branch of the Los Angeles Public Library before leaving the city.

"Thanks for pitching in, Fran."

"I'm happy to help, Jimmy," she said, "and happy you're giving Vinnie something to keep him occupied. If I strike out here, I can check the bookstores. I'll let you know how I make out."

Pigeon drove back to Santa Monica. He decided to get dinner out of the way before hooking up with Nathan Archer, so his first stop was Meg's Café.

"I was thinking about the Dennis Hopper movie," Meg said when she brought the special to Jimmy's table.

"What about it?"

"They feed in a taped video loop of the bus interior so Hopper won't see the passengers leaving the bus."

"Yes."

"And when they change from live feed to tape, Hopper just happens to be in the bathroom and misses the switch."

"Yes?"

"Good timing or poor writing?" asked Meg.

"Luck. Something I could use a little more of."

"No luck with Vinnie Strings?"

"Vinnie did great. He chased Charlie Chan all the way to Stockholm."

"And?" Meg asked, taking a seat.

"And then the guy died," Jimmy said.

"Charlie Chan died in Sweden?"

"Warner Oland died there, the actor who played Chan in the thirties."

"Didn't more than one actor play Charlie Chan?"

"Yes, at least three, but it doesn't get us anywhere. Vinnie thinks it may have something to do with the Beverly Hills mansion Oland lived in. I'm inclined to agree. I'm thinking

Richards began researching Warner Oland or Chan for a book, ran across something more sensational and brought Lenny into it."

"Exactly what Al Hall said to me at Richards' funeral. Richards told Hall he was researching a Hollywood biography that led him to a story worthy of national headlines."

"I'd love to get my hands on Richards' laptop."

"Maybe you'll get lucky," Meg said, rising from the table. "Are you having dessert?"

"No, thanks, I need to meet someone at my apartment."

"Big Saturday night date?" Meg asked.

"Yeah," Jimmy said. "Breaking and entering."

When Jimmy left Meg's, he decided to make a quick stop at his office; wanting to check the phone answering machine in case Nate Archer had called to change plans again.

When he walked in he found the girl lying curled up on the Oriental rug in a fetal position, her back to the door.

"That can't be very comfortable," he said.

Angel quickly sat up and turned to Jimmy.

"Are you Pigeon?" she asked.

"Yes."

"The door was unlocked."

"I know," Jimmy said. "I was testing a theory. Can I help you up?"

"I can get up myself," Angel said, rising to her feet. "But I could use another kind of help."

"Sit," Jimmy said, offering her the client chair as he moved to his own seat behind the desk. "What can I do for you?"

"I need someplace to hide and I need someone to get to my mother and pick up my things," Angel said, settling into the chair. "If you can help me with that, I may be able to help you find out who killed your partner."

"Are you Angel Rivas?"

"Good detective work."

"What is it you know about my partner's death?"

"I won't say until I feel safe and I have enough money to disappear. My mother has the cash. I need someone to go get it for me. And no police."

"That's a hard bargain."

"Take it or leave it."

"You can stay at my apartment," Jimmy said. "You'll be safe there while I think it over."

"If the police show up, I promise you I won't say a thing about what I know," Angel warned.

"I understand. Do you have anything to carry?"

"No."

Jimmy looked over at the answering machine, happy to find there were no new messages.

"Let's go then," he said.

Pigeon was standing in front of his building when Nate Archer pulled up at nine. Jimmy had secured the girl in his apartment and didn't want Angel to be alarmed in any way by Archer's arrival. He decided he would wait until they were done at Richards' place before telling Nate about Angel.

They parked the car on Ocean Avenue and casually moved toward the Richards house. The street was quiet. They were soon at the back entrance. Archer took out his set of lock picks and they were through the back door in seconds.

"That simple?" Jimmy said.

"That simple."

They each pulled out small flashlights.

"How did you know there was no alarm?" Jimmy asked.

"I guessed the police screwed up the security if there was any," said Nate. "What are you looking for?"

"A laptop computer, maybe a few library books."

"Why don't you start upstairs, I'll look around down here. The quicker we get out the better."

Jimmy agreed and he headed up the stairs. He found a bathroom, a bedroom and a second smaller room Richards used for a study. He was back downstairs in less than ten minutes. He found Archer in the front living room.

"Anything?" Nate asked.

"Nothing," Jimmy said. "You?"

"Just this," Archer said, moving his flashlight across the room at a heap of broken glass, a busted up metal frame and an upturned folding table. "It looks like Richards was just setting it up, no water or fish yet."

"But an awful lot of that," said Jimmy, slowly waving his light over the fish tank bedding spread out across the floor.

"Lenny was killed before Richards was killed, right?"

"Yes," Jimmy said.

"And this mess must have been made while Richards was fighting for his life."

"I would imagine."

"Then whoever killed Richards was back at your office sometime *after* Lenny died and brought a little blue gravel along for the ride. Would the alleged *drug related* gunmen have had any reason to go back?"

"Not that I can think of, it wouldn't be too smart."

"How about a police officer or investigator?"

"The scenes were covered by two separate departments, SMPD was here and LASD was at our office," Jimmy said.

"So maybe someone with the County Sheriff's Department was here before getting to your office later that morning."

"That's a terrible thought," Jimmy said. "Maybe Angel can shed some light on the subject."

"Angel?"

"Let's get out of here," Pigeon said. "I'll tell you about Angel on the way back to my place."

"It's late, maybe we ought to wait until the morning before we press the girl," Nate said as they pulled up in front of Jimmy's building. "She's had a rough day; she's probably still pretty spooked and very tired."

"That's a good idea," Jimmy said.

"At the same time, if she has anything to tell us I'd like to hear it soon. I really need to get back home."

"Work?"

"My wife is about to give birth to our first child."

"No kidding."

"Any day. Listen, Jimmy. We didn't mean to shut you out of Lenny's funeral arrangements; we put him to rest in San Diego Bay. It was something I felt Annie and I had to do alone, together."

"I understand," Jimmy said. "I'll call you at Lenny's in the morning. We can try to decide what to do about Angel over breakfast."

Jimmy stepped out of the car and stood watching Nathan drive off. Pigeon wondered how far Archer would be willing to go, how far he could be expected to go, if the going got hazardous.

When Jimmy entered the apartment he found Angel asleep on the sofa, the TV tuned to the Dodgers post game show. The Cubs had defeated LA and the Padres beat the Giants. A push, LA was still in first by three games.

Jimmy turned off the TV, covered Angel with a blanket, picked up *Les Misérables* and went to his bedroom to visit Early 19th Century France.

Jackson Masters greeted his grandfather coming off the concourse at LAX. The old man was returning to Los Angeles from a weeklong trip to New York visiting the family of an ancient ally. As they drove out to the Beverly Hills home, Jackson told the old man about the events of the last week. His grandfather listened carefully, not saying a word until they arrived at the large house. After the old man stepped out of the car, he insisted his grandson accompany him into the mansion. Jackson followed his grandfather. He was constantly impressed by the stamina and the self-confidence of the man. The old man had survived all of his notorious associates and he seemed determined to live forever.

The old man poured two shots of twelve-year-old single malt Scotch, handed a glass to his grandson and took a seat in a leather armchair opposite the younger man.

"I'm not happy, Jack, the situation is troublesome and this police detective has only made it worse. The man is a loose cannon. I've dodged bullets all my life and I refuse to be brought down by a fucking insect," the old man swore. "It's not the three hundred grand, the money is no problem. The problem is that Raft is threatening us and he can't be trusted. And any payoff, no matter how big, won't make the problem go away. We need a more predictable solution."

The old man waited for a response.

"Raft doesn't know anything about you or about who the woman was," Jackson said. "The reporter may have been on to something, but the notes he passed to the PI didn't spell it out and that was all Frank Raft saw. All of the reporter's research was on his laptop and it's been destroyed. Raft can't hurt us without implicating himself, I think he would take the money and run."

"He is a man without integrity, if it meant saving his own skin he would give you up in a heartbeat and that would lead right to my door."

"What do we do?" Jackson asked, dreading the answer.

"You will take Raft's call tomorrow as arranged. Tell him the money will not be available until Monday. Tomorrow evening we will decide what to do about Frank Raft. Finish your drink and go, I'm tired and angry and even you aren't safe when I get this way."

"I'm sorry," Jackson said.

"Sorry will not quite cut it, Jack. Go. Think about it and come back tomorrow night with something more useful than an apology."

Jackson left the mansion and climbed into his car for the drive home, effectively reminded that his eighty-eight-year-old grandfather was still a man to be feared.

Jimmy was having difficulty reading. He was fighting to keep his eyes open and his mind focused. He closed the Hugo novel and set it down on the bedside table.

After nineteen years in a French prison for stealing a loaf of bread to feed his sister and her child, the convict Jean Valjean was at last released. He soon violated parole and was again a wanted man. Relocating to Monteuil-sur-Mer and taking on a false identity, Valjean came to be known as Monsieur Madeline. His hard work earned him the respect of the townspeople and the former criminal became a successful businessman. In time he was appointed to serve as Mayor of the town. After nearly ten years at Montreuil, an incident on the street threatened to destroy Jean Valjean's new life and prosperity. A crowd had gathered to watch as the Mayor single-handedly lifted a wagon off the body of a worker who was trapped under the wheel. Madeline displayed remarkable strength and he saved the man's life. Among the spectators was the police inspector, Javert. The brute physical power of the Mayor aroused suspicions in the inspector and Javert was convinced that Monsieur Madeline was in fact the wanted convict Valjean.

As Pigeon closed the book, he wondered how far Valjean would go to avoid being exposed as the condemned man he had worked so diligently to forever lay to rest.

Jimmy also wondered how far Javert would go to uncover Jean Valjean's long buried past.

Jimmy looked into the living room to check on the girl and found she hadn't moved. He realized he would need Ray Boyle's help; only Boyle could protect Angel Rivas now. Jimmy needed to convince the girl Boyle could be trusted. That he was her only hope of surviving the serious danger Ricardo Diaz had exposed her to.

And Jimmy also knew Ray would never stop until he found whoever was responsible for the shooting death of the young LAPD officer, John Billings.

Detective Boyle would be as relentless as Inspector Javert.

VIRGINIA HILL

Jimmy was awake at dawn Sunday morning. He looked in on the girl. She was still asleep on the couch. He shaved and took a quick shower and then quietly slipped out of the apartment.

Jimmy picked up a coffee and the *LA Times* and walked down to the Santa Monica pier. He took an empty bench and he gazed out at the bay, mesmerized by the vastness of the ocean. At times like these he wondered why he bothered to get tangled up in the lives of others, knowing he had little or no power to change fate. At times like these he saw human beings as small and insignificant and felt he was no exception. The human animal, like all others, was motivated by self-interest. Survival, power, riches, fame, love. Lenny, Richards, Ricky Diaz, Ray Boyle, Nate Archer, Angel Rivas, Jimmy himself, all with their own agenda, all capable of being hero or villain, victim or savior. For a handful the desire to help others was simply self-interest of another kind, an irresistible need to do good. And for the most part, the altruism went unheralded or was greeted with suspicion. Or, in the case of Jimmy Pigeon's father, greeted with four bullets to the chest.

And who was keeping score?

A bearded man in a Red Sox baseball cap walked up to the bench and asked Jimmy if he could spare some change.

"Thank you, brother," the man said when Jimmy dropped a dollar bill into the battered paper cup.

Thank you, thought Pigeon as the man walked off after rescuing Jimmy from the overwhelming vastness of the ocean and the Devil's playground.

Pigeon dove head first into the *Times* instead.

If Jimmy knew one thing for sure, he knew he was not equipped to be the scorekeeper.

***

Angel awoke to find herself on a couch. *Which couch?* Disoriented. For the third morning in as many days waking in a strange place, struggling to recall where she was and who she was with, who she could trust.

Her instinct was to run, run again, but she knew she had lost the strength, the will, to keep running. She was not sure who she could trust, but she was certain she needed to trust someone. If for no better reason than convenience, Angel Rivas decided she would trust her fate to Jimmy. So, when she found the apartment empty, instead of tormenting about where Pigeon had run off to or who he might return with, she simply sat and waited.

A small piece in the *Times* neatly summed up where the investigation into the deaths of Lenny Archer, Ed Richards, Bob Tully, Ricardo Diaz, Officer Billings and Carlos Valdez was heading. Diaz and Valdez were looking to inherit full credit for Archer and Richards, the timely demise of Diaz would earn Frank Raft a commendation, Billings and Valdez cancelled each other out and it was all about drugs.

Jimmy uttered an audible *no fucking way* and closed the newspaper. He couldn't identify the two voices on the tape recording of Lenny's final moments, but he felt damned sure that it wasn't a pair of Hispanic drug dealers. The two men who killed Archer weren't talking the talk. Jimmy left the pier and started home. He understood he would have to be extremely careful with the girl, bring her out slowly and unthreateningly or she would bolt before revealing what she knew or thought she knew about the murder of Lenny Archer. He would need to get Nate Archer past her defenses and then somehow convince the girl that meeting Detective Ray Boyle was her best bet. But first he had to find out what kind of shape Angel Rivas was in after a night on his sofa and see about dealing with her demands.

As Jimmy climbed the stairs to his apartment he could only hope the girl hadn't run already.

***

It was a balmy Sunday morning at the small cemetery in Sherman Oaks where LA County Sheriff's Department Detective Bob Tully was being laid to rest in the presence of family members, friends and a fairly large contingent of the LASD. Tully's widow and teenage son stood near the coffin as Commander Jefferson hailed Robert Tully as a hero slain in the line of duty. Kevin Tully tried to concentrate on the praise being heaped upon his father, but his thoughts kept drifting to the championship baseball game he missed the day before; a game his school could not win without him.

Detective Frank Raft glanced at his wristwatch, mentally counting the hours he would need to wait before giving Jackson Masters the afternoon phone call which would confirm his early and comfortably financed retirement from law enforcement. He looked up to find Tully's wife staring into his eyes, her own damp eyes filled with questions. He forced a consoling nod and quickly looked away as Jefferson was replaced at the gravesite by the pastor of the Sherman Oaks Catholic Church. Raft listened as the priest assured the congregation that Robert Tully had been taken by God to a better place.

Raft gazed out at the dark cloud over Los Angeles in the near distance and could find no argument.

Less than a mile from the cemetery, Peter Quince sat in front of his computer monitor in the front room of his bungalow looking at photographs from the copied files of the late journalist Edward Richards. Individual photos of two young women, juxtaposed side by side, the resemblance of one to the other unmistakable. On the left a brunette, a lady who may have been considered a bombshell during the period in which her clothing dated her. Early to middle 1940's. On the right a very attractive woman with lighter hair but clearly similar facial characteristics, smartly dressed in contemporary attire. In the background, behind each of the two women, the entrance to a large home, more a mansion. To Peter Quince, obviously the same home in both photographs. Typed below the photo on the left, the name Virginia Hill; typed below the photograph on the right, a date, June 2, 1994. Earlier that month. And below those two notations, a recommendation to see page seventy-three, *Homes of the Hollywood Stars, History and Mystery.*

Peter had spent a good deal of time the previous day, if somewhat guiltily, browsing through Richards' computer files. He opened files having titles which inspired his interest or curiosity and read an assortment of interviews of movie personalities, film reviews, historical anecdotes and classic Hollywood biographies. He found the material well written and fascinating. But this page, the photos, seemed out of place. The title of the file was *Virginia Hill/Granddaughter?* and Quince found it in a folder titled *Charlie Chan in Fiction and Film.* It appeared to the school teacher that Richards was in the process of writing a new book. The folder contained various documents concerning the Charlie Chan novels and the history of the movies featuring the Oriental sleuth and the three actors who shared the role in film. What Peter couldn't grasp was what Virginia Hill had to do with the Chan project. Quince knew who Virginia Hill had been; in fact he'd seen Virginia Hill portrayed by Annette Bening on cable TV several weeks earlier in a film, opposite Warren Beatty.

Peter knew Richards' files should be turned over to the police, should have been the moment he had learned of the writer's death. Quince wondered how Kevin Tully's dad had come by the laptop. He had made up his mind to bring the disc to Tully's partner, Frank Raft, and he kept procrastinating because he was enjoying the subject matter immensely. Looking at the two women on his monitor, Peter considered taking the disc directly to Raft and once again he put it off. Instead, he prepared for a trip to the USC library to learn more about Virginia Hill and to search for a copy of Richards' *Homes of the Hollywood Stars* and check out page seventy-three. Quince removed the disc from the CD drive, returned it to the jewel case, locked it in the top drawer of his desk, grabbed a notepad and pencil and drove out to the University of Southern California.

* * *

When Jimmy walked into his apartment he found the girl sitting on the sofa, hands clasped in her lap like a school kid on a bench in the principal's office. *She is just a kid,* he thought, *and as vulnerable as a doe in the crosshairs.*

"Waiting long?" Jimmy asked.

"There's no food here," Angel said.

"I don't cook much. There's a café up the street does a decent breakfast. My treat."

"I need you to pick up my things from my mother."

"I will. Let's dine first and chat."

"I told you I'm not going to talk until I get my things."

"I know what you told me. I'll try to change your mind over potatoes and eggs. You've got nothing to lose but your appetite."

"Okay, sure."

"I want to invite someone to join us."

"No cops," Angel said.

"If I wanted to give you up to the police they would have showed up while you slept. I want you to meet Nathan Archer. His brother was my partner, whose death you claim to know something about."

"Invite his whole family," Angel said, jumping up from the sofa. "You can all watch me eat, but I'm not talking."

Jimmy phoned Nate Archer and told him where to meet them and then led Angel Rivas out to the street and over to Meg's Café.

After receiving Jimmy's call, Nate phoned his wife. He gave her the phone number of the café and Jimmy's home phone number. He promised to call if he found himself somewhere else.

"Don't begin having that baby without me," he said.

"Wouldn't think of it," his wife assured him.

Nate ended the call, left his brother's apartment and went to join Jimmy and the girl.

Ray Boyle sat at his desk at Parker Center. Ray had been sitting there for nearly two hours, since eight that Sunday morning, trying not to think about the unbelievably fucked-up inter-law enforcement agency investigation which he had in no uncertain terms been exiled from by ringmaster Tanner. Boyle was scheduled to be on duty until three and couldn't think of a single place where he would *not* rather be with the possible exception of a front-row-center seat at a Cher concert. He was beating his fingers on a wooden cigar box that once held Cubans and now held an assortment of Sanford No. 2 pencils and stick pens trying to approximate an inspired Keith Moon drum solo from an ancient Who eight-track tape he and Sharon had listened to on the player in his 1975 Plymouth Fury on Mulholland Drive while swapping saliva and dreams of happily-ever-after before economic considerations forced him to become a cop during the day while studying Law at night until he became just a cop and then a homicide detective. Sharon Boyle grew tired of competing with murder victims for his attention and she left him with his corpses, No. 2 pencils and Scotch.

Ray was drumming and waiting; waiting for the word and the word was the law. He was waiting for the other shoe to drop; the shoe that would kick the Archer, Richards, Tully, Diaz case onto the endless list of solved homicides and off the endless list of open cases. The wait wasn't long. The coup-de-grace arrived minutes later in the guise of a short inter-office memo informing all participating investigators that a joint LAPD, SMPD, LASD Press Release was being sent out on the wire early afternoon to announce the successful resolution to the inquiry into the deaths of a Santa Monica private investigator, a journalist, a Sheriff's Department detective and an LAPD patrolman and boast about the deaths of the pair of drug dealers responsible.

Not a fucking thing, Boyle answered the little voice in his head that whispered the name John Billings and asked *what can you do?*

"Not a fucking thing," he said, this time aloud.

"You talking to me?" asked crime scene investigator Carl Harriman as he walked up to Boyle's desk.

"Unfortunately not," Ray said. "What do you know?"

"I know the tooth imbedded in Detective Tully's shoe once belonged to Leonard Archer and I also know the blue gravel was picked up after the tooth," Harriman said. "What do you know?"

"I know it doesn't fucking matter."

"It might."

"Oh?"

"I mean, if I were you I'd be wondering where the fish tank was."

"No. If you were me you would have been bounced off the case by Captain Tanner. If you were me you would have already read this memo from the brass telling it like it is. If you were me you would have nothing to say to John Billing's mother at his wake tonight except he was in the wrong place at the worst fucking time. If you were me you would be itching to get your hands on a bottle of Dewar's," Boyle said. "But you're not me, you haven't been kicked off the case and you haven't seen the memo yet so I guess if you were really curious you could do a little looking around."

"And if you were me, where would you begin?" asked Harriman.

"I'd begin at the Tully home and then check out the journalist's place; kind of unofficially."

"I'll see what I can do," said Harriman.

"Thanks," said Boyle. "I'll be here until three."

As promised, Angel Rivas was both hungry and resolute. Jimmy and Nathan sat opposite the girl in a booth at the window of Meg's Café watching as Angel attacked a large plate of scrambled eggs smothered in pinto beans and green chili, Meg's gallant effort to satisfy the girl's ardent request for *huevos rancheros.* Angel took a short breather and looked up at the two private investigators.

"You look like over-the-hill Hardy Boys," she said, "and you're wasting time. At least one of you could be on his way to my mother's house."

The two men glanced at each other; Angel smiled and went back to her plate.

"I'd say she's made up her mind," Nathan offered.

"I'll go," Jimmy said. "Bring her back to my place when she's done and I'll meet you there as soon as I can."

Meg stopped Jimmy on his way out.

"So," she asked, "where did you find the princess and the stoic?"

"That's Nathan Archer," Jimmy said. "But don't spread it around."

"I can see the resemblance," Meg said. "And the girl?"

"She's right in the middle of this recent crime wave somehow, says she can shed some light on Lenny's death and she's making the rules. Put the meal on my tab, I have to run an errand for the kid."

"Sure. Anything I can do to help? Engage her in girl talk?"

"I'll try this first," said Jimmy. "But I might need your help with her later."

"Just say the word."

"Thanks," Jimmy said.

Pigeon walked out of the café. Meg watched him move down Third Street and then she strolled over to the table where Angel ate and Nate seemed lost in thought.

"I'm Meg Kelly. I knew your brother. I'm sorry about what happened to Lenny."

Nate didn't know how to respond.

"Are you sure you don't want something to eat?" she asked, taking him off the hook. "It's on Jimmy."

"No, thanks," Nate said. "Maybe some more coffee."

"Coming up. And how about you, young lady? Can I bring you something else?"

"A beer would be nice," Angel said.

"How about pineapple juice?"

"How about a caffeine-packed non-diet Coke."

Peter Quince used a pay telephone at the library and called the LASD for Frank Raft. Peter felt it was about time to turn over Richards' files, information which could very well be considered valuable evidence in a murder investigation. He was told by a desk Sergeant that Detective Raft was presently unavailable and was expected back at the station the following day.

"Would you care to leave a message for the detective?" the sergeant asked. "He may check in."

Peter was about to leave his name and phone number and the reason for his call when to his own surprise he simply said, "I'll try reaching him tomorrow."

After replacing the receiver, Peter realized what had caused his sudden change of heart. He was waylaid by the question that had been nagging him all weekend. How had Ed Richards' laptop come into the possession of Kevin Tully just after the journalist's violent death?

Peter went through the library copy of the *Sunday LA Times* and found the latest report on the investigation. He decided he would wait until he had another look through the computer files before he gave them up. He would search for any references to Ricardo Diaz, Carlos Valdez, Frank Raft, Robert Tully or Lenny Archer.

Peter returned to his research at a table in the USC library to learn more about Virginia Hill and her infamous circle.

Twenty minutes later he was looking at page seventy-three in *Homes of the Hollywood Stars*, the photograph of a Beverly Hills mansion. A large mansion which Peter easily recognized as the one he had seen in the background of the photos of the two women in Ed Richards' files. He quickly scanned the history of the mansion and its past occupants, who included Charlie Chan portrayer Warner Oland, Benjamin Siegel and Virginia Hill. And Quince learned the identity of the mansion's current resident, who happened to be one of the most powerful men in California.

"Holy shit," he said aloud, turning a few heads at a nearby table.

Peter added the name Masters to his list of references to search for in the Richards' files.

It took Jimmy some time to convince Maria Rivas he was who he claimed to be, an emissary dispatched by her fugitive daughter to collect the tools of Angel's escape. Clothing, cash and passport.

"What about the car?" Maria asked, finally relenting.

"If things go the way I'd like them to, she won't need the car because Angel won't be heading anywhere except back here to you. Safe and sound with a very suspenseful story to tell your grandchildren."

"Promise me you will not let any harm come to my little girl," Maria Rivas said as Jimmy turned to leave.

Jimmy looked into the woman's eyes. He knew he could not make such a promise, should never even consider making such a promise.

"I promise Angel will be safe," Pigeon said.

FAMOUS LAST WORDS

Less than thirty minutes after Jimmy left Maria Rivas with a seat-of-the-pants promise to protect her daughter, Frank Raft arrived directly from the cemetery. He pulled into a parking space and sat watching the Rivas house.

Raft had time to kill before his scheduled afternoon call to Jackson Masters to iron out the details of the big pay-off. He thought if he could catch up to the Rivas girl and silence her, he might have it both ways.

The detective searched his pockets for a smoke and a match and realized he had left his pager at home. He cursed his absentmindedness and lit a cigarette.

At the same time the pager on Raft's kitchen table beeped, signaling a telephone call originating from Meg's Café.

Back at Jimmy's apartment Nate Archer paced, waiting for Pigeon to return with the bounty that would hopefully inspire Angel to start talking. He stopped occasionally in front of a tall bookcase to examine Jimmy's library, which for the most part ran to the classics. Dumas, Dostoevsky, Dickens. Angel Rivas sat on the sofa leafing through a copy of *The New Yorker*, silent except for the time or two when she felt obliged to report that this or that cartoon was not funny.

Jimmy walked into the apartment, a suitcase in one hand and a small hand purse in the other. The purse held Angel's passport, one thousand dollars in cash and a bank debit card. The girl dumped the magazine and jumped up from the sofa, looking at Jimmy as if he'd just walked in with a pardon from the Governor.

"Clean clothes," she said. "Thank God. Can I use your shower?"

"Sure," Jimmy said, holding out the suitcase. "But make it quick. You can use the bedroom to dress."

"How is my mother?" she asked, grabbing the suitcase.

"Very worried."

"Can I have the purse?"

"The bath is on the house, the purse is going to cost you," Jimmy said. "You can warm up your singing voice in the shower. If you aren't ready to tell us something we don't already know about Lenny's death when you come out, I'll give the police a shot at you."

"No cops."

"It's your call," Jimmy said. "Get moving."

Angel carried the suitcase into the bedroom and she slammed the door shut.

Nate Archer had stood quietly listening until the girl left the room.

"Think she'll use the fire escape?" he asked.

"Not without this," Jimmy said, holding up the purse.

"Do you think she knows who killed Lenny?"

"Not exactly. But she knows something that may help."

"Why is she so afraid of the police?" Nate asked.

"I can only guess there's a cop or two involved in the killings."

"There were two voices on the office tape recorder," Nate said. "Are you thinking Raft and Tully?"

"I'd say they're the odds on favorites, but we need to hear it from the girl. Something strong enough to get Ray Boyle to jump onboard."

"Why?" asked Nate. "Why would two LASD detectives assassinate Lenny and the journalist?"

"Tully's not talking, so someone needs to ask Frank Raft. I'd rather it not be me," Jimmy said. "That's why we need Boyle. Or Charlie Chan."

The old man phoned his grandson.

"When do you expect to hear from Raft?" he asked.

"Soon," said Jackson Masters. "Early this afternoon. I'll tell him he'll have to wait until morning."

"Tell him this instead," the old man said. "Tell him we only have one hundred thousand on hand, say we can get the rest for him when the bank opens in the morning and deliver all of the cash to him then."

"If Raft knows we're sitting on a hundred grand, he'll demand at least that much today."

"I'm counting on it. Arrange a time and place for delivery and tell Raft to expect a courier."

"Who will you send?"

"That is not your concern. Call me when you've made the arrangements," said the old man before hanging up and turning to the other man in the room.

"So?" asked Nick Sedway.

"We wait. When we hear where and when the drop will be, you'll go and kill Frank Raft and immediately return to New York. Be careful, Raft is a devious man. I appreciate your help, Nick. I didn't want to have to use someone from here in Los Angeles," said the old man as he poured Scotch. "While we wait, please join me in a toast to the memory of your grandfather; he was a dear and trusted friend."

"He spoke of you often, with great respect," Sedway said. "And don't worry about Frank Raft. He won't be any trouble to you after today."

Ray Boyle grabbed the receiver before the phone could ring a second time.

"Speak to me."

"It's Harriman. I found what you were looking for."

"Where are you?"

"I'm on my way back from Santa Monica; I'm ten minutes from Parker."

"Meet me in the coffee shop at Broadway and Temple in fifteen," Boyle said.

"Sure," said Harriman.

"Ricky shot Tully again, when Tully was already down. Raft stood and watched," Angel said. She was sitting on the sofa, drying her hair with a towel, Nathan and Jimmy hanging on every word. When the girl paused a little too long, Jimmy cleared his throat to get her going again.

"And then Raft shot Ricky and I ran like hell."

"Did you know Raft and Tully were Sheriff's Department detectives?" Jimmy asked.

"I wasn't sure who or what they were until I saw the newspaper the following day. I thought I might have seen Raft before, giving Ricardo some grief," Angel said. "But it didn't matter. I ran because I had no doubt he would have killed me without blinking an eye, whoever he was."

"And you're sure Ricardo had nothing to do with Lenny Archer's death or the reporter's."

"Absolutely positive."

"I need to call Boyle now," Jimmy said.

"Boyle who?" Angel asked.

"Detective Ray Boyle, LAPD," said Jimmy. "The man who is going to become your knight in shining armor as soon as I can vacate the position."

"You told me there would be no cops if I talked to you."

"I promised your mother you would be safe and only Boyle can protect you," said Jimmy. "I'll have to break one promise to keep another."

Jimmy went to the phone to call Boyle.

While Desk Sergeant Murphy was taking a message from Jimmy Pigeon at his post at Parker Center, a request that Detective Boyle return the call as soon as possible, Ray Boyle sat at the counter of a coffee shop in downtown LA with crime scene investigator Harriman.

"So, you're sure it came from the reporter's house," Boyle said.

"The floor of Richards' house was covered with it," said Harriman. "I could do a lab comparison if you want, but I'll tell you right now it's the same blue gravel we found on Tully's shoe."

"Which means Tully was at Archer's office sometime after Archer lost the tooth, but before he picked up the gravel at the Richards murder scene."

"I'd bet on it," said Harriman.

"And what about the chances Tully was in Archer's office at the time Archer was killed and in Richards' house when Richards was killed. Is that worth a wager?"

"And Raft, too?"

"Had to be. And it had to be Raft who set Ricky Diaz up to take the rap and then silenced both Diaz and Tully."

"The sick bastard set up his own partner."

"Can we prove it?" asked Boyle.

"From the evidence alone, I don't think so. We need a witness, or a confession. It might help to know why Archer and Richards were marked in the first place."

"Do you think Raft might have had a good excuse?"

"At least a reason," said Harriman.

"I'm a little curious," said Boyle. "But if I find out he killed John Billings, Raft is going to have to talk very fucking fast."

"Are you planning to track him down sometime soon?" Harriman asked.

"My shift is over at three."

"Want company?"

"Do you like your job, Harriman?"

"Love it."

"Then I think its best you sit this one out."

Frank Raft had run out of cigarettes and had run out of patience. He abandoned his stakeout across from the Rivas house and he cruised in his car until he spotted a pay phone in front of a corner newsstand. He telephoned Jackson Masters.

As Masters had predicted and as his grandfather had hoped, Raft was anxious to get his hands on the one hundred thousand dollar down payment as soon as possible. Masters objected just enough to avoid sounding too eager to comply.

"Four this afternoon, in Malibu," Raft said. "Come alone."

"I won't be coming at all, Frank. I wouldn't be seen anywhere near you, don't take it personally. We'll send a messenger. Where in Malibu? Your place?"

"What kind of messenger?"

"Some flunky who runs errands for the old man," said Masters. "He won't know who you are or what he's carrying. He's harmless. Where in Malibu?"

"Nobody is harmless, Masters. Tell your flunky to be in Malibu and to phone my pager at three-fifty. I'll call and give him the drop location then. Tell your harmless delivery boy to be punctual. If all goes well, I'll ring you tonight to arrange for the balance which I will expect as soon as the bank opens in the morning. If things don't go well, there better be a damn good reason."

Raft hung up before Jackson Masters could argue with the delivery instructions or react to the implied threat. He grabbed a pack of cigarettes from the newsstand and he glanced at his watch. He realized he hadn't eaten a thing all day. He jumped into his car and headed out to Malibu. He could grab lunch at his favorite neighborhood diner and have more than enough time to stop at his house to check his pager and his phone messages before the call from Masters' delivery boy at three-fifty. And plenty of time to make sure he was well prepared for the old man's flunky messenger, harmless or not.

Jimmy grabbed the telephone receiver after the first ring hoping to hear Ray Boyle's voice. Instead it was a woman's voice and the voice asked to speak to Nate Archer. Jimmy asked the woman to hold and placed the receiver down beside the telephone.

"It's for you," he said to Archer.

"Who?"

"I'm guessing it's your wife," Jimmy said. "And it sounds a bit urgent."

Nate rushed to the phone.

Back at Parker Center, Boyle stopped at Sergeant Murphy's desk.

"Sergeant."

"Lieutenant."

"I need a home address for Detective Frank Raft, LASD, right away," said Boyle. "And after you get the information to me, I need you to forget I ever asked."

"Is that all?" said the Desk Sergeant.

"Yes, thank you," said Boyle, turning toward the stairs.

"Lieutenant."

"Yes?"

"Jimmy Pigeon phoned for you. He asked that you get in touch with him as soon as possible."

"Thanks, Murphy. I'll be at my desk waiting for your call."

Boyle headed up to his office.

"Annie's gone into labor, she took a cab to the hospital," Nate said. "I should be there."

"Of course, you should be there," Jimmy said.

"But I should be here, help you follow this through for my brother."

"You can't be in both places, Nate. Your wife needs you more than we do right now. We'll be fine as soon as I catch up with Boyle. We need to drop this mess into his lap anyway," said Jimmy. "So get going."

"I'll be back up as soon as I can."

"Just call me after the baby comes, let me know how it went. Hopefully I'll have good news. Hopefully it will be over. Some kind of justice for Lenny. Good luck."

"You, too," said Archer.

"Well, looks like it's just you and me kid," Jimmy said after Nate took off.

"Can I call my mom?" Angel asked.

"Sure," said Jimmy. "Go ahead."

Boyle called Jimmy Pigeon at home. The line was busy. Before he had a chance to try again, Murphy rang him with Frank Raft's Malibu address. Boyle checked the time. It was close enough to three. He grabbed his jacket and he headed down to his car.

Jimmy telephoned Parker Center after Angel was done talking with her mother. Sergeant Murphy told Jimmy that Boyle had been in, had been given Jimmy's message and had left again.

"Fuck," Jimmy said aloud after hanging up.

"Now, now," said Angel from the sofa.

Back at his Malibu apartment, Raft went directly to the pager he had left sitting on his kitchen table. He returned the phone call originating from Meg's Café. A few minutes later Raft learned Jimmy Pigeon had been at the café earlier in the company of a young Hispanic woman with a ravenous appetite. He decided that after receiving his down payment he would take a ride to Santa Monica to look up Jimmy Pigeon. Raft telephoned Anthony Gravano at home.

"Tony, it's Frank Raft."

"What can I do for you, Frank?"

"I need the use of the barber shop this afternoon, around four. I'm expecting a delivery and I'd rather not take it at home."

"How about I meet you there at three forty-five and let you in. You can let yourself out and lock the door when you're through."

"Perfect. I'll see you then."

"Frank?"

"Yes?"

"How did that laptop work out for you?"

"Great, Tony. I'll see you at a quarter to four."

Ray Boyle pulled up across the street from Raft's apartment building on Fernhill Drive at three-thirty. He was about to leave his car when he spotted Raft coming out. He slid down in his seat, saw Raft climb into his own car and drive off. Boyle restarted his engine and followed.

Ten minutes later, Boyle watched from his car as Raft paced in front of Tony's Barber Shop on Greenwater Road.

Boyle decided to wait.

Soon a second man arrived. He unlocked the front door of the shop. Raft entered the dark storefront shop and the other man left.

What the hell is this all about? Boyle wondered.

He decided to sit and wait a while longer and confront Raft when he left the shop.

At exactly three-fifty, Raft's pager beeped. He went to the wall phone in the barbershop and called the number lit up on the pager display. Less than a mile away a pay phone on Cliffside Drive rang once before it was picked up by Nick Sedway.

"Yes."

"Where are you?"

"Down at the beach."

"Find Dume Drive and meet me at the barber shop at Greenwater Road in ten minutes."

"I'll be there," said Sedway.

The street was quiet and deserted Sunday afternoon. A few minutes before four, Boyle watched a rental car park a few doors down from the barber shop. A man left the vehicle and approached the shop entrance. Boyle saw the man rap on the door. The door opened and the man stepped inside.

What the fuck? thought Boyle.

Then he heard a gunshot, jumped from his car and rushed to the shop entrance.

Boyle drew his weapon as he reached the front door. He tried the door and found it locked. He looked through the glass pane and found himself face to face with Frank Raft who stood on the inside pointing a gun. Two gunshots rang out, shattering the glass between them and knocking Boyle backwards and down to the sidewalk.

He was lying there when the first police car arrived at the scene.

From our bench on the Santa Monica Pier, Jimmy and I watched the sun sink into the bay.

"I don't know why Raft came after me and the girl, but he did. He had to have believed Boyle was dead. If he thought Ray Boyle would live to identify him as the shooter, Raft would have run as fast as he could down to Mexico and laid low until he decided what to do about getting the three hundred thousand dollars he expected. When the Malibu PD arrived they found Ray on the sidewalk and a corpse in the barbershop who was later identified as Nick Sedway, a paid assassin out of New York City. We guessed Sedway had been sent to kill Raft, but Raft had been prepared for the contingency and turned it around."

"What happened to Raft?" I asked.

"He showed up at my place. The girl spotted him from the window as he came in. I locked Angel in the apartment and I waited on the landing, halfway up to the floor above mine. I was above and behind Raft when he came to the door of the apartment. I had a gun on him and I called his name. I wanted to take him alive but he turned on me and got off a few shots before I put a bullet into his chest from the stairs. A lucky shot, and fatal. I ran to Raft and asked him why he had killed Lenny Archer and the reporter and he said, *for the money.*

"Were those his last words?" I asked.

"No," Jimmy answered. "He said, *This is funny,* and then he died."

"Those were Doc Holliday's last words," I said.

"I'm not surprised. Are you as hungry as I am, Jake?"

"I could eat."

"So, let's eat. It's about time you met Margaret Kelly."

I followed Jimmy Pigeon off the pier and we walked in silence to Meg's Café.

Part Three

PIGEON HOLD

"Investigation is a lot like poker,
you need to choose what to discard
and what to hold."
—*Jimmy Pigeon*

TWO WOMEN

I sat opposite Jimmy and Meg in a window booth at the café. Meg Kelly was an extremely attractive forty-three-year-old redhead who could easily have passed for thirty. Even in a plain dress under an apron she looked elegant. Jimmy and I had just finished a huge meal and he had asked me to hold any further questions until we were done with our food. When we pushed our plates away, Meg took it as license to join us at the table. After complimenting the cook, I couldn't wait any longer.

"How did Raft know the girl was with you?" I asked.

Jimmy let Meg field the question.

"It was my assistant manager, Pamela Walker. The SMPD found the phone number of the café on Raft's pager and they questioned me and all of my employees. Pam finally broke down and confessed she had been taking money from Raft to keep an eye on Jimmy," Meg said, as a party of six walked into the café. "I need to get back to the kitchen. How about coffee?"

"No, thanks. We'll head back to my place for coffee," Jimmy said. "I think Jake is anxious to hear more of the story."

Meg ran off. Jimmy and I left the café and walked to his apartment.

I started in right away.

"What happened after you shot Raft in the hallway?"

"I tried reaching Ray Boyle, no luck, so I called the Santa Monica PD and we waited for Detective John Barnum to arrive. He invited us both to the station for questioning. Finally, he told me I could leave, but said Angel would have to remain to tell him everything she could about the deaths of Carlos Valdez and Officer Billings here in Santa Monica. Then she would be turned over to the LAPD to talk about the deaths of Ricardo Diaz and Bob Tully. I asked Barnum if he had spoken with Ray Boyle. That's when I learned Ray had been shot."

"How bad was it?"

"It was touch and go for a while. Ray had lost a lot of blood. I went to visit him at the hospital a few days later. I told him how sorry I was and he told me I had nothing to be sorry about. He said he considered himself one fortunate bastard. Getting shot that Sunday in June was the luckiest thing that ever happened to him."

"Oh?"

"Boyle was on call that night. If he hadn't been at the hospital recovering from three hours in the operating room, he would have been called to the double homicide on Bundy Drive. You know the one. He was very grateful he missed it. Boyle said he watched the beginning of the fiasco on TV from his hospital bed and he thanked God he was hooked up to an IV."

"And you never found out why Frank Raft and Bob Tully killed Lenny Archer and Ed Richards?"

"It was a dead end after Raft died. Nate Archer's wife gave birth to a son that day. They named the boy Leonard. Nate seemed satisfied. His brother's murderers had paid with their lives, although we still had no idea why they had killed Lenny and Richards. Discovering the motive became less a priority for Nate. He was much more interested in staying in San Diego to get acquainted with the newborn Lenny Archer than he was in coming back here to face what he guessed would be more unanswered questions surrounding the murder of the boy's namesake."

"So?"

"So, with Ray Boyle recovering from his gunshot wounds and Nathan Archer opting out, it looked as if nothing was going to help me discover exactly why my partner had been killed. And then, late that week, out of the blue, Peter Quince showed up at my office."

Jimmy Pigeon neatly folded the *LA Times* in half, folded it again and dropped it into the wastebasket beside his desk. All of the news was about O. J. Simpson and the double homicide in Brentwood. Pages and pages of articles and photographs of the Ford Bronco car chase and Simpson's subsequent arrest at his Rockingham estate. Hidden in the depths of section two was a short piece on the murders of Lenny Archer and Ed Richards with yet another conclusion.

Archer and Richards had been murdered by Los Angeles Sheriff's Department detectives, Frank Raft and Bob Tully. The motive? Investigator Archer and journalist Richards had uncovered and were about to disclose information that pointed to illegal activities linking the detectives to a convicted drug dealer, Ricardo Diaz, also deceased. Case closed, once again, with expedience and a strong emphasis on law enforcement damage control. No one appeared to be very interested in light of the recent public and media frenzy surrounding a certain former football player. And Jimmy disliked and disbelieved the latest incarnation of the official line as much as he had the assorted versions reported earlier. Jimmy was convinced there was much more to the story, but all Pigeon had to go on was a cryptic reference to Charlie Chan and the photograph of a very big house in a book of celebrity homes.

Jimmy's eyes moved from the discarded newspaper to the empty desk across the office. Lenny's desk. Then he looked over to the office door, it's newly replaced pane of glass, which remained untitled. *Not very good for business*, Jimmy thought. Then, again, in the past few weeks he was finding it difficult to remember what was good *about* the business.

A rap on the door brought him out of his reverie.

Jimmy opened the office door to find a tall man in his early thirties wearing a corduroy jacket over a t-shirt and jeans. In his extended arms he held a black plastic case.

"What do you have there?" Jimmy asked.

"A notebook computer."

"Salesman?"

"School teacher."

"Are you sure you're in the right place?"

"Are you Jimmy Pigeon?"

"Guilty."

"Then I think I'm in the right place," said Peter Quince. "I hope I'm in the right place."

"Come on in," Jimmy said. "Maybe we'll find out."

A few minutes later Jimmy was looking at the screen of the laptop. Gazing at two photographs, side by side, two different women, standing in front of the same large mansion, a house that looked strangely familiar to Pigeon.

"What am I looking at?" Jimmy asked.

"I'm not positive, but I believe you're looking at something that has to do with the death of your partner," said Quince. "And there's more."

"Show me more," Jimmy said.

The teacher had done his homework.

After hours of research at the USC library the weekend before, Quince had spent his after school hours attempting to make sense out of the deceased journalist's apparently disconnected files and trying to figure what Virginia Hill, Lenny Archer, Frank Raft, Bob Tully, Charlie Chan and one of the most powerful men in California could possibly have in common—other than a renowned Beverly Hills home and a slew of unexplained deaths and disappearances.

Toward the end of the week he had managed to arrange the files in order, somewhat like a classroom presentation. Arranged in a way Quince felt told a story, though he couldn't decide what the story was about. He also couldn't decide where to take his presentation. When the news broke about Frank Raft's death and Raft's complicity in the death of Robert Tully, Peter was reluctant to take what he had to the police. Had he been inclined to do so, he was not sure which of three involved police departments he should trust.

When Peter woke up Saturday morning, he finally made up his mind to take his chances with Lenny Archer's partner. So here he was a few hours later, giving Pigeon the show. A disjointed story spanning fifty years.

The curtain dropped. The show was over.

"That's it," Peter said.

Names, places, dates, photographs. Meyer Lansky, Joey Adonis, Virginia Hill, Moe Sedway, Jack Dragna, Alliance of Extras and Stagehands, Mickey Cohen, Teamsters Union, Las Vegas, Johnny Stompanato, Lana Turner, Cheryl Crane, North Linden Drive, House Un-American Activities Committee, the Kefauver Hearings, Monogram Pictures, the LAPD and the Los Angeles Sheriff's Department. A history of murder, graft, coercion, embezzlement, police corruption, strikebreaking, mob warfare, scandal and more murder spanning the forties and fifties in Hollywood. And in the middle of it all, a couple of men with the same insatiable ambition.

Benjamin 'Bugsy' Siegel and Reginald Masters.

"What the fuck was Richards on to?" Jimmy asked.

"I have no idea, and I've been through it a hundred times, but I'm sure this mansion is a clue," said Quince, bringing the photographs of the two women back up on the laptop screen. "The woman in the photograph on the left is Virginia Hill; the one on the right, standing in front of the same house, very recently, is someone who has more than a passing resemblance to Virginia Hill. Bugsy Siegel was gunned down in the same house in June, 1947. Reginald Masters was in Europe at the time, drumming up markets for his cash cow, the Charlie Chan film series; reestablishing overseas contracts that were severed during World War Two. When Masters returned, he moved into the mansion on North Linden where Siegel had been shot to death. The mansion once occupied by Warner Oland, the actor who portrayed Charlie Chan, before Oland vanished from Hollywood."

"I feel like I've heard this all before," Jimmy said, recalling his last sit down with Vinnie Stradivarius.

"The mansion is the key. I'm guessing that stumbling upon the young woman on the right is what hooked Richards and got him nosing around," said Peter. "And his snooping apparently put a huge scare into someone."

"So, you're saying we need to find the girl."

"I'm saying *you* might want to find the girl. That woman, whoever she is, puts a huge scare into me, too. I came here to get this off my hands. It's all yours if you want it. I've numbered all of the files and you can hold onto the laptop computer as long as you like. Just forget where you got it."

There goes another prospective ally, Jimmy thought.

All he could do was thank Peter Quince for the lead and send the school teacher on his way.

Alone again, Jimmy sat at his desk and looked at the laptop. The technology scared him. He doubted he could shut the thing down and start it again, let alone find his own way around the maze of files Peter had walked him through.

He needed someone who was comfortable with computers, who was somewhat familiar with post WWII Hollywood fact and legend and who would jump at the opportunity to help sift through the ashes.

Jimmy picked up the phone and called Vinnie Strings.

Assistant LA County District Attorney Jackson Masters sat at his desk in the Downtown Criminal Courts Building.

The building had been a madhouse for days.

He had found the short piece on the Archer/Richards case deep in section two of the *Times*. The double murder in Brentwood had made the resolution of the Raft debacle relatively insignificant and nearly invisible.

Masters closed the newspaper and looked at the front page. He thought about the DA. He didn't envy Garcetti, as much as he wanted the other man's job.

Masters wondered if Garcetti would consider him for the prosecution team if the Brown/Goldman case ever got to trial. He wondered how he would react to the proposal. It was a case that could make or destroy an Assistant DA, could make or break the DA himself.

The old man would strongly discourage his grandson's involvement. If Jackson wanted the DA's job, the old man would recommend a much safer route. Gain the DA's office with a very well-endowed campaign coffer and the years of political clout commanded by his family.

Masters expelled a sigh of relief. He had survived Frank Raft and was once again free to entertain thoughts of his political future. It had been a close call, a nightmare since the day the old man had given him the mandatory task of solving the problem of Ed Richards. Reginald Masters was not pleased with the death of Nick Sedway, but the old man seemed satisfied. His grandson had managed to make the problem go away and Jackson's father had been kept in the dark. It had been weeks since Jackson felt he could face his father without exposing the mess he'd been in.

Jackson telephoned his father, former Governor William Masters. He suggested a long overdue luncheon date, Sunday at his father's home.

The old man sipped his espresso after completing the arrangements for the flight east. He understood the trip to New York was necessary to personally handle the fallout caused by Nick Sedway's death. Unfortunate. He had sincerely liked the young man.

The old man was a survivor.

He had survived the unions, the movie studios, the politicians, the gangsters. For more than fifty years he had survived and triumphed in the most ruthless business in the most ruthless place in America. Hollywood. He had earned fantastic riches and unequaled influence. He had put William Masters into the Governor's Mansion and would see to it that Jackson Masters was the most powerful legal figure in the entire state. He would not be brought down by a two-bit private dick, a third-rate journalist or a crooked LASD detective. And certainly not by a blackmailer, the granddaughter of a whore. Silencing the woman had been the only acceptable course of action and covering it up had been the only way to protect himself and the family.

For the old man, it was simply necessary.

He glanced at the photo of the former football hero on the front page of the *LA Times*. Handcuffed.

"Imbecile," the old man mumbled into his demitasse.

LEG WORK

Jimmy found Pam Walker at home. A studio in a cinder-block apartment building on Eighth. Pseudo-art-deco.

The laptop sat locked in the trunk of his Chrysler. Vinnie had given him fail-safe instructions about how to transport the computer to LA without damage. Vinnie was elated by the prospect of helping make sense of Richards' research and deflated when he learned Jimmy needed to make a couple of stops along the way.

"Jesus, Jimmy, I've been waiting all week. I've been through *Hollywood Meets the Mob* so many times, I can quote chapter and verse," Vinnie whined. "I've got all sorts of juice for you."

"Keep your shirt on, Vinnie," Jimmy had said and then he packed up the computer and went to find Pam Walker.

Walker had been questioned by the Santa Monica police and the County Sheriff's department after Raft was killed. She admitted to being recruited by Detective Raft as a paid informant. She insisted she believed she was doing a good deed. The SMPD and LASD both talked with her briefly and let her go. And then Meg let her go. Jimmy was hoping Pam Walker knew more than the police were satisfied or interested in hearing about.

When she opened her door, Pam looked surprised to see Jimmy standing there, and very uneasy.

"Can I talk with you, Pam?" he asked.

"Jimmy, I'm really sorry. I had no idea I was putting you in danger."

"How could you? I'm sorry you were taken in by Frank Raft. He was bad news. And I'm sorry it cost you your job."

"I can't blame Meg. She cares a lot about you and I nearly got you killed."

"You couldn't know," Jimmy repeated. "Now you know better. Could I ask you a few questions?"

"Of course, Jimmy. Come on in."

Jimmy sat on a stool at the counter separating the kitchenette from the one-room living area. Pam stood on the other side of the counter and poured coffee.

"Tell me exactly how Raft approached you," Jimmy asked.

Pam Walker first saw Raft the day after Lenny Archer's body had been found.

Raft and his partner had come into Meg's Café, taken a booth and ordered lunch; arriving not long after Jimmy left the café late that Tuesday morning.

Pam served the two men. Raft had been openly friendly and she had been tipped well. Walking to her car following her shift, she was stopped by Raft. Walker recognized him from earlier that day and she was initially alarmed by his sudden appearance. Raft quickly identified himself as an LASD detective and he asked if he could have a few minutes of her time. Satisfied with his police ID, Pam agreed to walk and talk.

Raft claimed he was working a crime investigation for the LA District Attorney's office. He claimed no one in the Sheriff's Department, not his Commander or even his partner, was aware of his assignment. He reported directly to an Assistant DA since it was suspected that LASD police officers might be implicated. Raft asked Pam to watch and listen whenever Jimmy Pigeon visited the café. He claimed Pigeon was being uncooperative and unforthcoming in regard to knowledge he might have or might discover about Archer's death. There was money in the investigative budget for her service. Whether or not she decided to assist, she was not to tell anyone about this or subsequent meetings with Raft. Doing so would threaten to undermine the investigation and put Raft and his co-investigators in danger. Pam thought it over. It sounded exciting, she believed it would do no harm, felt it was her civic responsibility and she could use the money. She casually asked Pigeon about the progress of the Archer murder investigation, overheard conversations between Jimmy and Meg, took note of who came into the café with Jimmy and she reported it all to Raft.

Pam Walker's last tip to Frank Raft helped him finally locate Angel Rivas.

"Did Raft happen to mention a name, the Assistant DA he was working for?" Jimmy asked, just in case there was a morsel of truth in Raft's mountain of deceit.

"Sorry, no."

"Probably doesn't matter," he said.

But something in his voice told Pam it did matter.

"Was I any help at all?" Pam asked.

The woman appeared eager to help, as if she needed to help. It had Jimmy thinking about Vinnie Strings, who was probably going stir crazy waiting to help. But Jimmy had another stop before going to pass the laptop off to Vinnie. He needed to have a short talk with Ray Boyle.

"You were a great help, Pam," he said.

"More coffee?" she asked.

"I've got to get moving."

"Jimmy?" she said as he moved to the door.

"Yes."

"When you see Meg..."

"I'll put in a good word for you, Pam."

Jimmy walked into the hospital room to find Ray Boyle screaming at the television from his bed.

"Calm down, Ray, your head looks like it's about to explode."

"Fucking Dodgers. I don't know why I fucking bother. Every time I watch a game they lose."

"I think you're overestimating your influence, Ray."

"I've watched the last two games on that piece of shit they call a TV and the fucking bums lost both. I'll wager if I keep watching this game, Colorado will destroy them."

"You don't want to bet against the home team."

"A sure bet is a sure bet, Pigeon, and what does it fucking matter? If the Dodgers stay in first place, the player's strike is a sure thing."

"You need to get out of here, Ray."

"Tell me about it. The fucking food is deadlier than two gunshots in the gut. I'm guessing you saw the *LA Times*. It looks like you'll get a medal for killing a cop. What a fucking world."

"There are more bad guys out there, Ray. Raft had someone running him. You know it as well as I do."

"I don't know if I give a shit."

"Sure you do."

"What do you want, Jimmy?"

"What are the chances Raft was working some kind of covert investigation for the DA's office?"

"Slim to none. I can't think of anyone in the District Attorney's office who would give Raft the time of day. Why would you ask? Who tried selling you that bill of goods?"

"A little birdie told me Raft was trying to sell it. I figure it for another line of crap, but I thought it wouldn't hurt to run it by you."

"I don't see it, but I can ask around. Might as well take advantage of my currency. It won't last long. It seems like other cops and prosecutors are a lot more willing to help when you've just been shot."

"That's cynical, Ray."

"Truth often is."

"Does the name Reginald Masters mean anything to you?"

"Did your little birdie say Raft was snooping for Jackson Masters?"

"No. She didn't have a name. But I asked you about Reginald Masters, who is Jackson Masters?"

"Jesus, Pigeon, do you live in Santa Monica or on fucking Mars?"

"Somewhere in between."

"Reginald Masters is a legend. The man practically owned Hollywood for thirty years. His son is 'Big Bill' Masters."

"Former Governor Masters?"

"Yes, and Jackson Masters is the Governor's son; a fast-moving assistant DA with his eye on Gil Garcetti's seat. Do you have something that puts Jackson Masters into Frank Raft's cesspool?"

"No. I don't know. Not really."

"What's this all about, Pigeon?"

"Who was the man Raft killed before he shot you?"

"Nick Sedway."

"Any relation to Moe Sedway?"

"Don't know. Why? What the fuck is this?"

"I don't know, Ray. A bunch of random notes Ed Richards was putting together before he was killed and a few words on a postcard from Lenny. I'm hoping Vinnie can help me cut through the haze."

"Vinnie? Are you that desperate?"

"He's a smart kid, when he's not at the racetrack. He's been doing his homework. This whole thing is tied somehow to ancient history. Hollywood, after the war," Jimmy said. "Vinnie is a student of the period."

"You want to know about Hollywood in the forties, you need to look up your old friend Roger."

"Why Rollins?"

"He was with the Hollywood Division during the heyday. You've known him your whole life, worked with him. He never talked about his run-ins with Ben Siegel and Mickey Cohen?"

"It never came up. That's interesting."

"What's interesting is I'm watching the fucking Dodgers lose again. Find Rollins. He'll love the chance to reminisce. I'll see if I can tie Jackson Masters to Raft somehow. Let's keep in touch. With any fucking luck I'll be out of this fucking asylum in a few days."

"I think that's the first time you ever asked me to keep in touch, Ray."

"I'm so fucking bored, I'll probably start wishing my stock broker keeps in touch. Find Roger, bring a bottle of Scotch along and Rollins will talk all night. Fucking Colorado Rockies, can you possibly believe this shit?"

"Thanks for your time, Ray," Jimmy said, trying to work his way to the door before Boyle blew up again.

"All I fucking have is time," Boyle said, hurling a cup of water at the TV screen.

"That's Virginia Hill. I've seen her picture in a few of these books," said Vinnie, looking at the laptop screen. "Who is the woman on the right?"

"Don't know."

"Looks a lot like Hill."

"Yes, she does," Jimmy said.

They were sitting side by side in the dining room of the Stradivarius home. Vinnie Strings in his wheel chair, pushed under the dining table as far as it would go.

A number of library books, opened and closed, were scattered on the table around the computer.

Jimmy had patiently listened to the kid for thirty minutes, Vinnie had nearly a week's worth of reading to summarize for Pigeon. It was interesting from a purely historical point of view, but there was nothing there to answer the question Jimmy needed answered.

"From all I've read," Vinnie said, once Jimmy moved their attention to Richards' files, "Virginia Hill was a real piece of work."

"The school teacher gave me a quick bio," Jimmy said. "Hill supposedly skipped the country with two million Mob dollars the day before Ben Siegel was assassinated up in Beverly Hills. The popular opinion is that one thing led to the other."

"That murder case was never solved," Vinnie said. "No one cared. Everything I've looked at tells me Ben Siegel's death was celebrated from coast-to-coast. That was forty-seven years ago, Jimmy. Almost to the day, in fact. I'd say its ice cold."

"We're looking for Lenny Archer's killer. I couldn't care less about Benny Siegel, unless it relates. I need you to go through all of Richards' files, cross-reference what he was collecting with what you found in these books. We need to find whatever it was that Ed Richards found, or thought he found, that would move someone to stop him dead. And I need you to highlight any references to the Masters family, any of them. The movie mogul, the former Governor and the Governor's son, Jackson Masters. He's an assistant DA here in LA County."

"Governor and Assistant DA, what's that about?"

"I don't know. It may be nothing, but we need to find out if it's about anything that led to Lenny's death. Raft and Tully paid, but there's a bigger fish out there and we need to drag the pond. Work as quickly as you can without letting anything slip through the net."

"It sounds like you're not going to stick around."

"I need to drive out to Tahoe to see an old friend," Jimmy said.

"For help?"

"Yes. Someone who was around when the Bugsy Siegel murder case wasn't so cold."

"Okay. I'm on this, Jimmy."

"Stay on it," Jimmy said. "Find a motive."

Pamela Walker paced nervously, smoked cigarettes, drank coffee and paced nervously for nearly two hours after Jimmy Pigeon's visit. All that time looking to the telephone and away again, unable to decide whether or not to make the phone call.

She wondered why she had lied to Jimmy.

While she had been describing her contact with Frank Raft, Pam had suddenly felt a strong resentment; one she hadn't realized she was harboring. She had been hurt and castigated, treated like a criminal by interrogators and lost a job that had been extremely important to her, all because she had agreed to help an officer of the law.

She had begun to see herself as a victim as she talked to Jimmy; to see herself as proof of the adage that no good deed goes unpunished. Then, without warning, she found herself withholding information from Jimmy. Pigeon had asked for a name, anyone in the DA's office who Raft may have mentioned. Pam hadn't considered it important until she heard the urgency of the question in his voice. And she had said no, without really understanding why she had lied. Now she understood she had held back because she wanted something for herself, felt she deserved compensation, reward not punishment for her good deed.

Now, she thought she might have something of value.

It was the night when Raft first approached her. They had walked for a while and she returned to her vehicle.

She found the card on the ground, had spotted it under the car as she unlocked the door. She reached down to pick it up. A business card. She read the name on the card and guessed Raft had dropped the card when he took out his shield to identify himself.

She paced nervously, looking at the telephone, holding the business card, trying to decide whether or not to phone Assistant District Attorney Jackson Masters, to ask Masters what it might be worth to have his business card back.

Ray Boyle didn't know he had drifted into sleep until Sam Stephens' booming voice woke him. It was like a sharp smack across the face. Stephens, barging in, ranting.

"What a fucking week. Parker is a zoo. The jailhouse is literally crawling with fucking reporters. And you will not believe the scene I just came from."

"Try me," Boyle said to his partner.

"Picture this, if you will," Stephens began. "A guy calls in a delivery order to Fazio's Pizzeria on South San Pedro near East 2nd. Large pie. Sausage, onion and green pepper."

"I appreciate the attention to detail."

"It's important. The delivery kid knocks on the door of 4D, top floor of a four-story apartment building on East 5th, and the guy opens the door. He keeps the kid waiting in the hallway while he 'goes to get his wallet.' He comes back to the door with a slice of pizza on a plate, he holds it out to the kid and he says, 'Take a bite of this fucking thing and tell me if its sausage, onion and green pepper.' The kid says he's not really very hungry and he can tell just by looking that its pepperoni and mushroom. The guy pulls a .44 magnum on the kid and he insists the kid taste it just to be certain."

"He forced the kid to eat pizza at gunpoint? Is that a felony?"

"It gets better," said Sam. "The guy takes the poor kid into the apartment and ties him to a chair. Clothesline. Then he calls the pizzeria and he tells the manager it's the third time they've fucked up his order and if they don't get the correct toppings over to him in twenty minutes, he's going to blow the delivery kid's head off. So much for don't shoot the messenger."

"Unbelievable."

"What'd I tell you? The manager calls Fazio at home and Fazio calls it in to 9-1-1. So me and Stevie O'Brien, this is who they put me with because you had to go and get plugged, run over to the pizzeria. O'Brien throws on a smock covered with tomato sauce and we take a pizza over to 5th Street."

"I can't stand the suspense."

"Wait. We get to the place, O'Brien knocks on the door, I stand out of view of the peephole. The guy says through the door, 'You look a little old for a delivery boy.' Not to mention O'Brien looks less Italian than I do, his skin is the color of Elmer's Glue. Anyway, Stevie starts winging it, rambling about how he owns the joint and he's Irish, the name Fazio is a cover to make it sound authentic but don't tell anyone because it could hurt business and the hostage in there is his sister's son and she'll murder him if anything happens to the kid and the pizza, which absolutely has sausage, onion and green pepper and is on the house, by the way, is getting cold."

"I'm exhausted just listening to this. Does the guy make the exchange?"

"He opens the door. He's got the .44 pointed right at O'Brien's head."

"Oh, boy."

"I've got to admit Stevie stayed cool. He takes a step toward the guy and he starts to open the pizza box. The guy asks Stevie what the fuck he's doing and O'Brien says he wants to show the guy the pizza is as ordered so he can get his nephew the fuck out of there. Meanwhile, I've got my gun out and I'm wondering when this guy is going to take a look over and spot me. The next thing I hear is screaming. I jump into the doorway and this guy is trying to get hot mozzarella out of his eyes while O'Brien is tackling him to the floor, the .44 drops neatly into the pizza box, Stevie is trying to handcuff the guy, both their hands are slippery with marinara and I don't know whether to try to help O'Brien or grab a slice."

"You arrest the guy?"

"Oh, yeah. When I left the station they were still trying to figure out the charge. The gun wasn't registered, but it wasn't loaded either. If we call it a kidnapping, the FBI rubs our faces it in until the end of time. And all along this guy is yelling about how he is going to sue the city and county of Los Angeles for burning his face with melted cheese. I mean, the cat's cheeks look like they were used to buff a car. So, how are you doing?"

"My body aches. I'm glad I missed everything, except maybe the sausage pizza. I've got a funny lead to follow and it hurts when I laugh. Would you by any chance happen to know if Raft had any connection to the DA's office?"

"I'm pretty sure he was assigned to the Menendez case. Doing investigative work for the DA during the first half of last year."

"The two kids who killed their parents?"

"They weren't convicted. Mistrial, five months ago. A new trial probably a year away. Raft would have been on it between the indictment in early December 1992 and the start of the first trial last July."

"Was Jackson Masters involved in the prosecution?" Boyle asked.

"Masters is very careful to stay clear of high profile cases that have the chance of going south," Stephens said. "And the Menendez case was a crap shoot from the start. Two juries, good-looking boy defendants. Masters is ambitious; he tries to avoid losing. He knows when to duck. I'll bet he stays as far away as possible from the football player."

"Masters could have crossed paths with Raft during the Menendez investigation."

"Sure. If Raft was hanging around for six months, I'm sure they would have bumped into each other. Why? What's this about?"

"I'm hoping to be out of here in a few days, but I won't be dancing for a while and I want to follow up the funny lead I mentioned. Could you help me out with a little leg work, very quietly?"

"Sure."

"We want to find out if Frank Raft was involved with the District Attorney's office recently and if he had more than a casual acquaintance with Masters."

"I'm off tomorrow, Ray. I'll see what I can find out."

"Very quietly, Sam."

The pager on Stephens' belt began beeping. He called into LAPD dispatch on the hospital room phone.

"What?" asked Boyle, when Stephens put the receiver down.

"Corpse found in the basement of an abandoned apartment house in East LA. Some kids were playing where they didn't belong and literally tripped over the body. Young woman, early twenties, no ID. Two gunshots, back of the head, close range. I need to meet O'Brien at the scene."

"It never ends," said Boyle.

"Want to ride along?"

"Cute."

"I'll call you later, give you the gory details."

"I can hardly wait. Don't forget the other thing."

"Covered," Stephens said. "Jackson Masters. Frank Raft. Quiet as a mouse."

GHOST STORIES

Jimmy Pigeon and Roger Rollins sat together on the screened porch looking out onto Lake Tahoe. Rollins had retired to the house on the lake eighteen years earlier, after nearly thirty years as a patrol officer, detective and captain in the Los Angeles Police Department and ten years as a private investigator. Rollins was a widower, father of three grown children and grandfather of eight. When Jimmy's father was killed in the line of duty in 1958, it was Rollins who rescued the fifteen-year-old from recklessly destroying his life. Years later, Rollins took Jimmy into his PI business as a partner and then the former LAPD Captain turned a blind eye when Jimmy tracked down and executed Will Cady, his father's murderer. The two men had a bond as strong as blood and Jimmy visited the older man as often as possible. The last time Jimmy had been out to the lake house was less than a month earlier, at a gathering to celebrate Roger's seventy-seventh birthday.

Now, Jimmy was here to talk about the distant past, to bring Rollins back to World War II and post-war Hollywood when Rollins was a young detective, mobsters rubbed elbows with movie stars, power and fame were bought with dollars and bullets and Charlie Chan was still the rage.

"Why the sudden interest in ancient history? I've known you all of your life, we worked together for seven years and you were never interested in a thing I had to say about anything that happened before the Dodgers came out to California," Rollins said, when Jimmy asked about Bugsy Siegel. "Unless it had something to do with your father."

"I'm a much bigger fan of the nineteenth century than I am of the twentieth," Jimmy said. "In my humble opinion, Western Civilization has been going steadily downhill since Archduke Ferdinand was whacked in 1914. I'm looking for a motive for my partner's murder and Ben Siegel's name keeps popping up."

"It was a lifetime ago. I joined the LAPD when I was eighteen years old, fresh out of high school. I spent my rookie year patrolling Hollywood and Vine, 1936, middle of the depression, more homeless and transients then than now. It was like a circus sideshow. I grew up real quick."

Rollins poured more Scotch before going on.

"The first time I saw Ben Siegel was in February of 1940 at the Academy Awards' ceremony in the Ambassador Hotel. He was laughing it up with Clark Gable and Bette Davis and looked as if he were there to present an award, or to receive one. I was a twenty-two-year-old uniformed officer, four years in and still wet behind the ears, on security detail at the hotel, wide-eyed, awed by the movie stars and the likes of Ben Siegel. Siegel had been in LA for a few years by then. Jack Dragna ran just about everything illegal before Bugsy arrived, but Dragna had to step down to make room for Siegel. Direct orders straight from Lucky Luciano's prison cell. Ben Siegel became the arm of Murder, Incorporated in the West and he answered only to Meyer Lansky in New York. He controlled prostitution, the numbers racket, the wire services and he had a stronghold on the film industry through control of the extras' union. Throughout the forties, the LAPD and the County Sheriff's Department brass were up for sale to the highest bidders; until William H. Parker became the Chief of Police in 1950 and made the LAPD his own. But for nearly a decade, until he was killed in 1947, Bugsy Siegel was something like the King of LA"

"So, who decided the king must die?"

"I couldn't tell you who killed Siegel; it's been a mystery for forty-seven years, as old an open case as the Black Dahlia. But I can tell you who may have benefited most from his demise. Quite a few did."

"Let's start with the short list," Jimmy said.

Arnold 'The Brain' Rothstein was assassinated in New York City in 1928. Case unsolved. His death initiated a bloody war between Joseph Messeria and Salvatore Maranzano for control of the New York rackets. Three young hoodlums saw the conflict as an opportunity. Meyer Lansky, Charles 'Lucky' Luciano and Frank Costello worked each side against the other and by the early thirties both bosses, Maranzano and Messeria, had been violently killed. Cases unsolved.

Charlie Luciano became *cappo di tutti cappi.*

In 1936, Thomas Dewey successfully prosecuted Luciano; Luciano was handed a thirty to fifty year prison sentence.

Dewey then turned his attention to Meyer Lansky.

Lansky's Achilles heel was Ben Siegel, the mob's most prolific assassin. It was decided Siegel should get as far away from New York as possible. He was sent west.

Luciano was locked up and Meyer Lansky was protecting Luciano's interests. Lansky insisted Siegel be given charge of operations in Los Angeles. Luciano felt obliged to comply. When Ben Siegel headed out to California, Jack Dragna ran the show in LA. From his prison cell, Luciano sent word to Dragna that Jack would have to step down and answer to Siegel. Jack Dragna resented his demotion from the start. Dragna's second in command, Mickey Cohen, saw Siegel's arrival as a chance to move up the ladder.

Siegel landed in LA with Moe Sedway in tow. Sedway was a childhood friend and the level head. Benjamin Siegel was immediately bewitched by Hollywood. Bugsy sent word to Lansky that Dragna was welcome to continue running gambling and prostitution. Siegel was interested in the movies. The mob was bringing in a fortune controlling extras and stage-hands, extorting payment from the studios by threatening to bring productions to a halt. Siegel left Moe Sedway to the mechanics and he spent his own time rubbing elbows with the movie stars. Before long Benny Siegel was a fixture at the biggest Hollywood events. Mickey Cohen often at his side.

Siegel was on top of the world, it seemed as if nothing could bring him down.

Then he met Virginia Hill.

And stumbled upon Las Vegas.

By early 1947, Siegel was standing on feet of clay.

He had sunk millions of New York mob dollars into the Flamingo in Las Vegas, which opened on Christmas Eve 1946 with less than overwhelming success. Lansky dispatched Moe Sedway to Vegas to check out the deteriorating situation. And while Siegel and Sedway spent more and more time away from the coast, Jack Dragna and Mickey Cohen jockeyed for control of criminal operations in LA. When a few million dollars of New York money invested in the Flamingo turned up missing, Siegel was suspect. Ben was ordered back to Los Angeles to do some explaining.

On June 19, 1947, Virginia Hill and Ben Siegel both left Las Vegas. Hill was on her way to Europe, by way of New York, carrying a black briefcase which may or may not have held two million dollars cash. The briefcase may or may not have been turned over to Meyer Lansky in New York to buy her life. Siegel returned to Beverly Hills to wait for word of a meeting to discuss the Las Vegas fiasco.

On the twentieth of June, Siegel was assassinated.

By the following day, Moe Sedway had taken control of the Flamingo on behalf of Meyer Lansky, while Los Angeles became the battleground for a power struggle between Jack Dragna and Mickey Cohen.

"Who won that battle?" Jimmy asked.

"It was a tug of war, lines were drawn. Dragna had 'friends' in the LAPD, Cohen had allies in the Sheriff's Department. In Hollywood, there was a struggle over who would control extras and stagehands. Dragna backed the existing union, Cohen stood behind the Teamsters. Lansky stayed clear of it. Luciano had been deported to Sicily a year before Bugsy was killed, he probably didn't figure in the move on Siegel. Lansky had a very soft spot in his heart for Siegel, so it's doubtful he ordered the hit; though he may have looked the other way."

"It seems as if Dragna, Cohen and Sedway are at the top of the short list," Jimmy said.

"No one believed Moe Sedway was involved in the murder of Bugsy Siegel. The two men went back a long way. Dragna was actually better off with Siegel still breathing and he knew it. Siegel let Dragna control the gambling, drug and prostitution operations and Mickey Cohen couldn't make any moves against Dragna while Siegel was alive. On the other hand, with Bugsy gone, Cohen lost almost all of his inroads to the Hollywood power brokers. In time, Cohen and Dragna both gave up on Hollywood and concentrated their battle on controlling the more lucrative criminal pursuits. Drugs and gambling. For the first time in decades the film industry was free from gangland extortion and film studio heads were finally able to make some really big money."

"Including Reginald Masters?" Jimmy asked.

"Particularly Reginald Masters," Rollins said, "and he's outlived all of them. Why do you ask about old man Masters?"

"Because Masters *has* outlived them all, benefited from the demise of Warner Oland and Bugsy Siegel and moved into the mansion they both once resided in. And because a young woman who looks an awful lot like Virginia Hill was seen in front of that mansion recently," said Jimmy. "That's why."

"How old a young woman?"

"Twenty, twenty-five tops," Jimmy said.

"Virginia Hill died in sixty-six," Rollins said. "If she had a daughter, and I've never heard of one, the woman would have to be closer to thirty."

"How about a granddaughter? What if she ran to Europe in forty-seven to have a child? There could possibly be a granddaughter, twenty years old or early twenties."

"Are you thinking Benny Siegel's granddaughter?"

"It's feasible."

"At Reginald Master's mansion? Recently. Why?"

"That, my friend, is the sixty-four thousand dollar question. And Lenny Archer died trying to answer it."

Jackson Masters lay awake in his bed, his wife asleep at his side, his two children sleeping in rooms across the hall.

He had been at the Criminal Courts Building for most of the afternoon. He had been summoned in for a mandatory meeting of all members of the District Attorney's Office to discuss immediate strategies with regard to the arrest at Rockingham the day before.

It was the very last place he had wanted to be on a Saturday afternoon. He was at his desk, shortly after the meeting, when his telephone rang. A woman caller.

The woman would not identify herself. She claimed to have knowledge which tied Masters to Detective Raft of the County Sheriff's Department. She added that she had been questioned by a private investigator who had appeared very interested in any connection Raft may have had to the DA's Office. She had decided to withhold her knowledge until she had the opportunity to talk with Masters, to ask his advice about what to reveal. She said she was looking for good reasons to forget what she knew and she would give Masters sometime to think about it. She would call again on Monday to find out *how many* good reasons Masters could give her for keeping silent. Masters easily translated her message. How much money was it worth? Before he could say a thing, the woman had disconnected.

Masters' wife stirred beside him. He closed his eyes and feigned sleep. When she became still again, his eyes popped open. He stared up at the ceiling. He was fairly certain the woman was Pam Walker, a restaurant manager who had been brought in for questioning after Raft's death. He had warned Raft against using a civilian. He guessed it was Jimmy Pigeon who'd been asking questions. He was also fairly certain Walker knew nothing specific, but the last thing he needed was to have his name connected in any way to the name Frank Raft.

Masters stared up at the ceiling. He had no idea what he would do when the woman called again, or how he would be able to get any rest until she did.

The two men sat looking out at the dark lake. Jimmy had accepted Rollins' offer of the guest room for the night and would head back to Los Angeles in the morning. They had shared the best part of a fifth of Scotch over the past four hours, grilled a couple of steaks, baked potatoes and talked old cases as they worked on the bottle. Rollins now sat silently. He seemed lost in thought.

"What's on your mind, Roger?" Jimmy asked.

"I was in Sacramento this morning, got back here just before you arrived. A reunion of California veterans of the 79th Infantry Division for the fiftieth anniversary of our combat engagement in Normandy. June 18, 1944. We planned the event nearly a year ago. Thirty-seven veterans of the campaign showed up and we were virtually ignored. Little if any press leading up to the event this past week, no TV cameras or major daily reporters present. Hundreds of lives were lost in the weeklong assault on Fort du Roule south of Cherbourg, but the media is much more interested in the double homicide in Brentwood. Not to trivialize the loss of those two lives, but I'm guessing there were dozens of innocent people killed that same day who no one but family is going to hear much about. I don't know, Jimmy, I just don't get it. Maybe I'm getting too old, out of touch, but it seems odd to me. Celebrity victims have always stolen the headlines. Now celebrity suspects and perpetrators are going to do the same. I suppose what I'm saying is, don't expect much interest in the death of an anonymous private investigator or a local journalist."

"I think I can count on one LAPD detective and one Santa Monica newspaper editor to pay attention," said Jimmy.

"I hope you're right," Rollins said. "What now?"

"Try to find the girl."

A clock inside the house chimed twelve times.

"Jesus, where does the time go," Jimmy said. "I think I'll turn in. I can't remember what day it is."

"It's Sunday now," Rollins said. "Funny."

"What's that?"

"Monday is the twentieth of June. The anniversary of the day Bugsy Siegel met his maker."

* * *

Seth Cady sat on a worn leather armchair holding a baseball bat. The chair had been sloppily repaired, back and seat, with silver duct tape. The baseball bat dripped blood onto the cracked linoleum floor. The room he sat in was on the third floor of a run-down apartment building in downtown Oakland.

Cady had arrived an hour earlier, direct from nearly twenty-five years in a prison cell.

Time added for bad behavior.

In 1958, eighteen-year-old Seth Cady and two older men had robbed a jewelry store in Santa Clara. Steve Gold and Al Linger were apprehended with the stolen jewelry, fleeing the scene. Seth got away. The following day, Seth's older brother, Will Cady, turned himself in as the third man in the jewelry heist. Will Cady needed an alibi, something to put him a good distance away from the fatal shooting of a police officer in Los Angeles on the same night.

A few months before Linger, Gold and his brother were released from prison in 1970, Seth was convicted and locked up for shooting and nearly killing a clerk during a liquor store robbery in Nevada. Cady got word about his brother's death a month later. Killed, execution style, no suspects.

Less than twelve hours after his release, Seth Cady had found Al Linger in the seedy Oakland tenement.

It took less than an hour for Cady to learn Steve Gold had died of cancer five years earlier and to learn the name of the man who had visited Gold and Linger twenty-four years earlier asking questions about Seth's brother shortly before Will Cady was killed.

Seth stood, struck the dead body of Al Linger one more time, tossed the baseball bat onto the duct-taped armchair, grabbed the loaded handgun and the four hundred dollars in cash he had found in Linger's dresser drawer and left the apartment.

Cady walked the few blocks to the bus terminal and he purchased a one-way ticket for Los Angeles to search for Jimmy Pigeon.

LEAVING LAS VEGAS

June 19, 1947.
Ben Siegel and Virginia Hill both left Las Vegas, both for the last time, in opposite directions.

Forty-seven years later. June 19, 1994.
Jimmy Pigeon woke early Sunday morning. Disoriented at first, not sure where he was. He heard the distinct sounds of surf and wildlife coming off Lake Tahoe through the open window of a guest room in Rollins' house. He felt anxious, in a hurry to get back to Los Angeles to discover what, if anything, Vinnie Strings and Ray Boyle had learned.

Rollins was preparing breakfast when Jimmy came down. He insisted that Jimmy stay long enough to eat.

"Why do you seem so certain your partner's death has something to do with Siegel's death, a shooting that's never been considered anything more than a mob hit?"

"All I'm really sure about is that Lenny's death had nothing to do with drugs. Lenny's reference to Chan in a postcard, the photograph of the Virginia Hill look-alike, the fact that the man who Frank Raft killed in the barber shop was named Sedway. Something in or about the mansion figures in; it's too much for coincidence."

"And remind me, Jimmy, what's driving you, considering the fact that even Lenny's brother seems satisfied the men who actually murdered Lenny have both been killed?"

"It's not enough, Roger. You taught me that yourself. You don't have to pull the trigger to be guilty. Both you and my father taught me to never bail out, to follow up to the end. Lenny was beaten and tortured. Tully and Raft are not the end of it. And it's not just Lenny. At least five others have been murdered beside Tully and Raft. Ray Boyle was nearly killed and more may be in danger."

"Keep that in mind, Jimmy," Rollins said.

Twenty-four hours after leaving Las Vegas, Seth Cady ate breakfast at the counter of a greasy spoon in downtown Los Angeles, appropriately named the Terminal Diner, after the overnight bus ride from Oakland. As he worked on his bacon, scrambled eggs and potatoes, he leafed through the phone directory under private investigators.

The counterman refilled Cady's coffee mug and took a stab at being friendly.

"Looking for a good PI?" he asked.

"I'm looking for a certain PI. Jimmy Pigeon."

"You won't find him in there."

"Oh," Cady said, looking up from the book.

"Pigeon works out of Santa Monica, his name has been in the news lately. His partner was murdered recently. If you're looking for someone here in town, I could offer a few suggestions."

"I need to see Pigeon," Cady said.

"Old friend?"

"Never met him. I'm looking him up for my brother."

Jackson Masters skipped breakfast Sunday. He had not slept very well and he had no appetite. When he first made the lunch date with his father for that Sunday afternoon he had been looking forward to the visit. But after the phone call from Pam Walker on Saturday, he was again afraid he might betray his anxiety in his father's presence.

William Masters lived in a large home not far from the Rockingham mansion that had dominated the news for the past week. A uniformed officer stopped Jackson Masters' car as he rode toward the ex-Governor's house. Masters showed the officer his identification and stated his destination. The officer apologized for the inconvenience and waved Masters through the check point. Masters pulled into the drive and put on what he hoped was a convincing smile before climbing out of his vehicle and slowing walking to the front door.

* * *

Jimmy Pigeon pulled his car into the driveway shortly before noon. In less than thirty minutes, the streets of the neighborhood would be jammed with vehicles approaching Dodger Stadium for the last of a three game series against Colorado. The Dodgers had lost the day before, suggesting Ray Boyle had continued watching from his bed in the hospital. Jimmy had called ahead before leaving the house on the lake. Fran Stradivarius had answered the phone and reported her son had been up half the night in front of a stack of library books and the laptop and Vinnie was now rolling around the house, fidgeting in his wheelchair, ambulatory pacing, as he waited for Jimmy to arrive.

The front door flew open before Jimmy could ring the bell, as if Vinnie had been peering out of the window all morning. It took Jimmy a few minutes to calm Vinnie down long enough to locate and greet Fran.

He found Fran at the kitchen stove. Her back was to him, three pots sat on lit burners on the stovetop. She was stirring a large kettle of tomato sauce with a wooden spoon. For a moment, she reminded Jimmy of his mother at the stove, already preparing dinner when he returned from school on weekday afternoons, anticipating the arrival of Jimmy's father from his shift with the LAPD.

It was a Friday afternoon in April, 1958. Jimmy had raced back from school, turning down an invitation to play in a pick-up basketball game at the schoolyard. Today, he was in a hurry to get home, anxious to know what the 'big surprise' was; the surprise Nick Pigeon had promised his son the night before.

Nick had come up to say goodnight to his son. Jimmy's two younger sisters were asleep in the next bedroom. Jimmy was reading a book his father had given him, Dumas' *The Three Musketeers.* Nick was a lover of the classics and Jimmy had inherited his father's enthusiasm. Jimmy put the novel down and smiled when his father walked in.

"Hey, Pop."

"It's late, son, time for lights out."

"Can I finish this chapter, Dad?"

"It can wait. It's been around for a hundred years, it will be there tomorrow. Speaking of tomorrow, do you have any big plans for Friday night?"

"Not really," said the fifteen-year-old. "Why?"

"I thought we might go out together, after dinner."

"Where?"

"It's a surprise."

"C'mon, Dad, tell me. I'll go nuts thinking about it all day in school tomorrow."

"How *is* school?"

"Fine. C'mon, Dad, tell me."

"Tomorrow. Now, get to sleep."

"That's not fair."

"Things are not always fair, son. Trust me, this will be worth the wait. A little mystery is good for you, keeps you on your toes. Now, bedtime."

"Dad?"

"Yes, son?"

"Being a policeman?"

"Yes?"

"Is it like the Musketeers?"

"Just a little bit, son."

"That's what I want to do, Dad. Be a police officer, like you."

"You have a long time to decide."

"All for one and one for all."

"Go to sleep," Nick said, turning off the light.

Friday, Jimmy sat at the kitchen table after school, his mother at the stove. He had been badgering her for nearly an hour, trying to get her to reveal the secret.

"Jimmy," she said, turning from the stove, "you are driving me crazy. Your father will be home soon. Go up the street to your aunt's house and pick up your sisters."

"Mom."

"Go. Get the girls."

An hour later, Jimmy heard a car pull up in front of the house. He ran to the front door and opened it to find Captain Roger Rollins standing there. Jimmy's mother came to the door. Rollins asked if he could talk with her.

Alone.

Before leaving twenty minutes later, Rollins reached into his pocket.

"We found these on Nick's body," he said, handing her two tickets for the very first home game of the first year *Los Angeles* Dodgers. The 'big surprise'.

Jimmy still had those two baseball tickets; a reminder that things are not always fair.

The woman at the stove became Fran Stradivarius again. She turned to find Jimmy standing silently behind her.

"Jimmy, are you okay?"

"Yes, Fran. Looks like you're cooking up a storm."

"Sunday dinner. I hope you'll stay."

"C'mon, Jimmy," Vinnie called from the dining room table. "I've been waiting all morning to show you this."

"Maybe I will, Fran," Jimmy said. He left the kitchen to find out what Vinnie was all juiced up about.

"I found two files we hadn't looked at," Vinnie said, as Jimmy pulled up a chair beside him at the table. "They were in a separate folder titled *North Linden*, the name of the street where the Masters' mansion sits."

"Go on."

"The first is a history of the mansion which Richards put together. The place was originally owned by the Fox Studio. When Warner Oland was signed for five more Chan films in 1934, after the incredible success of the first eight, the contract included a huge salary and the house on North Linden. When a new contract was negotiated in 1936, Oland demanded lots more cash and artistic control of the material. The actor was having personal problems. He was drinking a lot and becoming extremely difficult to work with. Oland's services were getting too costly and far too messy for the studio and they were looking for a way to get out of the contract and replace the actor. The task was given to Reginald Masters. In 1937, Oland walked off the set of *Charlie Chan at Ringside* and never returned. Sidney Toler took over the role of Charlie Chan in the next film. Masters somehow solved the studio's dilemma and was rewarded with the deed to the mansion in Beverly Hills."

"Okay," Jimmy said. "So, how did Ben Siegel wind up living in the mansion?"

"Rumor had it that Siegel may have been instrumental in *encouraging* Oland to disappear and Masters might have thanked Siegel by giving him the keys to the mansion. Masters' career skyrocketed after Oland left. He took the Charlie Chan franchise to Monogram Pictures during the war in exchange for a large piece of the studio and by war's end he controlled the film company. When Bugsy Siegel was killed in 1947, Masters moved into the vacated mansion."

"So, Masters moved into his own house. Big deal."

"Unless Masters gained more than just a new street address when Siegel died," Vinnie said.

"What's in the second file you found?" Jimmy asked.

"It's just a few pages, but it may be the break we've been looking for."

Vinnie just sat there looking at Jimmy. The kid was wearing a goofy smile.

"Are you going to tell me or what?"

"Richards put these few pages together specifically for Lenny Archer."

"For God's sake, Vinnie, tell me what it is."

"The photograph of the woman who looks like Virginia Hill and a long note to Lenny. Take a look," Vinnie said, bringing the note up on the laptop screen.

Jimmy pulled the laptop closer and read.

Mr. Archer:

Thank you again for your help last week. The information you were able to collect about the ownership history of the house on North Linden will be very useful in the research for my book, *Chasing Charlie Chan.* As I mentioned on the telephone this morning, I'm hoping you can now help me find a woman. I have included a photograph. On Thursday, I drove out to North Linden to shoot pictures of the mansion. I saw the woman leave the house before she was picked up by a taxicab. I thought I recognized her, but couldn't place her. I snapped a photo and then, not knowing quite why, I jotted down the number of the cab. When I returned home and looked over my files, I realized why the woman looked so familiar. I tracked down the cab driver and, for a price, he told me he had taken the woman to the Beverly Crescent Hotel.

I went to the hotel on Friday morning with a print of the photograph, to try to find out who she was. Again, for a price, I was informed by a front desk clerk the woman's name was Natalie Levant and that she was not in her room. I left a business card with the clerk, Harry Sherman, with a note asking the woman to please give me a call. I waited Friday and Saturday to hear from her, but never did. This morning, I phoned the hotel and was told she had left the hotel on Friday evening and not returned.

I wish I could give you more to work with, but this is all I have. Please let me know if you have any luck. Thank you for agreeing to meet me away from your office. For the past few days, I have had the feeling I was being followed. I'm sure it's just my imagination, but you know what they say about being paranoid.

Edward Richards

"Being paranoid doesn't mean they're not watching you," Vinnie said.

"They *were* watching Richards and he led them straight to Lenny. Raft and Tully. They followed Lenny back to the office from the drop point to find out what Richards handed him and what he knew. They tried beating it out of him and he wouldn't talk. Then they found what they were searching for, grabbed it and they shot Lenny on the way out," Jimmy said. "It's all on the fucking tape. They slaughtered him and then went and did the same to Richards."

"Why? For trying to find the woman?"

"I don't know, but I'm going to find out. Can you print a copy of the woman's photograph?"

"No problem, but I'll have to take the disk over to my desktop computer," Vinnie said. "The printer is in my room. Give me a minute."

Jimmy went back into the kitchen, to tell Fran he couldn't stay for dinner and thank her for the offer.

Jimmy waited in the dining room until Vinnie came back with the photograph. He snatched it from Vinnie's hand and headed for the front door.

"Are you going to see Ray Boyle?"

"Not before I go to the Beverly Crescent Hotel."

Seth Cady stepped off the bus. It was his fourth bus trip in less than forty hours. Southern Nevada Correctional Center to Las Vegas to Oakland to LA to Santa Monica.

Cady walked up the Third Street Promenade looking for a phone book. He spotted Meg's Café, walked in and sat at a window booth. A waitress fixed him up with coffee, a pen and a phone directory. He found Jimmy Pigeon's office and home addresses and jotted both down on a paper napkin.

The waitress came back to refill his coffee cup. Cady quickly slipped the napkin into a shirt pocket.

"Can I help you find something?" she asked. "I know the town pretty well."

It was Sunday. Cady didn't expect to find Pigeon at his office. He would find him at home, but he would wait. He needed a place where he could lie down for a while. He had not allowed himself a moment's rest since walking out of the gates of the Nevada prison. And he needed a place to go after he dealt with Pigeon, where he could stay out of sight until heading back to Las Vegas in the morning.

"Do you know a place where I can get a room, not too expensive and not too far from here?"

"Everything is too expensive around here," she said. "But there's a motel on Broadway at Nineteenth that's not terribly bad. And you can easily walk it."

"Thanks," Cady said, placing a five-dollar bill on the table and rising to leave. "I'll check it out."

"Hold on, I'll get your change."

"Keep it," he said.

Cady walked to the exit. He turned and gave the woman a big smile before stepping out to the street.

The waitress carried the phone directory back to its place beside the cash register.

"Who's your new friend, Kim," Meg kidded from behind the counter. "I haven't seen him here before."

"Just a man looking for a motel."

"I wonder where he's from. He had a strange look in his eyes. Like someone who doesn't get out much."

"I don't know about that," Kim said, "but I can tell you he's a good tipper."

Another customer came through the front door.

"Well, what a surprise," Meg said.

"Who is he?" Kim asked.

"Someone I hadn't expected to see again so soon."

The man walked straight up to the counter.

"How are you, Meg?"

"Good, Nathan. How are your wife and the baby?"

"Annie is doing really well," Nate Archer said, "and the boy is amazing. I can hardly take my eyes off him."

"That's great. I'm glad everything went well. So, what brings you back so soon? It must be something important to tear you away from your family."

"I'm looking for Jimmy. He wasn't at home or at his office."

"I haven't seen Jimmy for a couple of days. Last I heard he was headed to LA. He said he planned to see Ray Boyle at the hospital and see Vinnie Strings also. If it's urgent, I can make a couple of phone calls, try to find him."

"It's not urgent. It's just every time I look at the baby, I think about Lenny, and how I left Jimmy holding the bag. I wanted to talk with Jimmy about it, make myself more available if he needs help."

"I have keys to Jimmy's apartment," Meg said. "Let me get you something to eat, if you haven't had lunch. Then you can go over to his place and wait for him. Just make yourself at home. I'm sure Jimmy won't mind. He should be back before too long. In the meantime, I *will* make a few calls and try to track him down."

"Thanks, Meg. I appreciate it."

"Hold your gratitude until after you've tried the lunch special," Meg teased.

Just as certain genetic diseases skip generations, the sins of Reginald Masters had been inherited not by his son, but by his grandson.

The woman had chosen to approach Jackson Masters. It was logical, he was much more accessible than a reclusive millionaire or an ex-Governor.

She had contacted Masters through the DA's office and was able to persuade him that a private meeting was in his best interest. At a café near the Criminal Courts Building, she told him just enough to convince him her determination was unshakable. She insisted he arrange a visit to the home of his grandfather. She told Masters she would wait at the Beverly Crescent Hotel for an answer, but would not wait long. If she did not get word of an appointment to speak to Reginald Masters by the next day, she would be talking with someone who might consider her information worthy of a sensational news story and a huge price tag.

Then she had left Jackson Masters sitting in the café.

He sat, stunned, debating whether to call his father or call the old man. He called his grandfather and told Reginald Masters about the woman and what she wanted.

"Bring her to me, and don't speak of this to anyone," the old man had said, in a voice that chilled Jackson Masters to the bone.

Seth Cady checked into the motel on Broadway shortly after two on Sunday afternoon.

He paid cash for a one-night stay and asked the clerk to give him a wake-up call at five.

"Do you think Simpson really did it?" the kid asked, handing Cady a room key.

Cady said nothing. He had no idea what the kid was talking about.

Up in the room, Cady stretched out on the bed. His fifty-fourth birthday was less than a week away. He had spent nearly half his life, nearly all of his adult life, behind bars. He had been raised by a domineering mother and an alcoholic father who gave him little attention and less love. He had done little that was right in his life. The only human who ever cared about him, had ever defended or protected or nurtured him, was his older brother, Will. He had no prospects, no place he needed to be, except at the desk of his parole officer in Las Vegas on Tuesday morning. No place at all. He wanted to do one thing he could feel good about, one thing that would have made his big brother proud of him. He'd had a very long time with very little to do but think about what that might be.

Seth Cady could only hope killing Jimmy Pigeon would do the trick.

Jimmy quickly identified Harry Sherman from the gold nametag on the front of his red sport jacket.

"Hello, Harry," Jimmy said from across the check-in counter of the Beverly Crescent Hotel.

"Do I know you?"

"I'm really hoping this won't take that long," Jimmy said. He placed the photograph on the counter and tapped it with his finger. "Tell me about this photo."

"Am I supposed to know who the woman is?" Sherman asked.

"I haven't asked you about the woman yet. I'm asking about the photo; about when you first saw it. When Edward Richards first showed it to you."

"Are you sure about that? Are you sure it wasn't someone else?"

"I'm absolutely sure. In case you haven't heard, Edward Richards was killed two days later. And you're not going to get any work done at all until we get this little chat over with. So, talk to me or talk to the LAPD."

"Are you trying to scare me?"

"Trying to waste as little time as possible fucking with you, Harry. I'm guessing that would suit you also."

"Good guess. Okay. The guy comes in, says he's a news reporter, shows me the photo and offers fifty bucks for an ID. I give him the woman's name and her room number. He heads off to use the house phone. He comes back, hands me his business card and a note for the woman. And that's the last I ever saw of him."

"Did you deliver the note?"

"No, I gave it to the cop."

"What cop?"

"Not long after the reporter left, a detective turned up asking about the same woman."

"Did he ask about her by name?"

"No, but he described her very well. Well enough. I said something like, 'She's a very popular lady.' When he asked me what I meant, I mentioned the reporter and showed him Richards' business card and note. The man had a large, impressive badge. I was interested in cooperating. I also told him the woman was not in her room. The cop took the card and note and he walked out."

"Did you get his name?"

"No, I didn't. He assured me it was none of my fucking business. I took his word for it," Sherman said. "The guy looked very dangerous."

"Did you see *him* again?"

"No."

"What happened to the woman?"

"I don't know. I went off at three that day, it was a Friday and I didn't come back to work until Sunday morning. The woman was gone. I never saw her again."

"Can you tell me who checked her out? Who may have seen her last before she left?"

Sherman scanned the hotel reservation records on the computer at the end of the counter.

"No one checked her out. She just left her key in the room."

"That's all of it?"

"That's all of it," Sherman said.

"Can you tell me about the credit card she used for the room?"

"You know I can't."

Jimmy did know.

"So, can I get back to work now or are you going to grab me by the lapels and try to shake it out of me?"

Jimmy picked up the photograph, refolded it, slipped it into his pocket and headed out to his car.

Minutes later he was driving out toward the hospital to see Ray Boyle.

***

Jackson Masters sat at one end of a long dining table. His father sat at the other. The housekeeper had cleared the lunch dishes and William Masters confronted his only son.

"What is it, Jackson? You've hardly said a word."

He had tried, time and again while they dined, tried to speak out, tell his father about how his life had been turned upside down in the past few weeks. He needed help; the kind of help only a father could provide. But he couldn't bring himself to speak. He couldn't make his father culpable for crimes the man had no prior knowledge of.

He would not expose his father to the disease that had mercifully skipped generations.

"It's just the madness downtown," he said. "The double homicide last weekend, the media frenzy and the pressure on the office to start building a case. Everyone from Garcetti down is afraid of screwing up."

"It's times like this I'm glad I am not Governor. Try staying clear of that one. It's bound to be messy. So, is that all it is, son? Is everything okay at home?"

"Great, Dad."

"Good. Now, maybe you should get back to your family. I appreciate your coming to see me today, but I'm sure your own children will want time with you on Father's Day."

Father's Day.

Jackson hadn't realized it was Father's Day. He had slept late, after the restless night thinking about the phone call from Pam Walker. His wife and his two children had already left for church and hadn't returned before he took off to visit the Governor.

His children. Would they be spared? Could he protect them from the disease?

"Son?"

"You're right, Dad. I should get home."

The two men walked together to the front door.

"I suppose I should give *my* father a phone call," William Masters said. "When he returns from New York this evening."

"I'm sure Grandfather would like that," Jackson said.

Much more than my grandfather will like the phone call from me, he thought.

"Happy Father's Day," the Governor said at the door.

"You too, Dad."

"I'm very proud of you, son."

Masters manufactured a smile and turned to walk to his car. He felt his father's eyes on him as he moved away.

And he felt the disease eating him up inside.

Nate Archer left Meg's Café after another huge meal. He decided to walk it off before heading over to Jimmy's apartment to wait for Pigeon. He walked the Third Street Promenade and then strolled out to the Santa Monica Pier.

Archer settled on a bench on the pier and looked out over the bay. It was Father's Day, his first as a father. Annie had done everything possible to make it a special day for him. She had dressed the baby in a tiny shirt with the words *I Love Daddy* across the front. She had fixed a large breakfast. Waffles, eggs, fresh fruit, shamefully expensive Hawaiian coffee, even a Bloody Mary for the man of honor.

Nate had appreciated the effort and the attention, and he had shown his appreciation. But Annie knew her husband, knew when there was something troubling him and had a good idea about what was distracting him.

"I have another surprise for you," she had said that morning.

"Oh?"

"A free trip to Santa Monica, no strings attached. I expect you back here safely, preferably by tomorrow."

"Are you sure?"

"I'm sure. Go talk to Jimmy. See what he's learned. It's Father's Day. Your father would have wanted you to follow up, to find out why *his* son Lenny was killed."

"I love you."

"I love you. I understand you don't want to leave me and the baby so soon, even for a day. And it means a lot to me that you feel that way. But until this is resolved, until you know why your brother was murdered and who else is responsible, I'm afraid a part of you will always be somewhere else."

"I'll be back tonight."

"If you can. Just be careful and call me."

A seagull landed on a bench across the pier, flapped its wings and took off again. A bearded man in a Red Sox baseball cap approached Nate, holding out a battered paper cup. Nate placed a five-dollar bill into the cup.

"Thank you, brother," the man said. "Happy Father's Day."

"How do you know I'm a father?" Nate asked.

"We are all fathers," the man said. "They are all our children."

The sun pushed out from behind a small white cloud.

The man tipped his hat and walked away. Nate watched the man move toward the end of the pier. Archer stood up, stretched, and began moving off the pier, headed for Jimmy Pigeon's apartment.

Jimmy rushed into the hospital room. Sam Stephens was there, visiting Ray Boyle. Ray was out of his bed, sitting in a chair, an IV slowly dripping painkiller into his arm. Jimmy quickly dispensed with the formalities and shoved the photograph at Boyle.

"We need to find this woman, Ray."

"Did the Dodgers win?"

"Yes," Jimmy said.

"What did I tell you, Sam? I didn't watch the fucking game and the bums finally won."

"Ray," Jimmy urged.

"What is this, Jimmy?" Boyle asked, finally turning his attention to the photo.

"Maybe a case-breaker, Ray. We need to find her and talk with her."

"Nice looking woman. I'm in no condition to do much for you, Jimmy," Boyle said. "And I really can't tell how much sympathy I can generate in the department."

"Let me see that photo," Stephens said. He took the photograph from Boyle. He looked from the photo to Jimmy and back again. "We've already found her, Jimmy. Killed. There wasn't much left of her face, but I'm sure this is the same woman."

"What?" Jimmy asked.

"We found her body yesterday in an abandoned building. Shot. Twice. No identification," Stephens said. "So, who is she and what case was she going to break?"

"Jesus," Jimmy said. "I think Raft killed this woman and the cover-up led to all the other killings, from Lenny Archer on. I think you'll find the slugs that killed this woman came from the same gun that killed Sedway and wounded you, Ray."

"What the fuck are you talking about, Jimmy?" Boyle said.

Jimmy ran the entire story by them, ending it with his visit to the Beverly Crescent.

"We're running the woman's prints now," Stephens said. "No hits yet. I'll run the name, Natalie Levant. Are you sure that was her real name?"

"The clerk wouldn't let me see her credit card info," Jimmy said.

"We'll get a court order to look at the hotel records, but it won't be until tomorrow."

"I need to see Hank Fellows at the *Outlook*. Richards worked under Fellows at the newspaper. I'm hoping there's still time; hoping Hank can get this photo into the morning paper. Maybe someone saw or knew something about the woman and will come forward," Jimmy said.

"Give me a minute to call in to Parker. I'll initiate a search on the woman's name and I'll talk with ballistics about comparing the slugs against Raft's weapon," Sam said. "Then I'll go with you to see Hank Fellows, help give your request a little extra urgency and legitimacy."

"And what do I do," Boyle complained, "while you guys are out having all the fun."

"You're doing it, Ray," Stephens said, before grabbing the telephone to make his calls.

* * *

Seth Cady was jolted awake by a hard slap across the mouth. A dream. A memory.

Seth was eight years old. It was a Sunday afternoon. His father was home for a change, sitting in his armchair, reading the Sunday paper, working on his third tall glass of whiskey. Or fourth.

Seth Cady saw very little of his father, who bartended in a downtown Oakland saloon, drank away his tips after his late shift, stumbled home in the wee hours to be greeted by his wife with profanities that woke both Seth and his older brother nearly every night.

Seth had pleaded with his father for a game of catch. His father had turned him down. The boy sat on the couch, tossing a baseball into the air, watching it drop into his leather mitt. The ball got away, bounced off a table and knocked the whiskey glass to the floor. His father jumped up and slapped Seth sharply across the face. The boy went down hard.

Seth's sixteen-year-old brother, Will, pounced on his father. Will brought the man down with two punches to the gut and landed on his father with both knees. He gave his father a left and right to the head and pinned him down on the floor. He pressed his forearm into his father's neck, until the man was gasping for breath.

"If you ever lay a finger on Seth again, I'll fucking kill you." Will stood up and took Seth's hand.

Seth was trembling, his father didn't move.

"C'mon, kid, let's go out and throw the ball around," Will said.

His father had never touched Seth again.

Seth heard a phone ringing. He reached out and picked up the receiver.

"It's five, sir," the desk clerk said. "I was told to call your room at five."

Seth Cady placed the receiver down. He sat up in the bed and lit a cigarette. He picked up Al Linger's handgun and checked the cylinder. Six chambers full.

"It's time, Will," he said aloud. "Get even time."

Pam Walker finally gave up the battle. Since speaking with Jackson Masters twenty-four hours earlier, Walker had been entrenched in an inner struggle; weighing the anger of her unfair treatment against her morality. Being misled by Detective Raft, recruited to inform on her friends, was one thing. Blackmail for personal gain was something entirely different. She wouldn't do it; couldn't do it. She liked Jimmy Pigeon, always had. Though she had been unaware, she had nevertheless put Jimmy in danger. And she had lied to him, without excuse. She had felt used, and rightfully so. But since talking with Masters, Pam had felt something much worse.

Dirty.

She would try to make it right.

Pam decided not to telephone Jimmy; she wanted to speak to him face to face.

She grabbed her wallet and car keys from the kitchen counter and picked up Jackson Master's business card from where it sat beside the phone.

She walked out of her apartment and down to her car.

She lit a cigarette to calm her nerves, started her engine and pulled away from the curb; on her way to tell Jimmy Pigeon the truth.

Nate Archer walked to the kitchen to refill his coffee cup. He was waiting for Jimmy to get back. He hadn't heard any word from Jimmy or Meg. He had called his wife, Annie, to let her know where he was. He was making himself at home at Jimmy Pigeon's apartment.

He carried his coffee cup over to Jimmy's bookcase and scanned the titles, again. He had leafed through a copy of *The New Yorker*, from cover to cover, and now he was looking for something else to pass the time as he waited. Something to keep him from wearing out the rug.

He took a worn paperback copy of *The Three Musketeers* down from the shelf and opened the book to the front page.

He found an inscription: *Jimmy, whenever I need a reminder about what courage is, I return to this book. I hope it does the same for you. Love, Dad.*

Nate thought of his own father, who had died fighting a California wildfire when Nathan was fifteen; leaving him to look after his eleven-year-old brother. The cost of his father's courage had been very high and Nate had taken his responsibility very seriously. He had cared for Lenny, had strived to provide a good example, had tried to protect the younger boy. He had done well. His brother had grown into a fine young man, a young man who would have made his father proud.

Then Lenny went to Vietnam and everything changed. Though Nate wouldn't recognize the extent of the damage until many years later. And, in the end, Nate couldn't protect his brother from the nightmares and he couldn't protect his brother from an assassin's bullet.

Nate had been roused from a deep sleep at four that morning, his infant son was wailing from his crib. Nate had jumped from bed, run into the child's room, took the baby into his arms and coaxed *his* Lenny back to sleep.

When he had returned to bed, Annie had turned to him, half-asleep. And with a smile on her face she had mumbled, "Happy Father's Day." At that moment he knew what he needed to do and later, at breakfast, Annie knew it also.

He needed to know *why* his brother had been killed.

Nate settled into Jimmy's reading chair and turned to Chapter One of the Dumas novel.

Out in the hallway, Pam Walker approached the door to Jimmy's apartment. She stopped to take a deep breath and raised her arm to knock on the door. A large hand covered her mouth, a gun was shoved roughly into her ribs and she was slowly eased back away from the door.

"Make a sound and I'll kill you," Seth Cady said.

DEADLINES

Seth Cady guided Pam Walker into the stairwell off the hall. He turned her around to face him, keeping her mouth covered and pressed the barrel of the gun to her cheek.

"I'm going to take my hand away. Don't make a sound unless I tell you to and then only loud enough for me to hear you where I'm standing. Understood?"

She nodded. She felt faint. He removed his hand from her mouth.

"Was that Pigeon's apartment?" Cady asked.

"Who are you? What do you want?"

"Shut the fuck up, just answer the fucking question," Cady said. It sounded much uglier whispered. He pushed the gun forcefully against her chin.

"Yes, it is his apartment," she said, softly.

"Are you a friend of his?"

"Yes."

"Do you want to stay alive?"

"Yes."

"Then you are going to help me get through that door," Cady said.

He quietly explained to Pam what he wanted her to do.

Jimmy had called ahead from Parker Center, telling a telephone receptionist at the *Santa Monica Outlook* that he had to speak with Hank Fellows immediately, insisting it was an emergency, finally being put through to Fellows, imploring the Editor to *Hold the Presses.*

Fellows' response was equally melodramatic.

"Shake a leg."

They decided to take one car. Sam Stephens lobbied for his unmarked police sedan.

"If we run into heavy traffic, we can slap the nifty red flashing light on the roof," he said.

"How did you get stuck working on Father's Day?" Jimmy asked while they rode. "What ever happened to seniority?"

"Actually, I've got the day off. Otherwise, I wouldn't have the luxury of a joy ride to Santa Monica."

"Shouldn't you be home with your family?"

"We all had brunch together. A late Sunday breakfast, according to my eldest son, the attorney. Two sons, their wives, two grandchildren, we couldn't get rid of them soon enough. After they all left, my wife chased me out of the house. 'Go visit Ray,' she said, 'if you keep playing with that TV remote I'm going to shove it down your throat.' I married the woman thirty years ago and it's just as if we met yesterday afternoon."

"Thirty years."

"Three zero. Ray said you were interested in finding out if Frank Raft was playing footsy with Jackson Masters recently. I told him I'd look into it. It won't be easy. The County DA's office is going to be tougher to penetrate than the Vatican because of the Simpson arrest," Stephens said. "I'll do what I can."

"I appreciate it, but don't go out on a limb," Jimmy said. "It's probably nothing."

"But, if it is something, it could be tied into the homicide I caught yesterday. The woman did come out of the Masters' mansion, so, it doesn't feel like nothing. It *is* circumstantial. If Raft murdered her, it could have nothing at all to do with her visit to North Linden Drive. Raft could have been Jackson Masters' bowling partner and it wouldn't necessarily mean a thing. I suppose *you* could go out and ask Reginald Masters about the woman, why she was there. I doubt the LAPD brass would like me going into Beverly Hills to hassle the old man. He has a good deal of clout and let's not forget his son was once Governor."

"Do you think Reginald Masters would even talk to me?" Jimmy asked.

"I doubt it."

"That's a great help. Maybe someone can tell us about the woman," Jimmy said. "Give us something we can sink our teeth into. If Fellows will run the photograph, who knows, maybe we'll get lucky."

Stephens rolled the car into the parking area in back of the newspaper office and both men climbed out.

"And this is all about what, Jimmy? I mean for you," Sam asked.

"It's about why Lenny and Richards were killed."

"Knowing who killed them isn't enough for you, is that it? You can't handle not knowing *why*. As Boyle reminds me whenever he gets the chance, motive isn't everything."

"I admit it bothers me, not knowing why they were murdered. What bothers me more, what's driving me is I don't believe *Lenny or Richards* really knew why they were murdered. That's what really fucking bothers me."

Pam Walker stood mute, directly in front of the door to Jimmy Pigeon's apartment. Seth Cady stood to the left of the doorway, leveling the gun at her chest. He nodded and she raised her hand to rap on the door. She wanted to warn Jimmy somehow. She wanted to survive. She needed to alert Jimmy and she could think of only one way she might be able to do it and live to tell.

"Jimmy," she called, as she knocked on the door. "It's Meg. Sorry I'm so late."

The sound of her voice made Cady cringe, he nearly squeezed the trigger of his handgun. He looked at Pam with murder in his eyes.

She glared back at him and she lip-synched the words, *He was expecting me earlier.*

In the apartment, Nate Archer sat frozen in Jimmy's armchair. Red flags waving.

He knew it wasn't Meg at the door. *That voice is not Meg's*, he thought, and the circumstance was all wrong.

Meg was aware Nate was there, waiting for Jimmy to return. She had sent Nate over with the keys. If she had talked to Jimmy after speaking with Nate, had expected Jimmy to be there, Nate would have heard about it from one of them before now.

No, it wasn't Meg. But who was it and why was this woman claiming to be Meg Kelly?

Nate softly placed the Dumas novel on the floor at his feet and quietly rose from the armchair. He looked over to the entry door, knowing it was unlocked. A baseball bat leaned against the wall at the doorway. He slipped out of his shoes and tried to imagine himself the world's greatest ventriloquist.

"C'mon in, Meg, it's unlocked," he called. "I'm in the kitchen."

Then he moved as silently as possible toward the front door.

Pam was confused. She had tried her best not to sound anything like Meg. She had raised the pitch of her voice to further contrast Meg's baritone. But the voice that replied was not Jimmy's and she wasn't sure what that meant.

Pam looked at Cady for a sign, he gave it to her with a wave of his gun and two whispered words, *Go ahead.*

Then he stepped behind her as she turned the doorknob and pushed the door in.

The door swung into the apartment. Nate stood behind the door with a Louisville Slugger gripped in both hands.

The woman walked in first. Definitely not Meg. She was staring straight ahead, unblinkingly.

She looked as stiff and as fragile as an icicle.

Then the gun, pointed at her head, less than a foot behind and the arm holding the weapon, coming into view from behind the door. Nate raised the bat and brought it down on the arm with all of his strength, swinging for the fences. The gun discharged. Nate heard a bone crack and heard the woman scream. Cady pounced on him and began beating him with the good arm.

Nate went limp, lost consciousness. Cady hit him once more, for good measure, a jail yard roundhouse to the head. Cady turned to look for the gun. He found it. He found it in Pam Walker's hand. He called her something she'd never been called before, growled like a wild beast and he started toward her. She squeezed the trigger, the shot deafening, the bullet knocking Cady to the floor. He tried rising, he growled again, a sound so vile and so terrifying she shot him again. And again.

Hank Fellows was an easy sell.

He would bump a display ad for a local restaurant from page two. Six inches, two columns. He could run the ad the following day.

"Papa Luigi won't complain," Fellows said. "He owes us money. I can run the photo with a banner. Something simple like *Do You Know Anything About This Woman?* A few lines below the photo. Who should we name as a contact? LAPD?"

"No, not LAPD and not the County Sheriff's," Stephens said. "And I wasn't here today. Use the phones here at the newspaper to field calls. If you get anything on the woman before we do, let me know. Only me."

"You'll do the same?" Fellows asked.

"Absolutely, you'll hear it first."

"Okay. Now beat it, I've got work to do," Fellows said.

"Can I use your phone?" Jimmy asked.

"Make it quick."

Jimmy phoned Meg's Café. Meg picked up.

"Jimmy, where have you been? Nate Archer is up from San Diego. I gave him your house keys. He's waiting there for you."

"I'd better get over there. I'll talk to you later."

Jimmy ended the call and turned to Stephens.

"Sam?"

"What's up?"

"Do you have time to stop at my place before we head back to LA for my car?"

"Sure, why not," Stephens said.

Nate Archer felt something cool against his forehead. He opened his eyes to find Pam Walker dabbing his face with a damp towel. He tried sitting up, felt dizzy, tried again, this time succeeding, using his arms for support.

Pam was trembling.

"He's dead. I shot him," she said.

"Who was he?"

"I don't know. He was here for Jimmy. He grabbed me in the hallway."

"Who are you?"

"Pam Walker. I was here for Jimmy also."

"Where's the gun?"

Pam pointed to the weapon, it was lying on the floor beside them. She wouldn't touch it again. Nate took the towel from her hand.

"Get out of here, now," he said.

"I need to see Jimmy."

"I'll tell him. He'll find you. You don't want to be here when the police arrive and they won't be long."

She didn't argue.

"Give this to him," she said, handing him a business card, "tell him it's important. Very important."

He glanced at the card. Jackson Masters' card.

"Go," he said.

Pam stood up, paused for a moment and rushed out of the apartment. She couldn't look at Seth Cady's body.

Nate picked up the handgun and wiped it down with the towel. He struggled to his feet, moved over to the corpse, knelt and wrapped Cady's dead hand around the grip and the trigger. Then he fired the gun once, into the wall behind him. He set the weapon on the floor and crossed the room to the telephone.

He dialed 9-1-1. An operator asked him to hold. Before she came back on the line there was pounding on the door with an admonition, "Santa Monica Police, open up and stand away."

"It's unlocked," Nate said. "I'm unarmed and I am well away from the door."

Two SMPD uniforms stepped in, weapons drawn.

Nate stood near the telephone, arms raised high above his head. Feeling dizzy again. One officer pointed a gun at Nate. The other stared down at Seth Cady's body. Into Cady's eyes, wide open, filled with surprise.

Nate made eye contact with the officer covering him. He was older, calmer. His arm, pointing the gun, steady.

Nate might have felt relieved, if his head weren't spinning.

"Self-defense," Nate said.

"Save it," said the older officer. "Tommy, call this in. Use the car radio. Homicide, try to find Barnum, the ME and crime scene techs. Go."

The younger uniform tore his eyes from the corpse and hurried out.

"I need to sit," Nate said. "I feel faint."

"Go ahead, take it slow."

Nate Archer collapsed onto the sofa.

Sam Stephens pulled the car up to the curb opposite Jimmy's apartment building. Two SMPD patrol cars sat in front of the building entrance. Jimmy watched Detective John Barnum walk into the building lobby. An ambulance siren screamed in the near distance.

"What the fuck is all this?" Stephens said.

"It has all of the characteristics of a bona fide disaster," Jimmy said, jumping from the vehicle.

Two hours later, Jimmy, Nate and Sam were left alone in the apartment. The dead body was gone. Barnum and his men were gone. Jimmy was mopping blood from the carpet.

Pam Walker had not been mentioned while Barnum and his men were there.

Cady was identified as a recently released convict. No one there connected him to Jimmy, except Jimmy himself.

Roger Rollins would have known why Cady had come; Ray Boyle could have guessed. Jimmy saw it in Cady's dead eyes. Cady had come thinking about settling the score. Jimmy knew it never worked that way.

It would go down as a random break in. Armed robbery.

Nate Archer had been waiting for Jimmy to return. He heard the sound of someone trying to break in and he moved toward the door. Cady entered, he saw Nate and he took a shot that missed. Nate grabbed the baseball bat, pummeled Cady's arm, the gun discharged again and it dropped to the carpet. There was a struggle for the gun. Nate prevailed, Cady attacked, Nate pulled the trigger...three times.

The forensics team found five slugs; three in Cady's chest, one in the wall, one in the floor. Barnum did not care for the story, but the victim was a lifelong felon, just out of prison, violating parole, caught breaking and entering with a loaded weapon. Nate Archer was a well-respected investigator and John Barnum was very anxious to get back home to Father's Day festivities.

Barnum signed off on Nate's testimony.

"I thought it best to let Pam go," Nate Archer said, more to Stephens, as if Sam, the law enforcer, needed an explanation or an apology for breaking the law. "It made no difference, he would have killed us both."

"Ray Boyle is going to love this one," Stephens said, his way of foregoing judgment.

"We should get moving, Jimmy, to see her, Pam," Nate said. "She told me it was very important."

"Did she say what it was about?" Jimmy asked.

"I think it's about this," Nate answered, handing the business card to Jimmy.

"Jackson Masters. You want in on this, Sam?"

"I'll leave you to it. I'm way overdue at home. My wife chased me out, but I don't think she meant it to be permanent. Can you get back to your car?"

"I have *my* car," Nate said. "We're covered."

"Watch your backs and keep me in the loop."

Stephens left.

Minutes later, Jimmy and Nate took off to speak with Pam Walker.

JACKSON MASTERS

Jackson Masters was at his desk early. Another nearly sleepless night, tossing, turning, his wife bothered by his restlessness, her complaining, intensifying his uneasiness, because her concern was about her, not him.

Reaching downtown, the Criminal Courts Building overrun with media, the double homicide in Brentwood, cameras everywhere, microphones, questions called out for which he had no answers, hounds, barking up the wrong tree.

At his desk, staring at the telephone, expecting it to ring, expecting the worst. Toying with a thought, thinking about grabbing the receiver before the phone rang. Call the old man, tell the old man it wasn't over, it would never be over.

The joke was Jackson Masters had no idea, no clue who the woman had been. How she had scared the old man. The old man who, in Jackson's experience, had never shown fear. Never. And when his grandfather demanded his help, insisted on his loyalty, no questions asked, he had acquiesced, with no hesitation, not so much to honor his grandfather, but to protect his father who had somehow, mercifully, been passed over, been spared. If he had to protect the old man, to spare his father, he would.

That was the joke. To have come so far, to have come so close, headed for big things. The head DA's office, a desk in the Governor's Mansion or a seat in the Senate. Only to be stopped cold, doomed to go down, fall, alone or doomed to keep clawing at the walls of the pit, deal with another accuser, deal with Pam Walker, try to breathe again before another pointing finger jabbed him, left him breathless.

He couldn't do it. Wouldn't do it. He would call the old man. Tell the old man he was defeated. He would throw in the towel. Keep the old man out of it. Fall on the sword.

Masters reached for the telephone. Too late. It rang angrily.

Pam Walker, calling for a meeting, suggesting how many reasons he might need to give her to keep quiet about Frank Raft. Twenty thousand reasons.

He agreed to meet her.

Pam Walker placed the receiver down.

Nate Archer switched off the tape recorder.

"I don't like it," Jimmy said.

They were at Jimmy's office. Pam made the phone call, suggested a modest twenty thousand dollars and arranged to meet Masters at a coffee shop in Westwood. One hour.

"What's not to like?" Nate asked.

"We could be putting Pam in danger."

"We'll be right there. It's a public place."

"Let's use this tape. Confront him with the telephone conversation."

"There's nothing here," Nate said. "He hardly said a word. We need him to hand over the cash, to admit what the money is for. Pam will be wired, we'll hear every sound. We'll have some real ammunition."

"Masters is one of the smartest lawyers in the state," Jimmy said. "It's entrapment. He'll know we can't use it against him in court."

"It's not about court. It's about innuendo and the reputation of his family. The man is terrified that his name and the name Frank Raft show up in the same sentence. He tells us about Raft or we throw it to the press. Or we threaten to bring it to his father, the Governor."

"I still don't like it," Jimmy said, up against the ropes, but not ready to give up the argument.

"I need to do this, Jimmy," Pam said.

That was the argument Jimmy knew he couldn't win.

"We have state of the art equipment right here in this office. Lenny only used the very best," Nate said. "We will get every syllable, every sigh."

"What if Pam can't get him to talk?"

"She'll have to bluff," Nate said.

"Bluff?"

"Claim Raft told her more than he did. Pam?"

"Yes, Nate?"

"Can you lie with a straight face?"

"I want to keep the twenty thousand," she said.

Jimmy looked at her with disbelief and disappointment. "Pam," he said, "that isn't possible."

"I'm kidding, Jimmy," she said.

"There you go," said Nate. "Let's get you wired up. You'll need to remove your blouse."

"Sure I will."

An espresso bar downtown.

Jackson Masters at a small table, Pam Walker seated opposite.

A shopping bag on the floor at their feet.

Jimmy Pigeon and Nate Archer, sitting in a car across the street. Nate wearing headphones, turning dials, fine tuning the equipment, recording every word.

A short meeting. Pam doing most of the talking before leaving with the shopping bag, filled with cash, walking to the street corner. Nate and Jimmy arriving moments later to pick her up. In the car, reviewing what they had on tape.

> Masters: *What do you want?*
> Walker: *Compensation.*
> Masters: *What does it have to do with me?*
> Walker: *Detective Frank Raft enlisted me to help him in an investigation he claimed he was doing for the DA's office, specifically for you.*
> Masters: *He said he was working for me?*
> Walker: *Yes. He showed me his Sheriff's ID and he gave me your business card, to sell his case. Look. Raft used me, and he hurt me. I want to get out of LA, that's all. I can use some cash to get started. I don't know what you had to do with him and I don't care. The bastard is dead, he was a one man crime wave; and whether you're involved or not, I'm sure you would rather avoid any speculation.*

Masters: *How do I know you won't bother me again?*

Walker: *Because I won't.*

Masters: *I'm going to leave. Wait a few minutes before you get up to go. Don't forget your shopping bag.*

"Well?" Pam asked.

"You did good, Pam," Nate said.

"Was it good enough?" she asked.

"It will have to be," Jimmy said. "What now, Nate?"

"We play the tape for Masters, clue him to the woman's photograph in this morning's *Santa Monica Outlook*, tell him our next move will be a trip to visit his father. Then we cross our fingers."

"When?" Jimmy asked.

"We'll wait a few hours, give him time to settle in at his office, to savor the belief he dodged the bullet," Nate said. "It'll give us time to take Pam home."

"We'll drop you at Meg's Café, Pam," Jimmy said. "I'll feel better about your safety there."

"The café?" Meg said.

"I spoke to Meg. I told her what you did last night and what you were going to do this morning. She wants to see you. It's going to be okay, Pam," Jimmy said.

Jackson Masters was holed up in his office, doing all he could to avoid the commotion that permeated the entire Criminal Courts Building.

His grandfather had phoned while he was meeting with Pam Walker. The old man would want to know why his grandson had failed to pick him up at the airport the previous evening, had sent a limousine instead.

Masters put off returning the old man's telephone call.

Instead, he leafed through the newspapers, a morning ritual that had been interrupted earlier by Pam Walker's call. He read all of the Los Angeles newspapers and the *Santa Monica Outlook*, which he had asked his secretary to pick up each morning for the past few weeks. Fairly deep inside the *Los Angeles Times*, a short piece on the body of a woman found in an abandoned building, the victim not yet identified. Then the photo of the woman on page two of the *Outlook* stopped Master's heart and the text below the photograph destroyed his hope. The *Outlook* believed the woman could have knowledge related to the murder of Ed Richards, a staff reporter. A reward of one thousand dollars was offered for information about the woman. Who, what, where.

The phone on his desk rang loudly, startling Masters.

"Jimmy Pigeon is on the line," his secretary said. "He would like to meet with you today. Mr. Pigeon said he had questions about Frank Raft, Pam Walker and a shopping bag."

"Please tell him I can't see him today, make an appointment for tomorrow morning."

Masters booted up his desktop computer and he opened a new text document.

Occasionally, he looked down at the woman's photograph as he typed.

"He's stalling," Nate said.

"Maybe. Probably. He might be tied up, need time to think. He got the message, he agreed to a meeting tomorrow morning. We don't have much choice. We have to wait," said Jimmy. "There's no way we'll get into that building to see him without an appointment. The place is like the Bastille, surrounded by hungry, storming reporters. I think you should get back to San Diego. Cady did quite a job on your face. Your wife needs to know it's not as bad as it looks."

"You'll call as soon as you're done with Masters, or if you hear anything from Sam Stephens or Hank Fellows?"

"First thing," Jimmy said.

The gunshot had Jackson Masters' secretary screaming from the office into the hall. Two LAPD officers reached her quickly.

The uniforms entered the reception area with weapons drawn and moved slowly toward the closed door to Masters' private office. One of the officers swung the door in and both entered with firearms extended. Jackson Masters was in his chair, his head on the desk, blood flowing from the wound at his temple, a gun on the floor near his seat. A copy of the *Outlook*, open to page two, was on the desk at his head. On top of the newspaper sat a sealed envelope.

Sam Stephens caught the call and he was standing in Master's office fifteen minutes later looking down at the body. His temporary partner, Stevie O'Brien, was out in the reception area interviewing Masters' secretary. The two officers first on the scene were outside in the hall, keeping everyone out until the medical examiner arrived.

Stephens spotted the envelope immediately. He pulled on a pair of latex gloves, removed the sheet of paper from the envelope and read.

He took the note to the copier, made a copy, put the note back into the envelope, placed the envelope into an evidence bag and placed the copy into his inside jacket pocket.

Later that afternoon, his shift over, Stephens phoned Jimmy Pigeon from Ray Boyle's hospital room.

"Jackson Masters put a bullet into his head earlier today," he told Jimmy. "His secretary told us you called Masters not long before he checked out."

"Fuck," was all Jimmy could say.

"I'm with Ray at the hospital. I have something here. I'm so certain you'll want to see it, I bent the rules a bit so you could see it soon."

"I'm on my way," Jimmy said.

Jimmy and I had been in his apartment for hours, since leaving Meg's Café after dinner. Drinking espresso, smoking cigarettes, sipping brandy. Jimmy talked, I listened.

I tried to imagine the life he had led...did lead.

I was the son of radical college professor and a grade school teacher. I grew up in Brooklyn, but had avoided the darker, more violent corners of the city. And as an actor, my brushes with crime and punishment, deception, danger and revenge had all been pretend. Jimmy's story fascinated me, even excited me.

And it frightened me.

"It was a suicide note," I said.

"Yes."

"And?"

Jimmy walked over to a desk in the corner of the room and pulled a sheet of paper from the center drawer.

"Read it yourself," Jimmy said, handing the note to me and reaching for the Brandy bottle.

Jackson Masters' parting words.

> *I met Natalie Levant in Sacramento. I was attending a week long California Department of Justice conference. We began a sexual liaison. I saw Natalie two more times afterward, in Los Angeles, before finally deciding the affair had to end. She did not take it well. Ultimately she called me, threatening to make our relationship public if I didn't pay for silence.*
>
> *I arranged a meeting at my grandfather's mansion in Beverly Hills. He wasn't home at the time. I bowed to her request, telling her the money would be provided. I used Detective Frank Raft to hand over the cash. I had met Raft when he was investigating the Mendendez case for the DA's office. Raft was an ambitious man and was very willing to assist me. He saw me as the future chief DA and himself as my lead investigator. He was asked only to carry the money. All of his subsequent actions were results of Raft's madness, but I realize I'm responsible. I attempted to hide my infidelity to protect my career, to save my wife, children and my father from the damage, the embarrassment and the disappointment my selfish acts would bring about. In the end, I have hurt and disappointed those I love so much more.*

"Was that the end of it?" I asked.

"Disappointed, Jake?"

"I don't know if that's the word for it. But to think all those people were killed, and so many others suffered, because Jackson Masters couldn't control his libido. Well, it seems like there should have been a better reason."

"There are never good reasons, it's always senseless," Jimmy said. "But I admit I felt the same way. I *was* disappointed. I wanted it to be something huge, wanted to uncover a monumental secret. I wanted to solve the mystery Lenny Archer had died trying to unravel. I was seduced by visions of grandeur, allowed myself to forget that solving a crime does not diminish its effect, does not control its infectiousness. I had forgotten this before, when I killed Will Cady. I read Masters' note again, later that evening, here alone in this room. I felt great sadness, a sense of loss, but the anger and the disappointment lost hold."

I thought at first that Jimmy was giving me a warning; attempting to tell me something about the business he was in, the work that intrigued me, that had brought me to see him. I came to know, in short time, that this was not Jimmy's way. He was not a preacher. He taught by example, good and bad. And he was not talking about the life of a private investigator, he was talking about the life of an imperfect being; a human being.

"So," I said. "That *was* the end of it."

"Not quite," Jimmy said, "but it is for tonight. I'm tired. I haven't talked this much in years. You're welcome to spend the night. The couch opens to a bed, it has clean sheets and I'm told it's very comfortable. It's had a lot of use."

"Angel Rivas and Nate Archer."

"To name a few. We can pick up where I left off over breakfast."

I took Jimmy up on the offer.

The next morning, Jimmy told me the rest of the story.

And Jimmy was right.

Although the secret concealed was much more explosive than Jackson Masters' final words had professed, neither its concealment nor its revelation were any nobler.

THE KEY

On Tuesday, the day after Jackson Masters took his own life, Jimmy Pigeon received a phone call from Hank Fellows.

"Jimmy, I just paid one thousand dollars for a locker key. The locker is at Los Angeles International Airport."

One of the young boys who had stumbled upon the body of Natalie Levant in the basement of an abandoned building had picked the key up from the ground near the corpse. He had seen the photo of the dead woman in the newspaper and he delivered the key to the *Santa Monica Outlook* hoping to collect the reward.

"Have you checked it out?" Jimmy asked.

"I thought you might want to ride along. I can come to get you."

"Give me thirty minutes," Jimmy said. He told Hank Fellows where to pick him up.

The locker at the airport held a journal, handwritten by Virginia Hill, describing events in her life from early childhood. Of particular interest to Jimmy Pigeon and Hank Fellows were entries for the dates leading up to, and those immediately following, June 20, 1947. The day Bugsy Siegel was killed in the mansion on North Linden in Beverly Hills.

> June 15
>
> Joey Adonis came to see me today. Joey said he's worried about me, he still loves me. He warned me to stay away from Ben. Ben is still in Las Vegas, I'm supposed to go back to join him in a few days.
>
> "Charlie Luciano wants Ben Siegel out of the picture, " Joey said. "Charlie thinks Benny is a liability, can't be trusted. "

"Meyer would never allow it. "

"Lansky is over a barrel. He has his hands full in New York and Siegel is not considered a good bet. Meyer can't afford to back a loser, he may have to look the other way. "

"Charlie will have a hard time reaching Ben from that pile of rocks in Sicily he calls his family estate, " I said.

"Luciano has very long arms. Jack Dragna would love to see Ben disappear. Mickey Cohen could go either way. "

"How about Moe? He'll watch Ben's back, always has. "

"Moe Sedway is not stupid. He knows if he's standing too close to Siegel, he could get caught in the crossfire. "

"Where do you stand, Joey? "

"As far away from Siegel as possible, and I'm begging you to do the same. I think it's too late for Ben, I don't think anyone can save him. And I know you can't save him, Virginia, but if you're careful you might survive him. "

June 16

I phoned Reggie today, he is in London promoting the latest Charlie Chan film. I have been seeing him in secret for a few months, once or twice a week, when I'm in LA and Ben is in Las Vegas. He is intelligent, refined and funny in ways Ben could never be. At the same time, he has the same movie star looks. He is so like Benny physically, they could be brothers. Height, weight, eyes, smile. The same rugged handsomeness, commanding voice and take charge attitude. His wife divorced him nearly ten years ago and left California with their infant son. He has been married to his work since. It is his uncanny resemblance to Ben that has made the affair so difficult. When I look at Reggie I see Ben and realize how much I still love Benny. Reggie had planned to return from Europe at the end of the month, I phoned to tell him I had to see him as soon as possible. I told him I couldn't wait. I said Ben was leaving for New York on the nineteenth, he would be gone for two weeks and we could be together the entire time, could use the house on North Linden. Reggie said he would meet me there on the twentieth. I told him not to announce he was cutting his trip short, so no one would be competing with me for his time. I told him I wanted him all to myself.

June 17

Moe Sedway and I drove out to Las Vegas today. It was a terrible trip, as usual, made worse by the fact I barely said a word and Moe kept asking me what was wrong. I couldn't help wondering if Moe knew anything about what Joey had told me on the fifteenth.

When we arrived, Ben was in a hurry to talk with Moe. Talk about the mess the Flamingo was in. I begged Ben to talk with me first. I told Ben about what I'd heard from Joey Adonis. I told Ben he was in big trouble.

"Adonis is a liar, " he said. "He would do anything to put distance between you and I, so he could slip right in. "

"Joey wouldn't care if you fell out of a plane, would probably throw a party, " I said. "But I do believe him, he does care about me. He came to warn me, not to help you or hurt you. Let's leave, Ben, run away. Far away. There's enough cash lying around here to keep us hidden for a long, long time. "

"I'm Ben Siegel. No one is going to make me run. "

"Please, Ben, they'll kill you. "

"If I can't be in Los Angeles, I would rather be dead. It's the only place where I've ever felt at peace, the only place that's ever really excited me. LA and Hollywood. "

"What if you could have it both ways? "

"What do you mean? "

I handed Ben an eight-by-ten glossy press photograph of Reggie Masters.

"What's this about? " he asked.

"I have an idea, and as crazy as it might sound, it just

might work. But first, I have to tell you something that could end it all for us, here and now. "

I told Ben about my affair with Masters.

The look in his eyes was terrifying. I had seen that look before and it was usually followed by violence.

"How can I trust you, Virginia? " he asked, displaying self-control I had never seen in Ben Siegel.

"I love you, Ben. It took this fling with Masters to remind me just how much you mean to me. You have to trust me, at least listen to what I have to say. There may be a way for you to get out of this and I'm willing to help you even if it means we can't be together. "

"I don't understand, " he said.

I told him what I had in mind.

He looked hard at the photograph of Reginald Masters.

"And he'll be back in LA on the twentieth? "

"Yes, he'll be at North Linden to meet me. "

"I need to talk to Moe, alone, " Ben said.

June 18

Ben was awake most of last night, lying beside me in bed, staring at the ceiling in silence. I tried to talk to him, asked him what he had on his mind. I asked him what, if anything, he and Moe Sedway had decided. He told me to keep quiet, be patient and let him think.

Mickey Cohen and Johnny Stompanato arrived late today. They met with Ben and Moe in Ben's private office in the casino. I went down to the swimming pool, hoping I would be distracted, stop wondering what they were talking about and how it was going to affect me. It didn't help. I was a bundle of nerves. They were at it for hours. Finally, Mickey and Johnny left, straight to their car and back to LA. I was sitting at the bar when Moe walked out of the office soon afterwards. Then Ben came out and joined me.

"How about dinner? " he asked.

I wanted to know what was going on. Joey's words haunted me. It's too late for Ben, no one can save him now, no one can be trusted. Not Mickey Cohen. Not Moe Sedway. But I couldn't bring myself to question Ben. If he wanted to fill me in, he would, in his own time.

To ask would only anger him.

"Sure, I could eat, " I said.

June 19

Last night, alone in our hotel room, Ben told me what he wanted me to do. He handed me a briefcase, it held two million dollars.

"You'll stop in New York City first, " he said. "Give half of this money to Meyer. Tell him to get in touch with Mickey and Johnny, to let them know I meant what I said to them, that if they spoke a word about our meeting today to anyone at all, there is no place in the world where they would be safe. Take the rest of the cash with you to Paris, the plane tickets are in this envelope, with the photo. Bring fifty thousand dollars and the photograph with you to the address I've written on the photo. Give it to Brandeau, tell him to expect me in a couple of days and to be ready. I'll come to you at the hotel in Paris when I'm finished with the doctor. I'll be driving you to the airport in LA today. Don't tell anyone where you're going. Don't count on being back here in the states anytime soon. "

"Is this going to work, Ben? " I asked.

"I guess we'll find out, " he said. "Find out if Ben Siegel is as invincible as he thinks he is. "

At the airport, I imagined I was seeing Ben's face for the last time.

June 21

I saw Meyer Lansky in his New York office yesterday. I brought the briefcase. He took half the money and placed it into a small shoulder bag, then handed the bag to me.

"This is yours, " he said. "Consider it goodbye money, start a new life and don't come back money. If you show your face again or talk to anyone about the past few days, no one will be able to protect you. "

"Will Ben be alright? " I asked.

"Ben Siegel is no longer your concern, " Lansky said. "Now, go. "

I was nauseous during the entire flight to France, had been sick every morning for the last three days. I didn't need a doctor to tell me I was pregnant and I didn't need anyone to tell me the father of the child was Reginald Masters.

I delivered the fifty thousand and the photograph to Brandeau this afternoon and returned to my hotel.

I read the news in an international edition of the New York Times left at my room door. Ben "Bugsy" Siegel, born Benjamin Siegelbaum in Brooklyn, New York in 1906, was shot to death in Beverly Hills. Siegel was forty-one years old.

All I can do now is wait.

The next entry in the journal was dated more than two weeks later. Only a handful of entries followed for 1947, dealing mostly with the pregnancy, leading up to the birth of a daughter, Anna, in February 1948. Virginia had moved to Vienna, Austria and raised the child there.

After the child was born, Anna Hill became the primary focus of her mother's journal. It became an account of the girl's life; first words, first steps, first day of school, first signs of adolescence. Virginia Hill said very little about herself in the pages. Ben Siegel and Reginald Masters were never mentioned again.

Her final entry was on the day following Anna Hill's eighteenth birthday.

Virginia Hill died in Vienna a few days later.

"What do you make of it," Hank Fellows asked, after they had reached the end of the tattered diary.

"I don't know what to make of it," Pigeon said. "Who double-crossed who? Did Hill set Ben Siegel up, by telling him he would find Masters at North Linden on the twentieth? If Natalie Levant was Anna Hill's daughter and she recently discovered Reginald Masters was her grandfather, did she go to Masters to claim her birthright? I'd love to have been a fly on the wall when Siegel and Sedway met with Cohen and Stompanato at the Flamingo Hotel and to have been in the car with Cohen and Stompanato when they drove back to LA. We'll never know. They're all dead now."

"Reginald Masters is alive."

"What good does that do? He would deny he ever had anything to with Virginia Hill or that he ever knew she was pregnant with what she *claimed* was his child," Jimmy said. "And the suicide note doesn't implicate him."

"It's extremely doubtful there was any romantic encounter. Jackson Masters may not have known who Natalie Levant really was, but *she believed* they were related by blood. And I can't believe their meeting in Sacramento was accidental. Levant must have tracked Masters down and somehow convinced him to arrange an audience with Reginald Masters. I believe the suicide letter was Jackson Masters' attempt at diverting attention from the old man."

"That note, those were the man's dying words. Hill's journal is too incomplete, too ambiguous. If push came to shove," Jimmy said, "the note would carry more weight, win the day, discourage further police investigation."

"Maybe Anna Hill is alive; her married name could be Anna Levant."

"Sure," Jimmy said. "We can look her up in the Vienna phone book."

"How about the doctor in Paris, Brandeau?"

"Do you really think he's still alive?"

"Probably not," Fellows said, "but we might at least be able to find out what kind of doctor he was. I can put a couple of my best researchers on it. What do we have to lose?"

The question plaguing Jimmy was *what did they hope to gain?*

Jimmy's father would have answered, *you hope to find the truth.*

And the search for truth is a noble quest.

Noble, perhaps, but not without its complications.

Not without its responsibilities.

Since the day he first discovered the identity of the man who killed his father, Jimmy had come to recognize the dark side of truth; had learned that knowing the truth and knowing what to do with it were two very different things.

On Thursday, two days after finding the journal, Hank Fellows phoned Jimmy again.

"We've located George Levant, a Viennese businessman. His wife Anna passed away six weeks ago, cancer. Natalie was their daughter; she was living in New York. When she went to Austria for her mother's funeral, Levant gave her Virginia Hill's journal. He said his wife wanted Natalie to have it. He said he had never read it, knew nothing of its contents. I spoke with him personally. I had to tell him his daughter was murdered."

"Horrible news to have to deliver," Jimmy said.

"I make my living delivering horrible news," Fellows said. "We located Brandeau's son. He is a physician also, joined his father in the Paris practice and took over the practice when his father died in nineteen-eighty."

"What kind of medical practice?" Jimmy asked.

"Plastic surgery," Fellows answered.

A FLY ON THE WALL

Later that Thursday morning, a light drizzle fell on the small crowd assembled at Forest Lawn Cemetery in the Hollywood Hills. They had come from the memorial service to the gravesite where Jackson Masters would be buried.

A few opened umbrellas were scattered throughout the congregation, but most of the spectators sat unprotected, letting the gentle rain wash over their hands and faces.

A minister stood beside the casket reading verse from the Bible. A few rows of metal folding chairs had been set up nearby. Jackson Masters' wife and his two children sat in the closest row of seats. William Masters, the former Governor of California, who less than two weeks earlier had become his party's candidate for a seat in the U.S. Senate, sat beside the widow.

Directly behind them sat the old man, still strikingly handsome at eighty-eight. He had a full head of thick gray hair covered by an ancient Fedora, the wide brim pulled low across his brow. He also wore a full beard, neatly trimmed, as he had since first allowing it to grow during a trip to Europe in 1947. And he wore the thick framed, dark tinted eyeglasses that had long been one of Reginald Master's most familiar physical trademarks.

William Masters stared blankly at the casket that held the lifeless body of his only son, trying to comprehend the senseless waste of such great potential.

The old man stared only at William.

In 1937, two events changed Reginald Masters' life.

Throughout most of the previous year, Masters' career and his home life were both overly demanding and stressful.

The studio had dumped the problem of Warner Oland into his lap. Do or die. Oland was threatening to kill the goose that laid the golden eggs, the Charlie Chan film series.

The actor's demands for additional salary and for more artistic control, combined with his erratic temperament and behavior, had virtually eliminated the handsome profits the popular series had always earned. Oland literally held the studio hostage and it was left to Masters to negotiate its release.

Success or failure would determine his future.

At the same time, his pregnant wife was becoming very unhappy about Masters' long hours away from their home; his distraction and inattention to her condition and her needs.

When his absence and disinterest continued after the birth of their son, Masters' wife gave up all hope for a normal, loving family life.

In 1937, Warner Oland walked off the set of the latest Charlie Chan film and never returned. His departure opened a door that would lead Reginald Masters to unimagined power and riches.

Just a few days before Oland's disappearance, Masters' wife filed for divorce and left California with their four-month-old son. William. Masters never heard from his wife again.

In 1952, his former wife died. Masters gained custody of the fifteen-year-old boy and William Masters came out to California to live with the father he had never known.

The rain had stopped falling as the casket was lowered into the ground. Soon, the small crowd dispersed. The old man walked alongside his chauffeur to the car and when they reached the limousine, Jimmy Pigeon was waiting there.

"I need to speak with you, sir," Jimmy said.

The chauffer began to move, stepping to place himself between Jimmy and the old man.

The old man stopped him with a hand gesture.

"Who are you?" the old man asked.

"Jimmy Pigeon, sir, and I need to talk with you about your granddaughter."

"I don't have a granddaughter."

"Then I need to talk to you about Natalie Levant," Jimmy said. "Virginia Hill's granddaughter."

The chauffer began to move again, threateningly. The old man held him off again.

"Can you come to my home, Jimmy? You may enjoy seeing the place, it has quite a history."

"I'm familiar with some of its history," Pigeon said, not very surprised that the old man had called him by his first name.

"Well, then, how about this afternoon?" the old man asked. "Can you be there at four?"

"I'll be there."

Nathan Archer jumped into his car ten minutes after Jimmy's phone call and raced up to Santa Monica from San Diego. With the equipment they had used when Pam Walker met with Jackson Masters, Nate would turn Jimmy into a walking microphone. They would take separate cars. Pigeon would drive right up to the mansion; Nate would park his vehicle as close as possible without being noticed, where he would monitor every word spoken by Jimmy and the old man.

They sat in Jimmy's office, Jimmy at his desk, Nate at Lenny's desk, both looking up at the wall clock, waiting.

The old man stood at the sink in the bathroom off the Master Bedroom in the mansion on North Linden.

He picked up one of the large gelatin capsules he used daily to help control his cholesterol and he pulled the two halves of the capsule apart. He spilled the garlic extract into the sink. He re-filled both sides with a grainy, salt like substance from a small glass bottle, pressing as much of the substance as he could into each side and pushed the two halves together again. The old man dropped the filled capsule into his shirt pocket.

He walked downstairs to his library and he sat to wait for Jimmy Pigeon.

The old man thought about Jackson Masters.

Jackson had taken his own life, believing if he placed the burden on his own shoulders alone he could save the day. The old man could have told him it wouldn't work. He had seen the photo of Natalie Levant in the *Outlook*, he knew that sooner or later someone would learn who she was; sooner or later she would lead someone to his door.

The old man had no illusions about Jackson's motive; Jackson did not act to protect the old man. He had acted to protect his father. The man Jackson loved and admired most, the man who would likely be the next junior Senator from the state of California, William Masters.

William deserves to be protected, the old man thought as he waited for Pigeon. William was innocent. He did not know what went on in Beverly Hills before his mother died and he was returned to California. He knew nothing about Virginia Hill or Mickey Cohen or Natalie Levant or Frank Raft. But he would be tainted by the sins of the old man, possibly ruined, and that is why Jackson had tried to take it entirely upon himself. Jackson understood a father is less likely to be ruined by the sins of his son.

The old man knew what he had to do, see to it that Jackson Masters had not died in vain and save William's reputation and future.

If it wasn't too late.

The doorbell rang.

The old man was alone in the house. He rose from his chair in the library and he went to the front door to let his guest into the mansion. He would try his best to sell his case. He opened the door for Jimmy Pigeon, measuring the younger man as he spoke.

"Jimmy, I like a man who arrives on time. Would you care to join me for a Scotch in the library, or would you rather see the rest of the house first?"

"A drink would be good," Jimmy said.

* * *

The old man handed Jimmy a tall, thick-bottomed glass, generously filled with twelve-year-old, single malt Scotch. The old man sipped his own drink and he sat in an armchair opposite Pigeon.

"What can I do for you, Jimmy?" the old man asked.

"Lenny Archer was my partner and my friend. He was brutally murdered by Frank Raft and Bob Tully. I need to know why he was killed. It's important to me."

"Why come here?"

"Because Lenny, and the others, died to keep the truth of the crime buried."

"What crime is that, Jimmy?"

"The murder of Ben Siegel."

"And you believe you know what happened."

"I think I do, but I want to hear it from you. I need to know *how* it happened."

"And what is it worth to you, the truth?"

"I won't know until I hear it."

"Then I'll help you, and afterwards I'll ask you to do something for me in return. Before I begin, you'll have to turn off any recording device."

"In that case, you'll have to allow Nathan Archer to join us. He should hear this also; Lenny was his brother. Nathan is here, outside, listening. Can I call him in?"

"Sure," the old man said, "go ahead."

"Come up to the house, Nate," Jimmy said, and then he removed the microphone from under his shirt.

A few minutes later, Nathan Archer joined them in the library. The old man fixed a drink for his new guest.

"Where to begin," the old man said.

"Begin where Joey Adonis warned Virginia Hill that Ben Siegel's head was on the chopping block," Jimmy said.

Siegel sat with Moe Sedway in the casino office after Virginia Hill told him about her talk with Joey Adonis.

"Charlie Luciano wants me dead," Ben said.

"You need to disappear, Ben. You won't know when it's coming, you won't know who."

"Virginia has a wild scheme that just might work. Can I trust you, Moe?"

"You know you can, Ben."

"I need to call Meyer."

"Meyer, its Ben."

"Benny, how are you, kid?"

"Charlie Luciano is gunning for me, Meyer."

"How do you know?"

"That's not important. I need your help."

"I don't know, Benny. There's two million missing and Luciano is very unhappy. Charlie wants you dead and he wants his half of the money back. Nothing short of that is going to make Charlie happy again."

"I have an idea that could make Charlie happy," Siegel said. "I'll need Mickey Cohen and one other man to make it happen, but Mickey won't go against Charlie unless he hears it from you."

"What kind of idea, Ben?"

Ben told Lansky what he had in mind.

"It's crazy," Meyer said, "but I don't see any other way. I guess it's worth a shot."

"I'll send the two million to you with Virginia; do whatever you need to do with it."

"Virginia has to disappear too, Benny. I'll let her keep my half of the money, but she will have to leave the country and stay gone."

"Fine."

"I'll call Mickey; tell him to meet you in Vegas. He can bring Johnny Stomp along, if you need a second man."

"Thanks, Meyer."

"And we never had this conversation," Lansky said, "Good luck, kid."

* * *

Cohen and Stompanato arrived in Las Vegas the next day and they immediately met with Moe Sedway and Ben Siegel in Ben's office at the casino.

"If anything we say here today leaves this room," said Ben Siegel, "we are all dead men. Meyer Lansky will see to that. Understood?"

Everyone understood very well.

"Can you buy an LA county coroner, Mickey?"

"I know just the one," Cohen said.

Ben told them his plan.

"When?" Mickey asked.

"On the twentieth. I want the body to be virtually unidentifiable. Use a shotgun, close range, to the face. Get the coroner in right away, to ID the corpse and rush his report. I want to read it in the newspapers the next day. I want to read that Bugsy Siegel is dead. If it all plays out, you will forget Benny Siegel ever existed. LA is yours, Mickey. You'll have to slug it out with Jack Dragna. Moe, you get Vegas. Good luck, she's a bitch."

Siegel paused. He looked from one man to the other, waiting for any questions. There were none.

"Try not to fuck up the house too much," he said. "I like it the way it is."

Jimmy and Nate followed the old man into the front room of the house.

"They made a real mess here," the old man said. "The front window was blown out, bullet holes in nearly all of the walls, destroyed an Italian leather couch and covered a very expensive Oriental carpet with blood."

"And no one ever realized who was actually killed here that day?" Jimmy asked.

"Those who knew took it to their graves. Those who didn't, never figured it out. Brandeau did an expert job on my face and the beard did the rest. Reginald Masters and Benjamin Siegel were both very intimidating men, most people who faced them were reluctant to delve very deeply into either man's eyes."

"So, you became Reginald Masters."

"Yes. Ben Siegel was dead."

"And Virginia Hill?" Nate asked.

"I never saw her again. Lansky had been very clear about that. We both understood the consequences."

"And Natalie Levant?" asked Jimmy.

"She suspected I wasn't her grandfather, that I wasn't Masters. I agreed to pay for her silence. I never ordered her killed, or the others. It was Raft, he was insane."

"But you are responsible," Jimmy said.

"Yes, I am. And I involved Jackson Masters and I am responsible for him also. But William Masters is innocent. He came to me when he was fifteen years old, the son of the man I had killed and replaced. The boy changed my life. I have loved him as my own. I have caused the death of his son. William is a good man, a great man and he should be spared. Ben Siegel spent his entire life never apologizing for anything, I have never pleaded for a thing. But now I beg both of you to keep history unchanged. To believe Ben Siegel died in this room forty-seven years ago."

Siegel reached into his shirt pocket and he pulled out the capsule he had prepared earlier. He placed it between his teeth and bit down hard. "Save William," Siegel said, and he collapsed to the floor.

Nate knelt and brought his face to Siegel's face.

"Cyanide," he said.

"Can we do anything?" Jimmy asked.

"Nothing. He'll be gone in ten minutes."

"Should we call it in?" Jimmy asked.

"No. Let's get out of here," Nate said. "Let someone else find Reginald Masters dead. I'm sure they'll find the cyanide salts somewhere in the house. A lonely old man in a huge, empty mansion. Another suicide."

"Are you sure?"

"Yes, I'm sure. And I believe my brother Lenny would have done the same. We should take our Scotch glasses away with us."

"So, Bugsy Siegel was gunned down in 1947."

"I would say so," Nate said. "What about Hank Fellows? He saw Virginia Hill's journal and this would be a very big story."

"I think I can convince Fellows we were mistaken."

"That would be untrue."

"Truth is sometimes overrated," Jimmy said. "I have always admired Governor Masters. Too many have suffered already."

"How about the old man, do you think he got off easy?" Nate asked.

"No, not at all. The old man died never knowing what we would do."

PIGEON AND DIAMOND

"We left the mansion with drinks in hand," Jimmy said. "I came back here to watch the Dodger game. Nate went back down to San Diego. I haven't spoken to him since."

Jimmy and I had walked to the pier after breakfast at his apartment. It was late Sunday morning, the fourteenth of October. Nineteen weeks after Lenny Archer's death.

"Do you have any regrets?" I asked.

"Regrets?"

"About not officially closing the Bugsy Siegel murder case?"

"None," Jimmy said. "William Masters is far ahead in the polls. He's a shoe-in for the Senate seat. He will be good for the state. In this business you have to move on, Jake. You do the best job you can do and then you tackle the next investigation. I'm sure it's just about the same in any business, even in the acting business. You do your best and then you move on to the next role."

"If you can get one," I said.

"Do you have any film work lined up?"

"Not really. My agent has a long list of clients and my name is nowhere near the top of that list."

"See the man over there, Jake?"

I looked down the pier to where Jimmy was pointing.

"The bearded man with the Red Sox cap and the paper cup?" I asked.

"Yes. The man was a high-powered Santa Monica lawyer less than a year ago. He might have been a former private investigator or a movie star. I'm working on a case right now and I could use some help, nothing too dangerous, just a little leg work. I could tell you stories all day every day, but you'll only get a feel for the work I do by doing it. If you're interested, you can get your feet wet."

"Sure, why not. I have plenty of time on my hands."

"Tell me about free time," Jimmy said. "I simply can't accept the fact that the baseball season is over and there won't be a World Series this fall. I hardly know what to do with myself. What kind of world has this become, Jake, when our heroes trade baseball bats for picket signs or are indicted for murder."

"A complicated world, Jimmy," I said.

The bearded man in the Red Sox ball cap approached our bench on the pier.

Jimmy and I both reached into our pockets.

Jimmy and I sat in the Santa Monica office.

It was late January, 1995.

The Simpson murder trial had just begun.

Newly-elected Senator William Masters had been sworn into office.

There had been no World Series, but two California football teams were set to battle in the Super Bowl.

Vinnie Strings had just left the office after hanging around all morning going on and on about the huge wager he had placed on the San Diego Chargers.

"Is there anything you don't bet on?" Jimmy asked.

"Winners," Vinnie said, before skipping out.

Vinnie gone, Jimmy got down to business; tackling the end-of-month paperwork.

I was staring at the office door.

The glass pane in the door had been replaced more than six months earlier, but the words on the pane were freshly painted and still hard for me to get accustomed to.

PIGEON and DIAMOND
Private Investigation

The telephone rang.

Jimmy and I looked at each other.

"Your turn, Jake," Jimmy said.

I reached for the receiver.

ABOUT THE AUTHOR

J. L. ABRAMO was born in the oceanside paradise of Brooklyn, New York on Raymond Chandler's 59th birthday. Abramo received a BA in Sociology and Education from City College of the City University of New York and an MA in Social Psychology from the University of Cincinnati. He has been a long-time educator, a producer and director of theatre, and an actor on stage and in film; with a number of television credits including roles on *Homicide: Life on the Street* and *Law and Order*. Abramo's first novel, *Catching Water in a Net*, was recipient of the St. Martin's Press/Private Eye Writers of America Award for Best First Private Eye Novel, and was followed by two additional Jake Diamond mysteries, *Clutching at Straws* and *Counting to Infinity*. A stand-alone thriller, *Gravesend*, was recently published by Down and Out Books; and a fourth novel in the Jake Diamond series is in the works. Abramo is a card-carrying member of the Screen Actors Guild, Private Eye Writers of America, Mystery Writers of America and International Thriller Writers.

For more information please visit:

www.jlabramo.com

www.facebook.com/jlabramo

www.downandoutbooks.com

OTHER TITLES FROM DOWN AND OUT BOOKS

By J. L. Abramo
Catching Water in a Net
Clutching at Straws
Counting to Infinity
Gravesend
Chasing Charlie Chan
Circling the Runway (*)

By Trey R. Barker
2,000 Miles to Open Road
Road Gig: A Novella
Exit Blood

By Richard Barre
The Innocents
Bearing Secrets
Christmas Stories
The Ghosts of Morning
Blackheart Highway
Burning Moon
Echo Bay (*)
Lost (*)

By Milton T. Burton
Texas Noir

By Reed Farrel Coleman
The Brooklyn Rules

By Tom Crowley
Viper' Tail (*)

By Frank De Blase
Pine Box for a Pin-Up (*)

By Jack Getze
Big Numbers (*)
Big Money (*)
Big Mojo (*)

By Keith Gilman
Bad Habits (*)

By Darrel James, Linda O. Johsonton
& Tammy Kaehler (editors)
Last Exit to Murder

By David Housewright & Renée Valois
The Devil and the Diva

By David Housewright
Finders Keepers

By Jon Jordan
Interrogations

By Jon Jordan & Ruth Jordan
Murder and Mayhem in Muskego
(Editors)

By Bill Moody
Czechmate: The Spy Who Played Jazz
The Man in Red Square
Solo Hand (*)
The Death of a Tenor Man (*)
The Sound of the Trumpet (*)
Bird Lives! (*)

By Gary Phillips
The Perpetrators
*Scoundrels: Tales of Greed, Murder
and Financial Crimes* (Editor)

By Lono Waiwaiole
Wiley's Lament
Wiley's Shuffle
Wiley's Refrain
Dark Paradise

(*)—Coming Soon

www.ingramcontent.com/pod-product-compliance
Lightning Source LLC
Chambersburg PA
CBHW051257210726

48287CB00002B/551